Double Jeopardy

by

Donna Schlachter

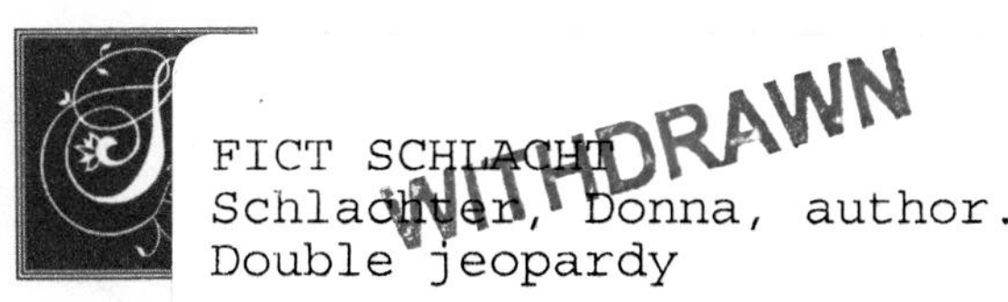

DOUBLE JEOPARDY BY DONNA SCHLACHTER
Smitten Historical Romance is an imprint of LPCBooks
a division of Iron Stream Media
100 Missionary Ridge, Birmingham, AL 35242

ISBN: 978-1-64526-083-7

Cover design by Hannah Linder
Interior design by Karthick Srinivasan

Available in print from your local bookstore, online, or from the publisher at:
ShopLPC.com

For more information on this book and the author visit:
historythrutheages.blogspot.com

Brought to you by the creative team at LPCBooks:
Eddie Jones, Shonda Savage, Denise Weimer, Pegg Thomas, and
Stephen Mathisen

Library of Congress Cataloging-in-Publication Data
Schlachter, Donna.
Double Jeopardy / Donna Schlachter 1st ed.

Printed in the United States of America

Praise for *Double Jeopardy*

"*Double Jeopardy* is a delightful historical romantic suspense novel set in 1880 Colorado. With a feisty heroine and a secret knight-in-shining-armor hero, both positive and negative sparks fly in their relationship. Interesting secondary characters add richness to the story. Surprise plot twists kept me guessing. And the realistic setting added so much to this wonderful read. I had a hard time putting the book down."

~Lena Nelson Dooley
Editor, speaker, and author of fifty Christian novels

"An engaging story that grips you from the first page, filled with characters who come alive through the vivid descriptions and narrative. Set in a small mining town at the foothills of the Colorado Rockies, this story of intrigue and redemption will draw you into the rough and tumble world of mining and the Old West."

~Tiffany Amber Stockton
Author of over twenty-five novels, including *A Fair to Remember*

"Donna Schlachter has created an engaging story with characters I cared about and enjoyed spending time with. I rooted for Zeke to get the woman of his dreams who could be an equal partner for him. And for Becky to get her heart's desire to marry for love. A delightful read."

~Mary Davis
Bestselling, award-winning author of The Quilting Circle Series and *Newlywed Games*

"Prepare for intrigue, adventure, and romance in late-nineteenth century Colorado. *Double Jeopardy* hooked me in and held me fast even though I've never cared much for Western fiction. An undercurrent of suspense kept me turning the page, and intriguing characters came to life. Many of the protagonist's predicaments and challenges made me want to scream, scold her, and cheer for this strong-willed woman until she finally meets her match in a handsome cowboy. Go ahead … get yourself lassoed by Donna's story. You won't sleep a wink."

~Susan G Mathis

Multi-published author of *Katelyn's Choice* and *Christmas Charity*

"In *Double Jeopardy*, Becky and Zeke find love and silver in the Colorado Rockies, while author Donna Schlachter weaves romance, humor, and mystery into a delightful tale that strikes gold. I loved every twist and turn along the way!"

~Margaret Mizushima

Award-winning author of

Burning Ridge: A Timber Creek K-9 Mystery

"What a fun read. I felt like I was in an old Colorado mining town. Donna's vivid descriptions brought the story to life without bogging things down. I loved the way Becky never backed down from a challenge. She's my kind of heroine."

~Suzanne Norquist

Author of *Mending Sarah's Heart* in the *Thimbles and Threads Collection* and *A Song for Rose* in the *Bouquet of Brides Collection*

Acknowledgments

First and foremost, to God the Father—without Him, no story is worth telling.

To my agent, Terrie Wolf, who believed in me before I believed in myself.

To my husband, Patrick, my biggest fan. I am so blessed to be married to you.

To Karen Burden Comerford and Trixie Orembt, who graciously provided me names for the donkeys.

To my editor, Denise Weimer, who made the story so much better.

They that trust in their wealth, and boast themselves in the multitude of their riches; none of them can by any means redeem his brother, nor give to God a ransom for him.
Psalm 49:6–7

CHAPTER 1

1880 Silver Valley, Colorado

Dead. Dead as her dreams and her hopes.

Dead as a doornail, as her mother would say.

Just thinking about the woman drove a steel rod through Becky Campbell's slumping back. Perched on a chair in the sheriff's office, she drew a deep breath, lifted her shoulders, and raised her chin a notch. She would not be like the woman who birthed her. Pretty and pampered. A silly socialite finding nothing better to do with her days than tea with the mayor's spinster daughter or bridge with the banker's wife.

No, she'd much rather be like her father. Adventuresome. Charismatic. Always on the lookout for the next big thing.

Now her breath came in a shudder, and down went her shoulders again. She tied her fingers into knots before looking up at the grizzled lawman across the desk from her. "There's no chance there's been a mistake in identification, is there?"

He slid open the top drawer of his desk and pulled out a pocket watch, a lapel pin, and a fountain pen, which he pushed across the desk to her. "He was pretty well-known around here. I'm really sorry, miss."

Becky picked up the timepiece and flicked open the cover. Inside was a photograph of her family, taken about ten years earlier when she was a mere child of eight and Father stayed around long enough to sit still for the portrait. Her mother, petite and somber, and she, all ringlets and ribbons. She rubbed a finger across the engraving. *To R. Love M. Always.*

Yes, this was his.

And so was the lapel pin, a tiny silver basket designed to hold a sprig of baby's breath or a miniature rosebud—a wedding gift from her mother twenty years before.

She looked up at the sheriff, tears blurring her vision. "And his ring?"

The lawman shook his head. "No ring. Not on his body or in his shack."

"But he always wore it. Never took it off."

He shrugged. "Maybe he lost it. Or sold it."

"I doubt he'd do either. My mother gave it to him when I was born."

She peered at him. Had he stolen her father's ring?

Or maybe Sheriff Fremont was correct. Maybe something as important as her birth hadn't meant much to her father. Maybe she didn't either. Was that why he left?

Because surely his absences couldn't be explained by any rift between her parents.

Although, what Matilda Applewhite saw in Robert Campbell—Robbie to his friends and family—Becky had never understood. Her mother, who ran in the same circles as the Rockefellers and the Astors, with presidents and admirals—yet much to the consternation of her family, chose a ne'er-do-well like Becky's father.

Becky set the two items side by side on the scarred wooden desk, next to the fountain pen. The same one he'd used to write his letters to her. Signing them, *Give your mother all my love too. Your devoted father*. She needed no more information. No more proof.

Dead.

Not what she'd hoped for when she'd left New York a month prior, against her mother's wishes, with little else to direct her steps than a ticket to Silver Valley and her father's last letter. Written a year before, but as full of life, promises, hopes, and wishes as ever.

She collected the only three material evidences of her father's existence and dropped them into her reticule, then stood. "Thank you for your time, Sheriff. I appreciate my father's death must be a difficult business for you."

He stood and dipped his head. "Yes, miss."

"Do you know how he died?"

He cleared his throat, not meeting her gaze. "Still investigatin', miss. Lots of things to look into."

She bit back a groan. Unlike in the city, where manpower and resources seemed limitless, out here, there was just the sheriff and sometimes a deputy. "Thank you again. Please keep me updated." She turned to leave but paused. "Where is he buried?"

"Over by the church. Just ask the preacher. He can show you."

Not as if she was in any rush to see her father's final resting place. Picking up her carpetbag which she'd left inside the sheriff's door, she stepped outside and scanned the street. Surely the man who was more gypsy than family man would hate to think of his physical body buried here in this town.

A morose sense of humor invaded her. At least it was a way to get him to stay in one place longer than it took to eat a meal.

Sheriff Fremont joined her on the front step. "You'll likely be returning home now, I 'spect."

She looked up past his dimpled chin, his bushy mustache, his aquiline nose, into eyes as dark as coal. "No, sir. I have no plans to return."

"What will you do?"

"Do?"

She blinked several times as she pondered the question, which was a very good one indeed. She'd not thought beyond the ache building in her bosom for the father she'd never see again. At least when he went off on yet another adventure, she had the unspoken promise of his return at some point, in the distant future. And always a letter. Or a postcard. Never many words on either, but confirmation he was alive and she was still important to him.

At least, important enough to sit a few minutes and pen a few words.

She stared at the dusty mining town. More tents than wooden structures. More mules than horses. More saloons than churches.

Two men tumbled onto the boardwalk opposite her, rolled down the two steps to the street level, and lay prone in the dirt littered with horse apples. The barkeep, a barrel-chested man, his formerly white apron now stained beyond redemption and a dingy cloth slung over his arm, burst through the swinging doors. "And don't come back. We don't need the likes of you in here bothering our customers."

The man turned on his heel and disappeared back into the saloon. Within ten seconds, the tinny notes of a piano filtered to her ears.

The two in the street lay still.

Had he killed them?

A pack of boys ran from a nearby alley, grabbed a hat from one the men's heads, and raced down the street, jabbering and hollering as if their britches were on fire. Three mongrels loped after them, tongues lolling and tails held high.

She turned back to the sheriff. "Is there a decent boarding house in town?"

One eye squinted as he peered at her for a long moment before nodding slowly. "So you're going to stay?"

"I have no reason to return."

She glanced at the two men in the street. One climbed to his feet, swaying unsteadily, while the other vomited into the dust without even lifting his head. The acrid odor wafted across to her, and she wrinkled her nose, breathing through her mouth. Until the smell coated her tongue. Then she snapped her mouth shut.

Maybe this wasn't the town for her …

No. She would never give her mother the opportunity to say *I told you so.*

"Well, we got us a hotel above the saloon over yonder, and just about every drinking establishment in town rents out rooms, but I wouldn't recommend those places. Mrs. Hicks over at number fourteen Front Street rents out a few rooms in her house. Tell her I sent you." He added the necessary directions.

"Thank you, Sheriff." She took a couple of steps, her drawstring bag banging against her thigh as she two-handed the carpetbag. "I'll also need directions to my father's claim so I can get that transferred into my name. As his next of kin."

"You'll need to check with the Land and Assay Office, two doors up from the mercantile. But I don't know what kind of a title he bought. Some can be transferred, but most who come out here can't think past their next pay lode, so they don't spend the money to buy that kind."

She tipped her head. "You mean I might need to buy my own father's property?"

He shrugged. "Not that I know much, but that's what I've heard. I wish you luck, miss. You'll need it if you plan to stay." He tipped his hat to her before closing his door.

Becky drew in a breath of the warm May afternoon, then released it in a sigh. First the cost of the train ticket, then her meals and occasional hotel rooms along the way. And now this. Was there no end to the ways her dwindling cache of gold coins could disappear like snow in July?

First things first—a proper place to stay tonight. She walked in the direction the lawman had indicated toward the home of Mrs. Hicks. Her heels beat a rhythm like a drum corps in a parade. She nodded to women and couples she passed but averted her eyes from the solitary men.

And there were many of those. Of all sizes and shapes, ages, and deportment. Several ogled her from the chairs they occupied outside the six—no, seven—saloons she passed, and that was only on her side of the street.

She glanced down at her wrinkled outfit—the dusty hem of her pale gray skirt, the cuffs of her shirtwaist stained from days on the train, and her boots, desperately in need of cleaning and polish. She tucked a strand of hair behind her ear, wishing she'd taken time for a bath. Or at least a sink wash.

Her mother would be mortified.

A lone barber lounged in one of his three chairs, not a customer in sight, testifying to the fact that the men hereabouts were more interested in cards, booze, and loose women than in personal hygiene.

A fact she confirmed when one lout stood his ground and refused to let her pass. Cheap perfume, rotgut whiskey, and sweat mingled to create an odor that made her eyes water.

Another man stepped up behind the drunk. "Micky, are you troubling this young lady?"

Micky swayed in place, twisting the brim of his hat in gnarled fingers. "She one of your flock?"

"Doesn't matter. Apologize and move on."

The drunk tipped his hat to her in apology and stepped back against the building, allowing her to continue. The preacher, his collar white against the severe black suit, nodded, and she acknowledged his courtesy with a tiny smile. "Thank you. Reverend?"

The clergyman dipped his head. "Obermeyer, Pastor Obermeyer."

She held out her hand. "I'm Becky Campbell."

He blinked a couple of times, then his brow raised. "Oh, you're—"

"Yes. Robbie Campbell's daughter." She glanced over her shoulder. "The sheriff told me you could show me where my father is buried."

He held her hand and sandwiched it between his own. "Please accept my condolences on your loss, Miss Campbell."

"Thank you." That now too-familiar ache swelled in her bosom. Would it never ease? "If I may call on you another time? I'm off to find lodging."

He tipped his head to one side. "Oh, you're staying?"

Why did everybody think that because her father was dead, she would leave?

Or was this wishful thinking on their part?

If so, why?

She nodded. "I am."

He shook himself like a hound dog awakening from a nap. Had he stretched and yawned, she would not have been surprised. "Good. Good." He pointed down the street. "The church is there. The parsonage is the tiny house behind. I'm in my study most days. Come by any time." He tipped his hat. "Perhaps I'll see you in church tomorrow?"

"We shall see. Thank you for rescuing me from that horrible man."

His shoulders slumped. "So many have too much time and money on their hands." He quirked his chin toward the others walking along the street. "Many work all week, then come into town and spend it on a Saturday, only to go back and repeat the same cycle next week."

Sounded hopeless. But what could she do about it? Nothing. If she wanted to make it on her own here, she had her work cut out to stay out of the poorhouse. She surely wouldn't ask her rich-as-Midas mother for assistance. Maybe once she got on her feet … "Thank you again. Good day."

She gripped her carpetbag and continued on her way, pleased that at least two men in this town—the sheriff and the parson—were raised by genteel women. She should count herself lucky she'd met both today. Having even one on her side might come in handy at some point. And having two—well, that was just downright serendipitous.

Three blocks through the business section, then a right for two blocks, and she found the house she sought. Narrow but well-kept flower gardens lined both sides of the walkway. She unlatched the gate, headed for the door, and knocked. Her gloved hands sweating, she longed for a cool drink of lemonade or sweet tea. As she raised her hand to knock again, the door swung open and a tall, thin woman of indeterminate age peered down at her.

Becky tossed her a smile and introduced herself. "The sheriff said you might have a room for rent?"

"How long?"

"I'm not certain. I plan to stay until I settle my father's estate, at least. Possibly longer."

The stern look on the woman's face eased. "Sorry for your troubles. Four dollars a week including meals." She peered past Becky. "And I only take respectable women. No children. No men. My name is Joan Hicks."

While the amount seemed high, Becky had little choice. "My name is Becky Campbell."

"Oh, you'd be—"

Becky sighed. Either her father was famous, or infamous. The former, she hoped. "Yes. His daughter. And yes, I'm staying in town until I get his claim sorted out."

The wrinkles around the landlady's eyes deepened, and her mouth lifted in a smile. "Actually, my next question was if you want dinner tonight?"

"I would. Thank you. What time?"

"Dinner's at five. Perhaps you'd like to see your room and freshen up."

She was going to like this obviously kindly, no-nonsense woman. So unlike her own mother. "Thank you."

The interior of the house was dark but cool, and Becky followed Mrs. Hicks up two flights of stairs to one of three doors that opened off the top landing. The landlady stood aside and held out her hand, palm up. "Payment due in advance. Pot roast for dinner."

Becky dug the four coins from her reticule and handed them over. "Thank you."

"No keys for any of the rooms. I got the right to inspect the room with an hour's notice. No cooking or smoking in the rooms. Privy is out the back door."

Becky swallowed back a lump of disappointment. She'd

expected indoor plumbing, just as she enjoyed in New York, but the modern conveniences hadn't made their way this far west.

Or at least, not to this house in Silver Valley.

She entered what would be her home for at least the next week, longer if she could figure out how to make her remaining money stretch further. She set her bag on a dressing table, and then she closed the door. When she sank onto the bed, the springs creaked beneath her weight. She sighed.

A pang of—of what? Homesickness? Missing her father? Wishing things were different?—caught her off guard, spreading through her like a flooding river, threatening to wash away all hope. So much for her dreams of prospecting with her father in the mountains of Colorado. Of catching up on all the years they'd missed.

Rather, that she had missed.

She doubted her father had lacked any adventures or excitement.

His life had been so different from her own.

She dumped the contents of her drawstring bag onto the bed and sorted through them. Sixty-three dollars which, along with the hundred or so in her carpetbag, should tide her over for a while. If she didn't have to buy her father's claim. If she didn't have to pay top dollar for every single thing she needed.

Because if there was one thing still alive in her, it was the desire to understand her father. To understand what drove him to leave the comforts of home and travel to this remote place. Was it the lure of silver? Was he simply tired of his refined life? Of his wife?

Of her?

Ezekial Graumann saddled up his best horse and headed for town. After three weeks pent up on the ranch, he needed a break. His parents needed a break from him. And he sure needed time away from his two sisters, two brothers, and their wives.

The late afternoon sun beat on his back and head, almost

cookin' him. He took a few slurps of water from his canteen, then swiped at the sweat runnin' down his face. No matter how long he lived in Silver Valley—almost half his twenty-six years—he still wasn't used to the fluctuations in heat and cold. And didn't think he ever would be.

His mount, a bay gelding he'd hand-raised and saddle-broke himself, loped along at a comfortable pace, coverin' the twenty or so miles to town in an easy gait—not like some of those cow ponies his father bought last year. Those brutes would jar the teeth out of a man's head.

Zeke patted his shirt pocket, makin' certain—for about the tenth time—that his money packet was safe. Not that he had anythin' to spend it on. He didn't drink. He didn't smoke. And he didn't hold with carousin' with the soiled doves in the saloons.

He sighed as he spotted the town named after the valley ahead and slowed his bay gelding to a walk. A cloud of dust wafted past him and settled on the roadway. He slapped his pants legs with his hat, sendin' up another small cloud, then brushed off his sleeves. He'd avoid the saloons and the cards today and head for the mercantile. An hour porin' over the catalogs could prove distraction enough, and maybe he'd come up with an idea for a gift for his parents for their weddin' anniversary next month. A new stove for Ma? A new saddle for his pa? Maybe a new table for the kitchen.

He halted his gelding outside the store, dismounted, and gave the bay an extra pat on the neck. "Won't be long."

The horse snorted as though in answer, then lowered its head to drink deeply of the waterin' trough. After giving a half-dozen pumps on the handle to add fresh water, Zeke climbed the two steps from the street to the store level.

He paused just inside the open doorway, inhalin' the familiar scents of tobacco, leather, wood smoke, and somethin' more intriguin'—cinnamon, maybe? Ginger? Cloves? He didn't know much about cookin', but he was an expert at eatin', and his ma used those spices in her cakes and cookies. He'd pick up some as an encouragement for her to make another batch real soon.

He nodded to the storekeeper, who wrapped a package for a customer. "Good day, Mr. Dixon."

"Hey, Zeke. Out for your annual visit?"

He chuckled along with the old man. The storekeeper greeted him the same way every time—and Zeke made it a point to come to town at least once a month. "Funny one, Mr. D." He stepped up to the counter. "Don't rush. I'm just lookin'."

"All right." Mr. Dixon, the apron around his waist makin' him look like a ten-pound sausage stuffed into a five-pound skin, made change and bid his customer a good day, then came over to where Zeke stood. "What kin I do fer ya today?"

"I think maybe I'll get me a new shirt. And can I look through your catalog? Want to get somethin' for my parents."

"Sure thing." He peeked beneath the glass countertop under which various items includin' ladies' gloves, hair combs, and boot hooks were on display. "I know I got that cat'log here somewheres. Saw it just yesterday. Ah, here it is." He laid the thick book on the counter. "What kind of shirt?"

"Something to wear to church, maybe?"

Mr. D. chuckled. "You thinkin' a new shirt might nab you a woman, Zeke?"

He hoped not. There weren't many women under fifty in town. And the ones that were—well, that wasn't his reason for goin' to church.

"Miracles could happen."

The shopkeeper laughed and turned to the shelves, climbed a wooden ladder, and selected several boxes. "Here's one in white, one in blue, and another from a nice striped flour sack. Made by a woman here in town."

Zeke held up each in turn, then made his decision. "I'll take the white one. If you wrap that, along with a bag of whatever spices Ma needs to make a spice cake and a couple of batches of cookies,

I'd sure appreciate it." He picked up the catalog and gestured to the two chairs near the woodstove which, while not lit on this warm May day, was a good place to prop his feet and sit out of the way. "I'll take a look and let you know when I'm ready to order."

"Fine. Fine. Kick the door closed for me, would you? Keep the dust out."

Zeke did as asked, while Mr. D bustled off to fill his order. He sat, flippin' through pages, ponderin' the array of goods offered by Bloomingdale's, a fine department store in New York City. A store he'd likely never set foot in—except through this catalog—and a city he'd sure as shootin' never visit.

No. Silver Valley was all the civilization he needed. Even his occasional visits to Denver scared the pants off him. All those people. Fancy clothes. Houses of ill repute. Expensive restaurants. Tall buildin's that blocked out the sun. He'd heard of other big cities, of course—Chicago, Boston, Kansas City—but had no desire to go there either.

Nothin' there for a country boy like him.

The bell over the door jingled, announcin' the arrival of another customer. Zeke peered over the top of the catalog. Hopefully, it wasn't one of the town girls who thought he was fair game because he wore pants and had no other encumbrances.

He stifled a chuckle. Encumbrances. Meanin' a wife—either here in Silver Valley or in another town—and no children. Not even a mistress. That's what the one called Sally had informed him one time. Thank heavens the postmaster's assistant showed her some attention to let him off the hook.

He relaxed into his chair and dropped the catalog into his lap. He didn't recognize this young woman. Judgin' by the modest appearance of her dress, hat, and gloves, she wasn't from the saloon. Those kind of women tended to flaunt all their—uh, womanly features for every man to see. The display might be enticin' to the senses, but it wasn't the kind of woman he wanted for a wife.

Not that he had any strong desire to wed soon. He liked the

way things were. He sensed his parents were hopin' he and his brothers would take over the ranch and release them from the work and worry involved.

Except the pickin's in town were slim.

Apart from Sally—who'd snubbed him since the last barn dance when he wouldn't waltz with her and now walked out with that fellow named George at the post office—and the parson's daughter—who looked and snorted like a horse—there were none who captured his attention.

But this woman—no, she was too sophisticated, too mature for him. Likely had a husband and a passel of kids waitin' at home for her.

Still, no harm in lookin'. Long as it wasn't lustfully.

Dark hair framed her oval face, accented by dark eyes, a tiny nose surely too small to breathe through, and a set of bow-shaped lips just beggin' to be—he shook himself. What was he thinkin'? He had no right to imagine kissin' another man's wife. If that man learned of his sensual thoughts, he'd find himself on the losin' end of a thrashin'. And rightly so.

Still, she glided through the store as though borne up by angels.

Even Mr. D seemed transfixed by her appearance. The storekeeper ran a hand over his baldin' head and cleared his throat as he stepped toward the counter, Zeke's order apparently forgotten. "Can I help you, miss?"

"Thank you. I was wondering if you sold women's clothing?"

Mr. Dixon shook his head. "Only small things such as hankies, gloves, and the like. The rest we order through our catalog."

"May I see it?"

Mr. D blinked several times as though she spoke a foreign language. "It?"

"The catalog."

"Oh yes, of course." The storekeeper repeated the process of searchin' for the book, then straightened, his forefinger pressed into his chin. "I know I saw that yesterday."

Zeke stood and crossed the store. "I've got it here, Mr. D."

The old man's face brightened. "Right. Right. Silly me." He looked from Zeke to the young woman and back. "Are you done with it?"

"Not quite, but I don't mind sharin' and lettin' the lady get on with her shoppin'. I'm in no rush." He quirked his chin toward the other chair beside the stove. "Would you care to sit and look for what you need?"

She smiled at him, and his heart skipped a beat. "That's most generous of you, Mister—"

"Zeke. Ezekial Graumann, but my friends call me Zeke."

She nodded. "Well, thank you for including me amongst your circle of friends." She sat in the chair, tuckin' her feet beneath her skirt, and accepted the catalog. "I won't take much time. I know exactly what I need." She studied the cover. "Oh, Bloomingdale's. One of my favorite stores. I've been there many times."

His heart thundered in his ears, drownin' out her words. He should have known. A fine lady like this wasn't from around here. She wasn't likely to stay. She'd go back to New York City and not think of him again.

He'd do best to keep his distance—and his thoughts—far away from this woman.

Now, if he could just convince his head.

CHAPTER 2

"But that's ludicrous. You can't charge me for something that is rightfully mine." Becky drew herself up to her full height—which still only brought her nose even with the second button on the land office agent's shirt—and glared at him. "I have his letters to prove who I am."

The man, who'd introduced himself as Tom Wilkerson when she'd entered the rough-hewn structure passing as the Land and Assay Office, shook his head. "Sorry, miss. I b'lieve you. There's others as wouldn't. But I do." His Adam's apple bobbed with every word. "But your father didn't buy the claim in perpetuity. He bought a lifetime stake only. Means it's up for sale again."

"How much?"

Mr. Wilkerson blinked. "For what?"

"My father's claim."

He licked a forefinger and paged through a ledger book on the board laid across two sawhorses. "Let's see." He met her gaze. "A hundred and fifty dollars."

She peered at the numbers and notations scribbled in the columns. "Says there he paid seventy-five."

"He made improvements."

Did the man think her an idiot? "What kind of improvements?"

"Just the ones required by law. Built himself a shack to live in. Cleared and leveled about half an acre. Stuff like that."

"And you want to charge me for my father's investment?"

"Well, whoever buys the stake won't have to put the extra work and money in. Seems it should be worth somethin'."

Becky drew a breath, wishing she'd thought to delay her trip to the mercantile. If she paid his price, after paying for a few necessities today and her order from the catalog, she'd have less than three dollars left. At least her room was paid for through the end of the week. Still, what would she live on until the claim paid off? "Could I pay half now and the balance over time?"

Mr. Wilkerson snapped the book shut. "I have at least three other prospectors wantin' to buy that claim. I only put them off once I heard you were in town. Out of respect for your late father."

She harrumphed. Respect indeed. *Her* respect for Robbie Campbell was slipping away like sand through her fingers. And as for this money-grubbing land agent—but no amount of name-calling would change the situation. Buy the claim at the atrocious price mentioned, or buy another and take her chances, or return to New York City with her tail between her legs and admit her mother was right.

No, she really only had one choice.

She dug into her reticule and extracted the handful of coins residing inside. Separating three from the bundle, she plunked the balance on the table. Dust motes danced in the air as though celebrating the transaction, but rather than exulting in the moment, Becky swallowed back a lump in her throat.

Mr. Wilkerson stacked the coins as he counted, checking them twice. Several he picked up, studied a moment, and bit down on, checking their authenticity. Apparently satisfied, he returned them to the table.

Then he opened the ledger and made a notation before sliding a sheet of paper toward her. "The certificate of ownership. Lifetime only, mind you." He tapped the document. "On the other side, a rough map of the area shows exactly where the claim lies. Make sure you get the right one. They all look pretty much the same out there."

"And how will I know I have the right one?"

"Hear tell there's a sign over the door of the shack that reads 'The Becky Mae.' That, and if nobody shoots at you, will be all the proof you need."

She blinked back tears. Her ne'er-do-well father had named his mine after her.

Seems he wasn't trying to forget her after all.

Becky strode down the sagging boardwalk, her gaze fixed on Sheriff Fremont, who lounged on a bench outside his office. Her hands clenched into fists, and she rehearsed her scolding. The man would know she was no shrinking violet.

As would half the town by noon, judging by the folks gathered around him. He leaned back against the wall and tipped his hat back on his head. Laughter ran through the group, while a couple of women clapped hands over their little ones' ears and marched them away.

Apparently, not everybody wanted to hear what he had to say.

She waited on the fringe of the crowd, drawing deep breaths to slow her racing heart. Maybe she'd do better to wait until she could speak with him privately. Not that she really cared who overheard what she had to say, but the man had a job to do, and if he didn't hold the respect of the town, that might make lawlessness reign more rampant than it already did.

Then again, his lack of candor might bring the town to ruin anyway.

She shifted from one foot to the other as the sun rose overhead. Her stomach growled, reminding her she skipped lunch to confront him. He seemed in no hurry to conduct his official duties unless entertaining old men and young boys was in his job description.

So unlike the police officers in New York City. Uniformed. Billy clubs in hand keeping time with their steps or rattling along a fence as a warning for minor infractions. Badges and buttons glinting in the sunlight. Highly polished boots a sign of respect for their office.

Not so with this small-town sheriff. Dusty, sharp-toed boots with heels designed for keeping the foot in the stirrup. His tarnished tin badge—perhaps cut from the bottom of a can of peaches or beans—decorating his leather vest. A sweat-stained Stetson covering his chocolate-brown hair. Wrinkles like canyons at the corners of his equally dark eyes.

She pulled her gaze from him when heat ran up her neck. And why would she be thinking about this man in those terms? It wasn't as if she wanted—or needed—a man in her life right now. So far, all the men she met in this town—with the exception of Zeke Graumann and the parson—were nothing but frustration to her.

Including Sheriff Fremont.

She waited another moment, then pushed her way through the remaining handful of onlookers. "Excuse me. Pardon me. I need to speak with the sheriff."

One man stepped in front of her and eyed her up and down. "And I'd like to talk with a pretty filly like you."

She glared at him. "Sir, step aside."

Another man jabbed the first in the shoulder. "Look at that. Now she thinks you's a sir and all."

The first man took a half step closer. The odor of unwashed body, stale cigars, alcohol, and rancid perfume filled her nose. Disgusting. The man thought himself a Lothario when he was nothing more than a cheap womanizer. She jabbed the heel of her shoe into the toe of his boot. "Let me pass."

He howled and bent over to grab his foot, then straightened as she passed, grasping her hand. "Why, you—"

She whirled to face him, but he wasn't there.

She blinked.

What had happened?

The crowd parted like water before the prow of a sailing ship, and she spotted her assaulter sprawled on the ground. Out cold.

And the only man in town apart from the reverend who garnered any favorable thoughts from her stood over him.

Zeke Graumann.

She wasn't certain who she should be most upset with at the moment. The stranger for thinking she was anything but a lady. The sheriff for not doing his job. Or Zeke, for stepping in where he wasn't needed.

Or wanted.

Most of all, not wanted.

There'd been plenty of times in Zeke's life when he'd wished he was somebody else. The oldest son instead of the youngest. Rich instead of rock-hard poor. The King of England rather than the prince of a small, four-section, hardscrabble ranch in southern Colorado.

And this was yet another of those times.

He wished he was standin' alongside Miss Campbell, because that's where he belonged.

Rather than watchin' from a distance to avoid her wrath.

One thing was for sure, though. He was glad he wasn't the sheriff.

He leaned against the railin' outside the lawman's office and listened in on the conversation between the lovely New York City firebrand named Becky Campbell and the man wearin' the badge this week.

Only May, and already Fremont was the third sheriff this year.

Silver Valley wasn't exactly law-abidin'. Or friendly to the law.

Seemed right now Miss Becky appointed herself town spokesperson, the way she rode up one side of the sheriff and down the other, tearin' a strip off him as she went. Occasionally, her victim glanced his way as though askin' for help, but there was no way he was gettin' between this she-cat and her prey.

He crossed his arms and glanced down the street. The stage, pulled by four matched black horses, drew to a halt in front of the mercantile. Wells Fargo on time again today. A body could set his watch by that outfit.

Zeke returned his attention to the conversation goin' on beside him.

Miss Becky shook a finger in the lawman's direction. "Sheriff, I don't need you protecting me from the truth. You should have told me my father was murdered."

"Well, now, miss, we don't have any proof of that."

She planted her hands on her hips. Her very shapely hips. "Did he commit suicide by shooting himself in the back?" She shook another finger at him. "And don't try to deny it. Mr. Wilkerson, the land agent, told me. Let it slip, more like it, judging by how he tried to deter me from coming here and talking to you."

"Likely, he was tryin' to protect your feelin's. Same as me."

"In case you hadn't noticed, I'm no shrinking violet."

"No, miss, you are not."

Zeke snorted. The sheriff got that right.

Miss Campbell stretched up on her toes, the top of her head comin' to the lawman's chin. What might it feel like to hold her in his arms, restin' his chin there on the crown of that soft, dark hair? He jerked his thoughts back to the conversation.

No lustful thoughts.

He was on thin ice.

In May.

She narrowed her eyes at the sheriff. "Did he kill himself?"

At least Fremont had the good grace to drop his gaze and study his hands. "No, miss. I guess he didn't."

"Was it an accident?"

"No proof of that either."

"So why are you sitting here, blathering with idiots and children, instead of out solving his murder?"

"Done what I could. No witnesses. No evidence."

"What about a motive?"

He looked up and blinked at her. "Motive?"

She stomped a foot on the boardwalk. An old hound dog at the far end moaned in his sleep, then turned around and settled down again. "Yes, the reason he was killed."

"Couldn't find one."

She tipped her head to one side. "Maybe somebody wanted his claim."

The sheriff straightened. "Miss Becky, it's been nice palaverin' with you, but I got work to do."

Her top lip lifted in a sneer. "Why do I get the distinct impression you don't want to answer any more questions?"

He shook his head. "Tryin' to be helpful, that's all."

Her shoulders sagged. "Is there anything else you can tell me about my father's death? Who found him?"

"Fella named Wilson. Owns the claim north of his. Came home early one mornin' after a night in town. Said he found your father dead on the ground, starin' up at the sun."

Not a pretty picture to leave the little lady with, of her father dyin' out there all alone. Still, it was a wonder the coyotes or vultures didn't get to him first. A small blessin', Zeke guessed.

"Who paid to bury him?"

Fremont lifted one shoulder and let it drop. "The pastor suggested we take up a collection to buy him a proper coffin and a stone."

"I'll pay them back."

"No need. Folks liked your father. He was a good man. Talked a lot about you. Said as how you were just like your mother."

She huffed. "I am nothing like her."

The sheriff shrugged. "He thought you were. Beautiful. Cultured. Educated. Said you both baffled him. That's the word he used. Baffled. Said you were both too good for him."

"He said that?"

"On my mother's grave."

She turned away, her reticule gripped in one hand while she lifted the edge of her skirt and made her way down the steps. As she passed Zeke, the faint fragrance of lily of the valley met him.

Pink circles highlighted her cheeks, and her bottom lip trembled.

Perhaps the she-cat had a tender side.

Her father.

More importantly, was it what her father had said—or thought—about her?

If so, wouldn't that beat all?

CHAPTER 3

Two weeks later, Zeke wondered if Becky Campbell's father's opinion of her was her only tender spot. Since he'd answered the help wanted ad she'd posted in the mercantile window, the woman had turned into a hard-nosed tyrant.

Findin' help in the small town was no problem. Too many men came west in hopes of strikin' it rich, only to lose their stake in a card game, a shady claim deal, or robbery. For those lucky enough to buy a stake, most lost it within six months for failin' to make the required improvements.

Diggin' for silver required money. Improvements required money. Livin' required money. And a man couldn't dig and build at the same time. Which meant one or the other had to give. Usually the improvements.

Always certain the next pick strike would reveal the motherlode, they kept body and soul together by chewin' hardtack and drinkin' coffee.

But always the profitable veins eluded them.

If not for the couple of hard winters and dry summers, Zeke wouldn't be caught dead workin' in the mines either. But his parents' ranch couldn't support four families—not that he had a wife and children yet—so he sought work elsewhere. With enough money, he could buy water rights for his own section of the ranch. With more water, he could run a bigger herd of beeves. More cattle, more money. Then he could give up this Monday-to-Friday job and work his own land more than just two days a week.

Maybe then he could think about settlin' down. Find himself a woman, have some children. Make his parents proud of him, as his own brothers had already done.

But until then … well, he'd put up with Miss Becky's persnickety ways. Not to say everythin' was wrong about her. He admired her spunk, her drive, and her refusal to back down even when faced with huge odds. What he didn't appreciate was her mule-driver attitude, her sharp tongue, or her scathing looks.

Plus, she couldn't cook.

Although he'd hired on as superintendent for the Becky Mae Mine, in order to keep the men workin' and his stomach from thinkin' his throat was cut, he was also considerin' takin' on the cookin'. Which was women's work as far as he was concerned.

Not that he'd ever say that to his mother. She'd hide him for sure.

Well, at least he only had to face Becky durin' the week.

When he hired on, he told her he'd insist on two days off. At first, he thought she'd kick up a fuss, but after that first week, she simply nodded when he said he'd see her Monday.

Of course, he looked for her in church on Sunday but didn't catch sight of her. When he asked her about that, she said she had plenty to do and not enough time.

Still, cookin' wasn't somethin' she spent much time on, judgin' by the burnt biscuits and skimpy porridge. Or the gravy like wallpaper paste.

In truth, the best part of the weekends was havin' somebody else do the cookin' for him. His mother, appreciative of the spices he purchased and the new kitchen table delivered last week, always made certain his shirt buttons practically popped before he left the table.

When he married, he'd find one just like her. A good cook, able to squeeze a nickel into two dimes, hard-workin' and yet soft and gentle when the time was right. Like with kids. And kittens. And chicks.

And her husband.

Completely unlike Miss Becky Campbell.

The woman was inept when it came to buildin' a fire, cleanin' a fish, or skinnin' a rabbit. Burned boilin' water. Didn't know the difference between poison oak and wild strawberries, as evidenced by the signature rash she scratched for four days. Refused to go behind a bush, insistin' he build her a pit toilet with a small shed for privacy.

No, siree. Miss Becky might be well-suited for city livin', but she was surely out of her element here. Life was hard enough in Silver Valley. He didn't need an encumbrance like her.

In fact, he didn't need any encumbrances at all.

Almost a month after moving in, Becky scratched at the dirt floor of the shack her father built, the broom bristles sending more dust into the air—and her nose and hair—than she could corral. She sighed and swiped the perspiration from her forehead with the back of her hand. Seemed that the number of hours she put in made no difference at all to the cobwebs in the corners, the ragged curtains at the two small windows, or the ashes accumulating in the hearth. She turned at the sound of a horse's hooves walking down her road, then peeked through the curtain.

"Hello. Are you here?"

Zeke!

Riding down her road. To her shack.

She set the broom aside with trembling hands. Work could wait. She stepped outside, knees wobbling. Goodness, the sight of the man shouldn't cause this kind of reaction. She saw him every day of the week. Worked beside him. Fed him. Worried when he went into the mine. Thought about him when he wasn't in sight.

Just like a wife.

She drew a couple of breaths to calm her heart and pushed those thoughts aside. Just because he came by on the weekend meant nothing. Probably looking for a lost cow. Or maybe she'd shorted him in his pay packet.

Or—oh no—he wouldn't quit on her, would he?

She studied his weather-rugged face. Looked for a hint as to why he'd come all the way out here.

Had to be a reason.

And knowing Zeke Graumann, a good reason.

But would it also be good for her? Or bad?

She pasted on a smile and spoke past a mouth filled with cotton. "Hello, Zeke."

He dismounted and stood beside his horse, reins held loosely in his hands. "Looks like you're busy."

She nodded. "Always something to do. Can I help you?"

He tied his horse to the post on the porch, then leaned against the railing. Her breath caught in her throat. He looked almost like he belonged there.

But he didn't. And no amount of wishing would make it true. As much as she needed him to manage the mine and get the work done, he was a cowboy, not a miner.

No matter that he made her feel safe. He was capable, a hard worker—when he set his mind to it and didn't mind taking orders from a woman—but his heart wasn't really here.

He tipped his hat back on his head. "Thought I'd drop by and see if you needed any firewood chopped."

She glanced toward the back of the house. The pile of wood near the back door was low. Barely enough to keep her through the weekend. She gave a brisk nod. "That would be nice."

Nice? Nice was a pretty piece of cloth for curtains. Nice was a hot bath on a cold morning.

A man taking time away from his own business on a weekend was—the man was a saint.

"How much do you need?"

"Enough for laundry and cook fires next week."

He pulled a pair of gloves from a back pocket. "That's reasonable."

Becky sighed and sat in a nearby chair. "Even though the sun doesn't go down until well after supper, and despite the fact I work from sunup to its setting, I never reach the end of my chores."

His Adam's apple worked up and down. "Runnin' a mine takes a lot of time. And energy."

Becky nodded. "And money."

Now, why had she gone and said that? No point in scaring the man away by making him think maybe she couldn't keep paying him and the other two.

She tossed him a smile. "Not that you have to worry about that. I have enough to pay you."

He dropped his gaze, then looked up again. "I'm not worried."

"But you work here during the week to support yourself. I'm sure you could be doing any number of things besides mining." Should she take him into her confidence? She hadn't made any real friends to this point. Perhaps he'd have ideas on how to help. "I'm already a month here, and I haven't turned a profit yet."

He pursed his lips. "I hear some of the men who come to town never make any money. They end up sellin' out and goin' back where they came from. Compared to them, you're already a success."

Becky sighed. "If that is their definition of success, I want nothing to do with it. My back still isn't accustomed to—" She would not mention her bed. "Standing over a laundry tub. And my nose isn't used to the dust that's in the air all the time."

He climbed the steps, and for a moment she thought he'd sit with her. His eyes roved between her, the front door, and the empty chair. Then a slight shake of his head, and he stepped off the porch and disappeared around the corner.

She chided herself. Talking too much. She'd scared him away with her problems. Men didn't want women with troubles. They wanted women who were sweet, pliable, good cooks.

And she was none of those things.

And likely never would be.

Becky ducked inside and hurried through to the rear of the

cabin, where the thuds of the axe indicated his offer was already in action. When she reached the doorway, she froze.

He'd tossed his shirt on the laundry tub and now bent over the chopping block, axe raised in the air, long-john shirtsleeves rolled above his elbows. Muscular forearms rippled like waves on the water as he wielded the tool. Efficient movements belied the effort it took to cleave the wood, making it look as though he cut butter with a hot knife.

No doubt about it, he was a fine specimen of a man.

While she stood there, silent, twisting her apron into knots, he split the lengths of firewood and stacked them beside the cabin in neat, criss-cross bundles of four. Feeling guilty about her lack of contribution, she snuck inside and put on coffee. The least she could do was offer him something to drink when he was done.

When the chopping sounds ended, she poured a cup and headed to the back stoop. A stack of wood as high as her waist—more than enough for a couple of weeks—and a box of kindling resided where before there were but a handful of twigs and even less wood.

But no Zeke. What was he up to? Resting on the bench against the back of the cabin, shaded by the overhanging roof? No.

She gazed around the yard, pausing at the chicken roost.

He looked toward her, a basket in one hand and a watering can in the other. "You feed and water them today?"

No, she hadn't. Her shoulders slumped. So much to do and so little time.

"Thought so. That's what they were a-tellin' me."

She caught the grin in his voice. She straightened her shoulders and stuck out her chin. "So now you speak chicken, do you?"

"And cow. Dog. Some mule. Horse, though, is my first language." Zeke exited the wire enclosure and set aside the water and basket of grain. He quirked his chin toward her. "That coffee for me, by chance?"

"Yes." She held it up, nodding at the open door behind her. "Why don't you come in and rest a moment?"

"Don't mind if I do."

When he brushed past her on the threshold, heat rushed up her neck. As he accepted the mug with thanks, she attempted to downplay her reaction with a teasing tone. "Thanks for tending to my chores. Do you do laundry too?"

"Not me. That's women's—" He froze, the tips of his ears red. "What I mean is—"

"This is another one of those times when I regret I'm only a woman." She tossed him a half smile. "Then I could spend my time as I like." She studied his face, looking for a sneer, something—anything—that would indicate he really didn't mean what he'd started to say.

Otherwise …

He dropped his gaze. "Stupid. That was just plain stupid of me. I apologize."

He sounded genuine. He looked contrite. Still blushing, which, in her experience, few men did. So why did the words hurt so much?

Perhaps because her mother often reminded her of a woman's place in society. Dutiful wife. Nurturing mother. Keeping the house until her husband returned.

Becky swallowed hard. Except, in her mother's case, that wouldn't happen.

Zeke Graumann was a good man. But her father had been one also. And even though Zeke filled her doorway like a knight in shining armor, there was no way she'd let him into her heart.

She didn't need the pain his leaving would cause.

He set his tin cup on the table. "Mind if I sit?"

Becky nodded, granting him a measure of grace. "Although, if my father heard what you said …"

Zeke's smile slipped away. "I knew your father. Liked him. He never backed down from a fight."

From the doorway, she surveyed the area around her shack before turning inside, allowing an admission with the sag of her shoulders. "Sometimes I feel ill-suited for this life I've chosen. I don't know if I am strong enough to continue his dream."

"Things will get better."

Becky shook her head. "I don't know anything about surviving in this place. And now I have you and Miguel and Dakota depending on me. Supplies are expensive, and money disappears before it's earned. So far, you've managed to pull just enough silver from the mine to pay your wages and expenses, with a few pennies put aside each week. After a month, I've saved a grand total of fourteen cents." A broad sweep of her hands indicated the cabin and property—and her frustration level. "Not much for all the time and work I've put in."

"No, but that's not why you came here, is it?"

She turned to face him again. Had he looked into her soul? How else would he know why she'd traveled well over a thousand miles to get here? Or why she stayed when everything in her screamed for her to leave.

Was he laughing at her? She didn't see any evidence of mocking. The creases around his eyes refused interpretation. And his mouth didn't lift at the corners.

"No. And it's not why I stay." She tipped her head to one side. "So why do you keep working for me? And why do the other two stay? It's surely not my cooking."

Now his lips turned up. "If you asked them, they might say your cookin' is punishment for their bad deeds."

"Well, I appreciate them putting up with it." Becky pressed her lips together and stood with her back to the sink for a moment, collecting her thoughts. "My father said hard work and determination are always in short supply."

"I'd say he was right."

She exhaled. "I just wish he hadn't always been so right about the hard things and so wrong about the dreams and fancies he set his mind to."

"Like strikin' it rich in Colorado?"

She nodded. "Like saying he'd send for us when he made his fortune. Like filling my head with grand ideas of adventures and excitement." She pressed a hand into the small of her back. "There's nothing fun or fancy about this rugged terrain or the hard men who would kill one another over a dull yellow or silver vein in a rock."

He nodded. "You're right. It is a hard life. And not ever'body is a saint."

"You can say that again."

Zeke held up a finger, redirecting her. "But there are plenty of good ones. Your father was one of them. He saw the potential not only in this land but also in the people."

She gave a sad smile. "Sometimes I think he was blind to their faults."

"Sometimes. But he talked about you and your ma a lot. Wanted to share this place with you."

Becky swallowed hard, tears blurring her vision. "He did?"

"Sure. Said how he was savin' to send you money for train tickets."

She gulped. "Why did he wait? Mother had money. She didn't need his."

"Maybe that's why. He wanted this to be his gift to you both. Not hers." He reached toward her. "He deserved better than the end he got."

"He did."

She tore her gaze away. What was it about Zeke that made her tears threaten so easily? That dissolved her feelings of unworthiness and replaced them with images of hope?

As painful as the conversation was, though, some good came of it.

She'd do what the law couldn't.

Find the man who'd killed her father.

An hour later, Becky stepped through the open doorway of the mercantile. She slipped off her hat and stained gloves, tucking them into her shopping basket. Although it was still early in the year, the sun shone brighter and hotter here than it would in May in New York. She paused a moment to allow her eyes to adjust.

In the dry goods section, Mr. Dixon measured out a length of pale blue paisley for a woman she didn't know. Two children hovered near the jars of peppermints and honey sticks as an older woman behind the counter kept an eye on them.

Becky nodded in her direction. "Mrs. Dixon."

A smile relaxed the wrinkles in the woman's brow. "Good day. Miss Becky, isn't it?"

"Yes, ma'am."

Mrs. Dixon turned to another clerk organizing ladies' gloves in a case. "Sally, why don't you help Miss Becky here while I keep an eye on these imps." She waggled a finger at the two boys. "If you behave, perhaps I'll let you choose a candy."

The younger of the pair shoved his hands in his pants pockets. "Behavin', ma'am. We's behavin'."

Sally sidled down the length of the counter. An apron covered her blue cotton day dress, the cuffs slightly frayed. Her red hair, bundled into a now-untidy bun at the nape of her neck, suggested an Irish heritage. "Hello. I'm Sally Matheson. You're new in town."

"Yes, I am. Becky. Becky Campbell." She glanced at the woman and her children. "Their mother has her hands full."

Sally smiled. "Sure does. 'Specially since she has three more younger'n them at home. Thankfully, she also has an older girl who helps out."

Life could be demanding in other ways, Becky supposed. If others could survive, she could too. "Six children. The woman likely never has a moment to herself."

"It's the way things are out here."

She slid her list across the counter. "I can pay for some of this, but I was wondering ..."

Sally picked up the note. "Let's see what it comes to, then Mr. Dixon can figure how to handle it. He carries an account for most ever'body in town."

"He's very trusting."

"Says he's here to help folks. And I guess the good Lord pays his bills for him. Least, that's what he always says." She pushed the paper back. "Best you read that list out to me. Can't read nor write."

Becky couldn't imagine not being able to enjoy a good book or pen a letter—not that she'd had time to do either in her time here. In fact, she owed her mother at least a note to let her know she'd arrived safely. And to tell her of her husband's demise.

She swallowed back the dread of the onerous task and focused on the needs of the present. "Bacon. About a pound, please. A small ham if you have one. Some sugar, coffee, and flour."

While Sally scurried off to fill her order, Becky wandered around the shop. She ran a hand over the bolt of fabric from which the children's mother had made her purchase. If she had the money, she'd buy a length of that for herself. She held the material in front of her. Would that color look pretty on her?

Would Zeke notice?

She tucked the length back into the bolt and returned it to the shelf. She had no money—or time—for such a luxury.

And what Mr. Zeke Graumann—or any other man—thought of her clothes was of no importance to her.

She paused near the stove, where catalogs rested on a chair. Her cheeks heated at her naiveté of just four weeks before, when the world had seemed to settle itself around her. She'd ordered more than she could pay for, hoping to bring civilization to this rough-and-tumble world.

Her eyes roved the shelves behind the counter, then paused on a pale pink shirtwaist.

Exactly like the one she'd chosen.

Exactly like the one from the catalog order Mr. Dixon had said he'd canceled. Thankfully, he understood her predicament. Perhaps when the mine turned a profit—whenever that was—she'd come in and purchase the item.

If it was still there.

"Next?"

Becky turned to where Sally accumulated her purchases. "I think the last things are writing paper and a couple of envelopes."

Sally fetched the items, stroking the paper with one hand as she set it on the counter. "I surely wish I could read 'n' write." She tapped the sheet. "Who you sendin' a letter to?"

"My mother. She'll worry unless I let her know I arrived safely."

"My ma isn't worried about me, I'm sure."

An ache grew in Becky's chest at the thought of this delightful young woman not having someone to care for her. "Where are you from?"

"New York City. Not that I was born there. I was born in Buffalo, but my parents lost their farm, and we moved to the city. They're both in service. And that's what they had in mind for me too. Marryin' a groundskeeper."

Becky's heart leapt like a calf released in the spring. "I'm from New York City."

Sally leaned closer. "I was dead tired of being poor. Couldn't see nothin' ahead of me but more of the same."

"I actually came here to live with my father."

Sally's eyes misted over. "Right. I 'member that. Sorry for your loss."

Having lived without her father most of her life left a surprisingly small hole in her heart. What did hurt was not knowing why he really left her. "How did you end up in Silver Valley?"

Another shrug. "Worked a little here, a little there." Her brow drew down. "Only honest work, mind you. Met up with a family headin' west whose woman died, and the pa needed help with the young'uns. He decided Denver was far enough for him." She crossed her arms over her chest. "Not me. So I hired on as cook with another train comin' down here. Lots of men thinkin' they're gonna strike it rich in gold. But that ran out real quick. And silver takes just as much work for only ten cents on a gold dollar."

Guilt crept up Becky's spine like a spider in a web. She wasn't a man, but her father was one of those looking for a get-rich-quick opportunity, and hadn't she followed him out here for the same reason?

No, not quite. She'd have lived in a tent with him, mud to her knees and not two bits to rub together, just for the privilege of being near him.

The silver? A side benefit.

Mrs. Dixon sidled up beside Sally. "Did you get everything on your list, Miss Becky?"

Responding to the not-so-subtle hint to move along, Becky offered the older woman a smile. "I think so, Mrs. Dixon. Thank you."

A quick look tossed at Sally, and Mrs. D shifted away to greet another customer.

Sally giggled behind her hand. "She's mighty nice, but she likes to get her money's worth. If you know what I mean."

Becky, being much the same herself, understood. "I'd best let you get back to your work."

"Sure nice to meet you. The other women in town are either married or workin' at the saloon. The one worries I'll try to steal their husband, and the other worries I might give away for free what they're tryin' to sell."

Heat raced up Becky's cheeks. Would she ever grow accustomed to the rough lifestyle in the West? Such matters would never be discussed in New York.

Then again, perhaps a little honesty was refreshing for a change. Unlike those in high society who smiled to her face and talked about her behind her back. In her opinion, so-called breeding counted for little when it came to the value of a person.

Take Sally, for example. Helpful. Cheerful. Compassionate. Yet most of her own acquaintances in New York City—including her mother—would snub their noses at her because she wasn't of the right class.

Sally placed Becky's purchases deep in the recesses of a flour sack, then tallied the cost. "That will be a dollar and fourteen cents. How much do you have?"

"Four bits."

"I'll get Mr. Dixon to come over." She waved a hand in the owner's direction. He nodded and gestured that he'd be over presently. Sally handed her the sack. "He won't be but a minute. Do you have a beau?"

"N-no. I've only been here a month."

Sally waved off her words. "There are five men to every woman, and like I said, few single or of the marryin' kind. You'll have men fallin' at your feet in no time. Me, I'm courtin' George Newman. He's the postmaster's assistant. We've been talkin' about gettin' hitched, maybe in July." She touched her lips with an index finger. "He hasn't asked official-like, so it's still a secret. But I'd sure like my mother to know about him. So's if we do wed, it won't be such a surprise."

"That's nice, thinking of your mother's feelings."

Sally nodded. "Sure. And if'n I sent her a letter, broke the news to her gentle-like, I'm hopin' she could find a way to come to the weddin'."

"I would certainly think she'd want to see her daughter married to a nice man."

Sally gave a dramatic sigh and fixed Becky with a bright, hopeful, slightly teasing stare. "Then I need someone who can help me write her a letter."

"I will. I mean, if you trust me. You don't even know me."

Her new friend tipped her head to one side, her ringlets lying across one shoulder. "Know you? Sure, I know you. You live here in town, don't you? And what do you mean by 'trust you'?"

Impressed that Sally wouldn't look for an ulterior motive in her offer, Becky tapped the page. "To say things the way you want them said. Of course, you could always send a telegram."

"Well, it would get there quicker, but I do like the idea of givin' more detail in a letter. Seems like it would come across better."

Becky did a quick calculation in her head. "We have time, I think, so long as we do it soon."

"How about tomorrow after church?"

Becky swallowed hard. Church. Definitely not in her plans. She'd hoped for a quiet day to herself before the miners returned in the evening. She had no desire to waste time singing and praying to a God who wasn't listening to anything she had to say.

But now, between church in the morning and then writing the letter, her offer had turned into an all-day affair.

Apparently, her new friend took her silence as agreement, for Sally clasped Becky's hands. "Oh, that would be so fine. I know George would love to meet you. His boss always invites us over for dinner after service."

Ah, the excuse she needed not to put in an appearance at all. "I couldn't simply show up uninvited."

But her friend would not hear of it. "No worries. Half the church will be there. One more makes no difference."

Becky sighed. There was no getting out of it. She wanted to help her new friend write her letter. It was important to Sally, so it was important to her.

And she'd attend church.

But that didn't mean she had to enjoy it.

CHAPTER 4

Becky exhaled as she stepped outside the church. Well, that wasn't as bad as she'd feared. Every seat had been filled. She'd thought the morals of a mining town would be reflected in its church attendance. Apparently not.

Even Miguel and Dakota, who never expressed any particular religious fervor, joined in singing loudly and somewhat off-key about sinners coming home. And Mrs. Dixon, despite the fact she didn't like Sally lollygagging with customers, sang a lovely soprano part for the hymn about gathering at the river.

Although what any of these songs had to do with fire and brimstone—the only kind of preaching Becky recalled from her few childhood visits inside the house of God—she couldn't figure out. In fact, the preacher spoke kindly about God's plan for mankind—and womankind, too, apparently.

She hovered near the door, waiting for Sally and George, but the press of the crowd forced her into the yard.

A man pushed past, jostling her, and her ankle turned on a rock. Pain shot up her leg, and she thrust her hands in front of her, anticipating a fall.

How humiliating.

A strong hand gripped her elbow, and she accepted the offer of help gladly. Once she righted herself, she peered up.

Straight into the smiling face of none other than Zeke Graumann.

She narrowed her eyes. He looked like the cat that just swallowed the canary. A very handsome cat. And she the little yellow bird.

She released his arm. "Thank you, sir."

He doffed his hat. "Always pleased to assist a lady in distress."

She gritted her teeth. She was not in distress. She was simply pushed and almost twisted her ankle by an inconsiderate lout without a thought for anybody but himself.

Sally stepped up beside her. "I saw that man bump you. That wasn't very nice." She smiled at Zeke. "Why, you're one of the Graumann boys, aren't you?"

He nodded. "That I am. Nice to see you again, Miss …"

"Sally Matheson. I clerk at the mercantile. Do you have plans for dinner, Mr. Graumann? We're goin' to Mr. Porter's, and I know he wouldn't mind one more."

Becky sighed. Sally was a nice girl, but much too forward. Inviting a man she'd barely met to dinner was—well, it simply wasn't done.

He smiled. "Mr. Graumann is my father. I'm Zeke. And yes, I do have plans. I hoped to invite Miss Becky here to join me and my family. But I see she already has a prior engagement, so excuse me."

When he turned and headed for his horse, Becky grabbed Sally's arm. "Really, Sally. You don't even know the man."

"I know his family. That's all that matters—although he wouldn't give me the time of day at a barn dance once. Anyway, we don't stand on formal introductions and the like." She jabbed an elbow into Becky's ribs. "Besides, I was doin' you a favor. I saw how he was studyin' you in church, out of the corner of his eye and all. And how your cheeks turned pink when you saw him."

"They did not."

"Sure did. He was hoverin' so close behind you all the way out of church, I thought he was your new shadow. And you should have gone with him. He'd be a good catch."

Becky frowned at her new friend, although no real anger stirred behind the expression. "I am not fishing for a man. Despite what you might think."

"Just sayin', is all. He's got manners. And land. And he works hard."

"Yes, I know all that."

"So why wouldn't you choose him?"

Becky sighed. "Sally, it shouldn't be that way."

"Why not?"

"A woman shouldn't decide who courts her based on his assets or his manners. I certainly don't want a man to marry me because of my money."

"That's fine if you got money. You got choices." Sally blinked a couple of times. "What else is there? If he has manners, he likely won't beat you. And if he has money or land, you won't want for anythin'."

"What about love?"

Sally peered at her, then burst into laughter. "You're joshin' me, right? Why, love comes later. You can't choose a man based on love. You grow into that together." She looped her arm through Becky's. "You got a lot to learn about men and women."

Becky allowed her friend to pull her toward the postmaster's house as she considered her words. Is that why she'd never felt that strong pull of attraction to a man before? Because she looked for love before its time?

But hadn't her father told her that he fell in love with her mother the first time they met?

Then again, her parents weren't exactly the best example of a strong marriage, were they?

Maybe Sally was right. Make a match first, and let love grow in time. After all, weren't security and shared goals more important?

Her head said yes, but her heart wanted to continue the debate.

An hour later, Zeke passed the bowl of mashed potatoes to his brother and accepted the gravy from his father. As usual, his mother's cookin' was excellent. And plenty of it.

So why did his mind keep wanderin' back to the postmaster's meal? Were they eatin' chicken or beef? Carrots or turnips? Or both?

And did Miss Becky cut her food with her knife or her fork?

He stabbed another hunk of beef and shoved it into his mouth, hopin' to distract his thinkin' from the pretty woman. He chewed, relishin' the smokehouse flavors, grateful for the tenderness of the aged beef.

Otherwise, he was so distracted he might have chomped down on his tongue.

His sister-in-law kicked him under the table. "Are you feelin' ill, Zeke? Usually, by this time, you'd be workin' on dessert."

Heat rushed up his neck. "I'm fine. Thought I'd take my time is all."

"She's right." His father punched his arm. "You'd be three helpin's in and thinkin' about leftovers. You feelin' all right?"

His mother cleared her throat softly. "Leave the boy be. Maybe he has something on his mind." She eyed him down the length of the hand-hewn table. "Or some*body*."

Chuckles and giggles from his sisters and sisters-in-law. He pushed back his chair and stood. "Think I'll get me some dessert and take it outside where a man can have some peace."

More laughter followed him as he left the room and headed for the kitchen, where he set his plate on the sideboard and hacked off a slab of still-warm chocolate cake, his favorite. Food at the mine was scarce and meager, and his mother knew it. She complained he worked himself to the bone, but the truth was, Zeke wanted to make certain Miss Becky ate enough too.

He wouldn't overindulge to her detriment.

In fact, his idea about cuttin' his own wages to leave her enough to run her crew of diggers just expanded to eliminatin' his pay. She'd never notice. The plan to keep his own spread afloat by workin' this other job wouldn't exactly pan out if he did, but he could see no other alternative. If things didn't pick up at the mine, he'd either have to quit or start puttin' in his own money so she could at least break even. Showin' a profit was likely a pipe dream. Isn't that what they called it in those dens of iniquities he read about in them penny dreadfuls?

Because he worried that if she didn't soon make some money, she'd sell the mine. Or leave.

And despite his protests against his family's insinuations that he might have somebody on his mind, they were spot on.

One woman.

One Becky Campbell.

So different from just a few weeks before. Back then, even a fool could have seen she found nothin' in him of interest to her. In fact, if he'd been sensible about the entire matter, he'd have hightailed it back to his spread like a flash of lightnin'. She'd had nothin' but contempt for him. And distrust.

He'd seen it in her eyes every time she caught sight of him.

He'd heard it in her voice every time she gave him another order.

He'd recognized it when she stiffened every time he came near.

No, siree, two weeks ago he'd have sworn on a stack of Bibles that Becky Campbell wasn't the woman for him.

Why, she'd have kept air from him if she could.

But that was then, and this was now.

That talk they had gave him hope she might like him a little. Trust him a mite. Not mind so much spendin' time with him.

He sank into the rocker on the front porch and forked cake into his mouth, wishin' he'd stopped to pour himself a cup of coffee or even a glass of cold buttermilk from the spring behind the house. But instead of enjoyin' the treat, it turned to sawdust in his mouth.

Much like everythin' he did lately that didn't include Becky Campbell.

He mentally shook himself.

Wise up, Graumann. She's too good for you. She doesn't want a cowboy. And doesn't need you. Even today, she couldn't get away fast enough.

Double Jeopardy

His head knew the truth.
Now, to convince his heart.

CHAPTER 5

After dinner, despite her desire to return to her shack and sleep the afternoon away, Becky sank onto the edge of Sally's cot behind the mercantile. "Are you ready?"

Her new friend exhaled as she paced the room, twirling an errant lock of hair into curls around her finger. "As I'll ever be."

Becky recognized the trembling hands and shining eyes as something more than mere nerves. The evening before, George, the postmaster's assistant, had proposed marriage. And Sally had accepted.

According to Sally's account, it was the most romantic proposal ever and had included a long walk in the woods, a blanket spread on the ground near the lake, a full moon, and fresh flowers in a canning jar.

Sounded wonderful.

Becky patted the mattress. "Sit. You're making me positively dizzy."

Sally tossed her a smile. "Sorry." She sat on the bed with her knees drawn up and faced Becky. "Now, what should I say?"

Becky considered her own letter—as yet unwritten—to her mother. That was the question, wasn't it? What to say?

Sally surely didn't need to tell her mother about the hardships of life in a silver town. Or the rough men and rougher women who lived here. Or the arduous journey across country.

In her own case, she needed to disclose her father's death, but in a way that wouldn't shock her mother into a relapse. Matilda Campbell's heart hadn't been strong for several years. In fact, many times her mother had implied she'd gotten worse because of her husband's long absences. Which she always mentioned in her letters to him. And upon his rare returns.

And her daughter's decision to follow in his footsteps likely hadn't lessened her mother's medical issues. Had she truly been selfish, as her mother had implied, by not putting her mother first? Thinking only of her own dreams?

Tears pricked Becky's eyes, and she swallowed hard past the lump in her throat. Perhaps she was exactly like her father. Which, if someone else said that to her under other circumstances, would have thrilled her.

But not when put into the context of killing her mother slowly.

She shook off her morbid thoughts and returned to the issue of Sally's letter. She pulled a sheet of writing paper from her bag along with an inkwell, which she placed on the wide window sill, and her father's pen. Not one of those new metal ones, cold to the touch, but a hand-carved version her father had brought from one of his many trips. Warm. Fit her hand perfectly. Alive, as though eager to record her words.

"You'll need somethin' to write on." With an eager expression, Sally hurried to her side with a big, black book. "This is a Bible Pastor said I could give you, seein' as how you can read. For now, you can use it to bear down on."

"Oh … thank you." Becky smoothed the pages of the expensive leather book, touched by her friend's thoughtfulness. Good reader or not, she'd hardly know where to start in such a thick tome. And Sally was sure to ask about her progress. But she could worry about that later. Becky took a deep breath. "Let's start with 'Dear Mother.'"

Sally shook her head. "Cain't say that. She'll know somethin's up. Never called her nothin' but 'Ma' all my life. And 'Pa.'"

"Okay. 'Dear Ma and Pa.'"

"No. Stick with 'Dear Ma.' I don't partic'larly want him to know what's goin' on with me."

"Sounds like you and your pa don't get along."

Sally shook her head, vigorously this time. "He's a bad man. Mean as the dickens. 'Nuff said." She gestured to the paper. "Just sendin' this to my mother."

She scribbled the words. "'Dear Ma.' All right. Stop pacing and tell me what next."

"Tell her you're writin' for me. Don't want her to think I got myself all educated. Might make her feel small, you know?"

Becky scratched at the sheet of paper propped on the Bible in her lap. "'Dear Ma. A friend is writing this letter for me.'" She looked up and dipped her pen again in the ink bottle. "Probably you should say something about being well and happy and having steady work."

Sally leaned toward her. "Oh, that's good. Tell her about how good the Dixons are to me. And that they let me live here so I can save my money." She froze. "Reminds me. I want to send Ma money for the ticket to come to the weddin'. That'll be all right, don't you think?"

"I think that's a great idea."

Becky's mind cast to her own mother as she wrote what Sally wanted. Mother would love to hear *she* was getting married. Maybe not to anybody who lived in this town, unless it was the banker's son. Somebody respectable, although she wasn't certain even Carl Schmidt would qualify as suitable husband material for Matilda Campbell's only daughter.

After all, he was a big fish in a tiny little pond.

However, Master Schmidt was only twelve, so her mother had no concerns in that area.

"Got the bit about your job. What now?"

"Go ahead and tell her I'm gettin' married, and I want her to come out here."

How would her own mother react to receiving such unexpected news in a letter? "Let's tell her about George and what a wonderful man he is. How happy he makes you. How well he treats you. Then break the news about your wedding."

Sally nodded. "That sounds fine."

After several minutes, she straightened and waved the paper—now covered on both sides with Sally's words. "Let's see what you think."

She read the letter, then nibbled her lip while Sally paced the room again, hatching the remainder of her missive under her breath. Becky used the lull to her advantage. Perhaps she could share some news that would cheer her own mother's heart as surely as this engagement announcement would please Sally's mother. Nothing as dramatic as a wedding or even an engagement, of course. Such words would likely give her mother a conniption fit.

Or worse.

Sally stopped pacing and turned to her. "What about your mother?"

"What about her?"

"You haven't said much. Is she nice?"

Is she nice?

"In her own way. And by her own definition."

"Was it hard to leave her?"

Becky nodded. "Mother often complains of dizziness, clamminess, or her heart even sometimes skipping a beat. More than once, I wondered if she merely sought attention. Or used the symptoms to get me to do something I didn't want to do. But the doctors said that wasn't the case."

Sally's eyes widened. "So your ma is sick?"

"She is."

"I'm so sorry." Sally patted Becky's shoulder. "I'll pray for her."

Becky smiled. "Thank you." She glanced at the letter. "We have a little room left. Do you want to say anything else?"

"Tell her I have ten dollars to pay for her travel. And tell her to take the train to Chicago, then to Denver, and then here."

Becky wrote the instructions. She blew on the ink to make it dry more quickly. "Anything else?"

"We need to tell her when the weddin' is. And that I'll be so excited if she can come. But I understand if she can't." Sally planted a forefinger on her chin. "How long will it take for her to get the letter, do you think?"

Becky wallowed on the soft feather mattress, untangling her skirts from around her legs. Sally pulled her to her feet, and they both giggled.

A voice called from downstairs. Mrs. D. "What are you two gettin' into up there?"

"Nothin', Mrs. D." Sally laid a forefinger across her lips. "They like to nap on Sunday afternoons. It's their only day off."

"Then we'll finish and leave them be." Becky brushed down her skirts and picked up her reticule from the bed. "Let's say it takes a month. And then a month for her to travel here. So you should set a date in July, as you were thinking."

"How's about a Sunday?" Sally scrunched up her face in thought. "Maybe after church so's folks will already be there?"

"That's a very considerate plan."

Sally hopped in place like a child. "Let's go talk to the pastor now and make sure it's fine with him."

Becky smiled at her friend's enthusiasm. "Should you discuss this with your George first?"

Sally waved off the suggestion. "If'n he had his way, we'd wed tomorrow. But I said I must have my ma here. He'll complain it's too much of a wait, but we'll just have to make do." She sighed. "It is a mighty long time. Heavens, a cat could have kittens in the same length of time." She held out a hand. "Comin' with me?"

Becky nodded, and in less time than it took to boil a kettle for tea, the date was written on the pastor's calendar. July eighteenth. Which she would add in a postscript to the bottom of Sally's letter.

Sally hugged her when Becky stood at the end of the road to head back to her own home, Sally's letter in her pocket. "Thanks for all you did. And for the envelope. Here's the three cents for the stamp."

Becky dropped the coins into her bag. "I enjoyed spending the day with you."

Her words surprised her—because they were true. While just yesterday she rued agreeing to help her friend, in truth, the time had passed quickly.

"I sure had a good time too. Now, off to home with you to write your own letter. I'm sure you have lots to share with your mother. The weekly stage leaves tomorrow morning, so no dilly-dallying."

As Becky headed back to the claim, she pondered Sally's words.

Yes, she had much news.

The question was, how much could her mother take?

The next morning, in her own little shack, Becky stared at the almost-blank sheet of paper before her. She hadn't gotten any further than *Dearest Mother*.

She straightened and sighed, rolling her shoulders and bending her neck from side to side. If she didn't get this task completed soon, she'd end up a hunchback.

And at the very least, she had to get back to town to make certain Sally's letter left Silver Valley on the stage today, or Mrs. Matheson might not make it to the wedding on time.

She turned her attention back to the paper. Maybe she should simply start the way she had with Sally's letter. Tell her mother she'd arrived safely. Share a few stories of the train and stage travel. Her first impressions—the positive ones, of course—about Silver Valley.

She scribbled a few sentences, then sat back again, chewing on the end of her fountain pen. Too much white space stared at her. She tried to put herself in her mother's place. What would Mother want to hear from her only daughter? That she was happy? Contented? Fulfilled? Meeting plenty of society young ladies?

Becky snorted. That she was miserable and catching the next stage home. To please send money for her return ticket. Because none of those other things were likely to happen in this town. There wasn't much society to speak of, and what little there was certainly didn't recognize her as their equal. And why should they? She'd traded in her bustles and parasols for sensible walking shoes and simple day dresses. Two, to be exact. One now faded by hard work and harder washings. The other kept for church and shopping trips to town. She didn't attend the women's groups or social functions. Didn't have money to put into the collection plate at church. Her face sported a fresh sunburn, and her chapped hands defied her multiple slatherings of lard and honey lotion.

In fact, just the other day, watching Zeke working, she'd envied him his open-necked shirt and dungarees. Wondered how the material would feel against her bare skin without the three layers of unmentionables required beneath dresses.

Perhaps she would order a pair and try them on. In secret.

She sighed. What next? A line or two about the general store, the Bloomingdale's catalog—no mention of her inability to order more than the two items she'd already received—and perhaps a few words about the church and the parson. That sounded good.

Not that she'd been a regular attender in New York, her mother never having expressed religious fervor, saying she preferred to worship God in her own way and to allow her only child to do the same.

Perhaps she should tone down her enthusiasm so as to not completely shock her mother. So far, she'd only attended the one time, but words from the sermon from the previous day echoed in her mind. The pastor had taught from a verse in the book of Psalms about not trusting in riches. Is that what she was doing? Was that the mistake her father had made? Thinking money would be the answer to all his problems? Maybe she'd go again. Even if God wasn't interested in her, she might learn something.

She rearranged the inkwell on the desk. Of course, she didn't trust in riches. She had none of her own. And wanted no part of her mother's family wealth. No, she needed to make her mark through her efforts.

Just like her father.

She hesitated. Was that what had caused the distance between her parents? Most people looking at their family from the outside would have surmised they were the happiest of people. No worries over money. High social standing. A grand home. Servants galore.

Yet her father, over and over again, had left those cushiony surroundings and headed off into rugged and often dangerous terrain. First, there was his scheme to make his fame and fortune by photographing the Wild West. Then he managed to convince a museum in Philadelphia that he knew enough about indigenous peoples to be included in a tour of Africa, where he almost lost his head to a tribe of bushmen.

She sighed again. From as far back as she could remember, about every year or so, he'd set off on another hare-brained, get-rich-quick scheme. Always trying to prove himself to her mother.

And never quite measuring up.

Take this final trip, for instance. A silver mine in Colorado, when the only thing he knew about mining was what he read in a book or gleaned from some chance meeting at a local pub.

Becky swiped at a stray tendril escaping from the knot she'd twisted earlier in the morning, then straightened her shoulders. If she was to survive in this rough-and-tumble part of the country, she must be as strong as her father.

No, stronger.

She resumed her letter, speaking aloud as she wrote. "I am quite contented here in Colorado, although the work is hard and the rewards will likely be a long time coming. However, I've learned that money is not my only goal. I will consider myself a success if I can pay my employees, meet my own needs, and put aside a little for reinvestment."

Becky started a new paragraph. "I have made a life here for myself and made a few friends." Her heart lightened at the thought of Sally and of celebrating her friend's wedding soon. And Zeke?

Could she call him a friend? She hoped so. But best not to mention him right now. No point in her mother getting the wrong idea. "My home is a small shack Papa built. It's not overly large but is snug and warm. Soon I will buy material to replace the curtains." She glanced at the stove in the corner, a recent Saturday project. "You can even tell Cook that I managed to get most of the rust off a wood stove that I use for cooking, boiling water, and for heat on cooler nights. Thankfully, I haven't needed it often, as the weather here has been temperate."

There, those small domestic tidbits should please her mother. Although she'd likely be horrified at the idea that Becky might actually pick up a needle and thread and sew the material herself. Or cook. Or scrub the stove. Not that she couldn't. But women in New York society simply did not sew clothing or curtains. Instead, they frittered their hours away on yet another needlepoint cushion cover or a cross-stitch sampler.

She smiled, wondering how many covers or samplers she could count in Silver Valley.

Not many, she'd wager.

The sound of horseshoes clinking on the rock outside drew her attention as she signed off her letter: "Your loving daughter."

No need for her name. Matilda Campbell had but one daughter.

Zeke called through the open window. "I'm goin' to town to buy a new pickaxe. The old one just busted into about ten pieces. Need anythin'?"

She folded the letter, then rose and went to the door. He sat on his best horse, the saddle leather and metal parts shining in the early sun. Strong legs, long as the day, gripped the animal's sides. Her eyes roved up his length. Narrow waist. Broad chest. Homespun shirt brightened by a red kerchief. A mop of blond hair covered by his Western hat. Pure cowboy.

The sight of the man sent her heart beating faster.

Must be the altitude.

"Yes, I have a couple of letters. Could you mail them for me?"

"Sure. But I have to leave right away. The men are waitin' for me to get back so they can keep on diggin'."

"One minute." She hurried inside, tucked the letters into the envelopes, and returned. "Here they are. And the money for postage."

When she dropped the six cents into his hand, her fingers touched his palm, and a shiver ran up her arm. She snatched her hand back, heat racing to her face.

Thank goodness she hadn't mentioned Zeke to her mother. Even though he was easy on the eyes, there was no future for her and the cowboy. She might as well get that straight right now.

She was pure city, born and bred.

And he wasn't.

And never would be.

CHAPTER 6

Tuesday, just after noon, deep inside the mine, surrounded by darkness that the oil lantern barely pushed back, Zeke grunted when his shovel hit yet another rock. He swiped at the sweat runnin' down his forehead, threatenin' to blind him, leavin' a chalky gray streak on the back of his hand. His shirt clung to the small of his back and under his arms, and his tongue stuck to the roof of his mouth.

But he wouldn't quit.

Not when a man's life hung in the balance.

And certainly not so long as Becky worked beside him, matchin' him stroke for stroke.

A moan echoed through the cramped tunnel, filterin' around a rock as big as a yearlin' steer that kept them from reachin' the man on the other side. Miguel, one of their diggers, was trapped. Dakota, their other man, carried buckets of rocks and dirt out of the tunnel behind them.

Zeke straightened, hitched up his belt, then resumed diggin'. Becky paused to take a swig of water from the canteen before continuin' her scrabblin' at the rubble with her own shovel, eyes glued to the barrier before them.

He laid a hand on her arm. "Your hands are bleedin'."

She shrugged off his touch. "It's nothing a little salve won't fix up. Later."

"Here, tie this around your hands." He untied the bandana from his neck and tore it in half before pouring some water over the cloth. "It'll keep the dirt out. Give you some protection."

Her eyes narrowed as she looked from him to his offer before grantin' permission with a single, quick nod. She leaned the shovel against the side of the tunnel and held her hands out. He wrapped, then tied the cotton.

Her mouth lifted in a tiny smile before she quirked her chin toward the boulder. "We'd best keep going. You know how Miguel hates to be late for dinner."

He nodded, forcin' his expression to remain impassive.

But the fact she smiled at him—for him—was enough to re-energize him, and he attacked their task with new energy. Within minutes, they'd chipped and scraped away enough earth and smaller rocks to drive a fresh timber beneath the obstruction.

Zeke set his shovel aside. "Miguel, can you hear me?"

"*Si, señor*."

"Okay. Stand as far away as you can in case this thing rolls the wrong way." He turned to Becky and Dakota. "I want it to roll to the left here, toward us. So we'll jam the timber over here." He indicated the right corner near the wall. "Be ready to jump aside if the rock takes on a mind of its own."

He picked up the nearest timber—a three-foot section used to shore up the ceilin'—and jammed it into position. Zeke, Dakota, and Becky leaned on the length of wood, usin' a cabbage-sized rock as a pivot point. But even with all their weight and the groanin' of the lever, the boulder merely rocked a few inches, then settled into its former position like a hen back onto its nest.

Dakota muttered somethin' under his breath, then stood, pushin' his hat back on his head. "This ain't never goin' to work. We need somethin' else."

"Uh, Mister Boss?" Miguel's voice echoed through the chamber.

"Yes?"

"Sounds like the roof is getting ready to fall in here. Some stuff is coming down."

A knot formed in Zeke's gut. "We need a longer lever."

Dakota shook his head. "Longest ones we got are to shore up the walls. Nothin' more than five feet."

Words formed at the back of Zeke's throat that would have earned his mother's wrath—and the threat of a bar of soap. He bit them back.

What to do?

Becky looked toward the mine entrance. "Do you have a rope?"

"Sure. But we can't get it around this rock."

"My father taught me how to lash two boards together. He learned it on his voyage to Africa. Apparently, they sailed into a storm, and several spars broke off and—"

"Uh, can we wait on the story and just concentrate on gettin' Miguel out before this tunnel buries us all?" Zeke headed for his saddle. "Back in a flash."

He trotted toward the railin' where his tack hung, untied the rope, and hurried back, mullin' over her ingenious idea.

Becky Campbell never ceased to amaze him. While he'd never admit he'd thought her inept or inexperienced when it came to this kind of work, she had just come up with the perfect solution.

Maybe she was more than a pretty face encased in a dainty socialite's body.

Perhaps he'd underestimated her.

Perhaps she'd overestimated her ability to help the men out of a jam.

Or maybe her father had exaggerated his skill and experience.

Becky swiped at perspiration running down her face as she scrabbled dirt from beneath a chunk of granite. If they could move this one rock, the rest would fall like a house of cards.

As she offered suggestions, Zeke and Dakota worked on the two lengths of board, each one about five feet long. Dakota clamped the wood together in his ham-sized hands while Zeke wrapped his lariat around the overlapped portion.

She stood and dusted off her hands. "That should be long enough. Are you ready?"

Zeke nodded. "I understand how a lever works, but are you sure this is the way to go?" He glanced at the rock-fall blocking the tunnel. "Maybe we would spend our time better by diggin'."

She shook her head. "There's too much debris."

Dakota's brow pulled down. "De-bree? What is that?"

Zeke gestured to the rubble. "That stuff."

"Then why didn't she just say rocks and dirt? Fancy words to confuse a fella."

Zeke chuckled, sweat running down his face creating rivulets in the dirt streaking his cheeks, giving the impression of a kohl pencil in the hand of a child. "She's from *the city*, remember?"

The digger clapped his boss on the back. "Right."

Becky growled at them, then threw her hands in the air. "Fine. Laugh at me. But remember—I'm the one who came up with the idea for extending the lever."

"We'd-a come to it eventually."

Zeke's words held a ring of truth. He was well accustomed to working on a ranch, getting along with whatever was at hand. "Sure, but likely only after you wore yourselves out."

"Mebbe." Dakota jammed the end of the board into the depression. "This how you're a-thinkin' this is gonna work, Miss Becky?"

"Let's keep our fingers crossed."

He looked up at her from beneath dark brows. "Can't rightly work if'n I do that." He held up one hand and crossed his first two fingers, then gripped the board again. "Nope. Can't do it." He shook his head, casting a sly grin toward Zeke. "City folk."

Now Zeke laughed, the sound echoing off the walls and ceiling like the purr of a large cat. She exhaled. They could have their fun at her expense, but she'd show them …

After a few seconds, she gestured to the lever. "Miguel will be happy to know we didn't mind leaving him trapped in there while we all had a party out here."

The two men sobered, and Zeke's mouth turned down. "Duly

noted, Miss Becky. To work, Dakota."

Dakota leaned into the board and pushed with his shoulder, but the far end slipped out, and he fell forward. Cursing under his breath, he scrambled upright, brushing dirt from his hands. A quick glance at Becky, and his cheeks flushed. "'Scuse my language."

Zeke propped the lever into its niche again, then set his foot against it. "I'll push from down lower, and you work the far end."

Dakota nodded, and the men bent to their task. This time, the board didn't slip out, and the granite boulder rocked in its base.

Becky knelt beside the blockage. "If you shift it that way, I'll dig out the rubble from this side. Then you can move it this way, and I'll do the same over there. Back and forth."

Zeke licked his lips. "Sounds good. Watch out for your fingers."

They leaned into the weight, and she did as she'd suggested. When they eased the rock back, she moved around to the other side and repeated. First one side, then the other, scooping out the nest-like ring, holding the rock in place until the moment they allowed the hunk to settle. It slid down the face of the rock-fall and landed with a *thud* she felt up through her feet.

But the hoped-for outcome didn't occur.

The blockage didn't collapse and open the tunnel.

Dakota groaned, kicked a rock, and paced the small area, once again muttering under his breath.

Becky straightened and pressed her hands into the small of her back. Digging rock was hard work. "So far, so good. Now we dig a hole to get him out."

Zeke nodded. "Seems the only thing we can do." He stepped close to the debris. "Miguel, can you hear me?"

"*Si.*"

"How are you doing?"

"Air feels a mite thin. And there's something else."

Great. Something else they definitely didn't need right now. Becky glanced at Zeke. Heat emanated from him, no doubt generated by his exertion. His jaw worked as he chewed on a thought or worried over his digger's safety.

What would it be like to have him concerned about her like that? To have somebody—anybody—who'd spend time thinking about her? Sure, her mother no doubt did. But in a matriarchal, change-her-for-the-better kind of way.

Not like this. Not like—she shook the thoughts off. They were here to do a job. No matter how warm he felt, how much she wanted to curl up in his arms and have him take care of her—whoa. Where did that thought come from? She didn't need anybody—much less a man—looking after her. She was an intelligent, able-bodied, creative-thinking woman who could—who could what?

Wish for love and companionship?

Did her abilities mean she couldn't have both?

For perhaps the first time in her life, she hoped not.

For perhaps the first time in her life, she contemplated the outcome of giving up one for the other.

And she didn't like the picture generated.

But she had a job to do here. "Miguel, what is it?"

"I hear something. Like a buzzing in my ears."

She nodded. "Probably the effects of less oxygen. Hold on. We'll have you out in no time."

"I thought that at first too. But now I see a bunch of wasps on the ceiling. Buzzing around."

She shuddered. "Don't bother them, and they won't bother you."

"See, that's the thing. I got stung real bad when I was a kid. Doc said if I get bit again, it could kill me. Some kind of bad reaction."

Sting shock. She'd heard of that before. And yes, it could be deadly. She turned to Zeke. "We've got to get him out of there."

He nodded. "Let's dig."

The two men wielded shovels while she removed the manageable pieces and tossed them to the side.

Miguel shouted. "Stop. You're riling up these wasps." Another shout, then a slap. "One of 'em just stung me on the hand."

Dakota stepped back. "Now what? If we rouse them beasts any more, they'll attack him. And us when we open the wall."

Becky's heart thundered in her ears as she struggled to think. She pointed to the lever. "Let's use it as a battering ram." When the men didn't move, she picked it up and pounded at the wall. "Like this. Make a hole big enough for me to get through. Then I'll push him out, and hopefully, the wasps will go for me instead of him."

Zeke shook his head. "Why? You think you're sweeter than him?"

"No. Wasps don't go for sweet. They are carnivores."

Dakota frowned. "Huh? Speak English."

"They eat meat." When Miguel shouted again, she whirled around. "What is it?"

"Another one stung me. My hand is swole up, and now my eye is almost shut. And I can't hardly draw a breath."

She handed the lever to Zeke. "Do as I say, or he'll die."

The two men rammed at the wall until a hole the size of a large potato appeared, then they dropped the board and dug with their hands. Within a couple of minutes, the opening was large enough for Becky to shimmy through. Without ceremony, she stretched her arms over her head and did a mock-dive, plunging through the hole.

When she caught halfway in, she called to the men behind her. "Push me the rest of the way."

Somebody—Zeke? Dakota?—grabbed her legs and pushed, while the other put pressure on her feet, and she plopped to the floor of the tunnel. Scrambling to her feet, she brushed her hair from her eyes and looked around.

Miguel lay slumped near the far wall, propped up, his hands wrapped around his face, knees drawn to his chest.

She hurried over and knelt beside him. "Miguel?"

He moaned and turned over.

She gasped. His face was as swollen as a giant squash. His

hands, which had been stung repeatedly while he tried to protect himself, resembled sun-bloated fish, all pasty white and mottled.

She hooked an arm under his. "Come on. We've got to get you out of here."

Several wasps buzzed around her head, but she resisted the urge to swat at them. One landed on her arm, and she swallowed hard. In a reading she'd done about the insects, killing one sent a message to the hive to attack.

Miguel wouldn't survive any more stings. She'd take them for him.

A needle-like jab on her neck let her know her plan to act as bait was working. He rolled onto his hands and knees, and grunting with effort, she pushed, pulled, and half carried him as he crawled toward the opening. Sweat dripped into her eyes, almost blinding her. She maneuvered the digger up to the opening.

Pinning him in place with her hip, she called out, "Catch him when I get him in the hole. He's in bad shape. He needs cider vinegar on those stings right away. The bottle is on the shelf near the table in the shack."

Zeke's face appeared at the hole, the whites of his eyes gleaming in the semidarkness. "Send him through. We'll take him out and come back for you."

She shook her head. "Just take care of him. I can get out on my own."

Becky lifted Miguel's arms over his head, repeating the move which had brought her into this space. As she slid him through the hole, the ground beneath her rumbled. His feet disappeared from sight, and she tucked her skirt into her waistband, revealing a dirty and torn petticoat. If her mother saw her now …

Another rumble, and the roof timber directly overhead cracked with a loud noise before falling, landing on her leg. She cried out as dirt and rubble cascaded down on her. The wasps lifted from the ceiling in a mass of black, writhing buzz saws, heading for freedom.

And directly for her.

If she got in their way—the possibility was too horrible to contemplate.

She closed her eyes and dove for the hole. A sharp pain raced through her ankle and up her leg when she tripped on a rock, but she couldn't stop now. She had to get out of this cave.

And to safety.

Or certain death.

Two weeks later, Becky hurried back to the mining claim from town as quickly as her still-sore leg allowed, her brown-paper-wrapped bundle tucked beneath her arm. This was an exciting day, to say the least.

After contemplating the comfort and convenience of dungarees, following her experience of working alongside the men to rescue Miguel, she'd made a decision.

If she had to work like a man, she'd dress like one.

Still, she wasn't prepared for the expression on Mr. D's face when she told him what she wanted.

The smallest pair of men's dungarees he could order.

Even now, she slowed her pace as she recalled his response when she'd hobbled into his store the day after the collapse. First, questions about her physical condition and that of Miguel. Word had already spread around town, apparently. Once assured of their well-being in the face of near disaster, his shoulders had relaxed, and the wrinkles in his brow had eased.

Until she'd said what she needed.

Then he'd cleared his throat softly as if he had a bit of apple or a grain of rice lodged there.

He'd raised one eyebrow and tilted his head to the side, as he was wont to do when addressing a naughty child.

Finally, one side of his mouth had lifted in the tiniest of smiles before he spoke. "Miss Becky, I happen to know that none of the men at your claim could fit one leg into a pair of long pants that size."

His tone, gentle as though coaxing a horse from its stall, spoke low enough to stay between the two of them. He'd told her once before he had no intention of feeding the town's gossip mill.

She'd held his gaze. She would not back down. Before heading west, whenever she'd had a difficult discussion with her mother, she'd acquiesced to the woman's mortified response and the flutterings of her fan.

Not this time.

"Thank you for the information, Mr. Dixon. How long might that take to arrive?"

He'd held her gaze a moment longer before nodding and scribbling on the pad of paper he always seemed to keep in his apron pocket. "'Bout two weeks. Check back then."

And so she had. The shopkeeper was as good as his word. Fourteen days.

Now she headed home to try on her purchase. Mr. D had offered her the use of the back room where Sally lived, but she'd declined his kind offer. She wanted to do this in private, where she could move around freely, testing the fit under different conditions.

After all, if she was about to ruin her reputation—for what self-respecting woman wore men's clothes?—she wanted to be sure the choice was worth the risk.

When she reached her shack, she glanced around. Sounds of metal striking rock came from the tunnel about fifty feet away. Zeke's horse shifted its weight and lifted a hind leg, snuffling as she passed.

Good. Nobody would see if she made a complete fool of herself.

She entered the cabin and shut the door, then yanked the flimsy curtains closed. Someday she'd make good on her words to her mother and replace the window coverings with something heavier for the winter. In the meantime, the holes and tatters allowed the cool evening breeze to come in, and nothing, she felt certain, would keep the flies out anyway.

She crossed to her rough bunk in the far corner and sat on the edge of the thin mattress. Slipping off her shoes, she stretched her toes. Then slipped off the bloomers, petticoat, and underskirt. The plan was to pull the dungarees on under her skirt, in case they didn't fit.

She sighed. Even alone, her modesty constrained her.

There were families with three and more children in the area who lived in homes not much bigger than hers. However did they manage?

Throwing caution to the wind, she slipped off the skirt, then peeled off her shirtwaist and corset, breathing a deep sigh of relief as she tossed them on the bed. Clad only in her camisole and pantaloons, she untied the string encircling her purchase. Her fingers trembled so much, she considered simply cutting the cord, but such a length of string was not to be wasted.

She chuckled at her newly instilled frugality.

Her mother would be horrified to know her daughter saved such trivialities as used wrapping paper and string.

The long pants nestled in the paper as though reluctant to be released. She lifted the sturdy cotton piece by the waist, allowing the legs to unfold on their own. Surely much too long—perhaps she'd turn them up as she observed children in town do instead of hemming them.

Perhaps folding them at the cuffs would suffice. Although she was fairly certain she could sew a straight line for window coverings, she wasn't certain about pants legs.

And the waist, although the smallest available. She needed to find something to tie the pants up with. A rope? A length of leather strapping? A belt?

Oh well, she'd figure that out later. Once she decided if she even liked the strange-looking piece of clothing. Trousers sure looked all right on men, with their long legs and narrow hips and waists. But what about on her?

Would all her curves appear to be in the wrong places?

Thinking about how Zeke Graumann filled out his dungarees brought another rush of heat to her neck and cheeks. Why did the man affect her so? He was absolutely not for her. Yet there was something. His attention to detail at the mine? Or the way his eyes always seemed to smile when she spoke? Something sure had changed in recent weeks. He'd even mentioned several times his appreciation for the brave way she'd launched herself through the hole into the tunnel the day of the mine incident.

He no longer even expressed his amazement that she knew anything beyond cooking, cleaning, and keeping a house. Although cooking was debatable. What was it about this higher altitude that left everything either burned black or underdone and runny? At least she'd managed a passable pie once or twice recently.

Whatever the reason, there was no question: the man had an effect on her.

And that would never do.

When she sat again, the green and blue bruise—the reminder of her escape from the tunnel—appeared vivid against her skin. Miguel was back to his old self, thanks to the vinegar remedy she recalled reading about one time, but even the cicadas in the trees at night spooked him. She couldn't blame him, she supposed. If the old saying "once bitten, twice shy" was true, then surely being stung more than a dozen times would be enough to spook even the hardiest of souls.

She slipped on the dungarees and pulled them up into place. The sturdy material felt foreign on her legs and around her waist. She buttoned up the front and pinched about two inches of material at the side. That much excess material gathered at her waist wouldn't be comfortable. She'd have to take them in.

After rolling up the length about four inches, she paced the shack several times, enjoying the way the cuffs flapped around her ankles with every step as though announcing her arrival. A couple of deep knee bends, then she practiced sitting, kneeling, and lifting her leg as though mounting a horse.

These pants provided a freedom of movement she hadn't experienced since, as a young child, she'd often ditched her skirts and raced through the house in her pantaloons, much to her father's delight and her mother's horror.

Horror. A word her mother used liberally and sometimes injudiciously. Seemed everything horrified her. And whatever did was instantly taboo. "Don't want to upset your mother" was a phrase she learned early in life, and from several different sources. Her father. Her mother's doctor. Her mother's friends.

And always associated with when Becky misbehaved in some way.

Well, her mother wasn't here to be horrified by this sight.

Her mother was safe and sound in New York City and unlikely to ever darken her doorstep here in Silver Valley.

While the thought of perhaps never seeing her mother again caused a momentary sense of loss, she wouldn't miss the judgmental attitude. Or the unspoken rules of society that she never failed to transgress. Or the feeling that she was never quite good enough.

Never quite enough.

She twirled around the room, spinning wildly, holding her arms out to the side, then over her head like a dancer she'd once seen at the theater. Ballet, it was called.

Amazing what a pair of dungarees could do for the spirit.

Amazing what a pair of dungarees could do to a body.

Zeke stepped back from the window. Without intendin' to, he'd inadvertently caught sight of somethin' not meant for his eyes.

Becky Campbell, whirlin' around, almost out of control, like a child's top set loose on the floor.

While there was nothin' wrong with what she did, the problem was what she wore.

Men's pants.

And little else. Prancin' around in her flimsy cotton thing—was that a chemise?—and those dungarees. Scandalous. If anybody else saw her …

He eased into the shadows, takin' care not to tread on the loose step that creaked when bearin' weight. If she knew he was there, he'd never be able to face her again.

And while he thought about her—a lot—he never pictured her in this state of attire.

Always she wore her circumspect, long-sleeved blouse or shirtwaist and skirts that reached her ankles, her hair tied back into a braid or whatever she called that knot at the base of her neck or the top of her head. Perhaps a tendril escaping over one ear, despite her attempts to tuck it back or capture it with a hairpin. A bonnet encirclin' her face like a halo, deepenin' his impression of her almost-supernatural qualities.

But this.

He shook his head. No, this seemed cheap and common. Was her desire to wear men's clothin' part of a plan to assume a male identity? Another shake of the head. Not with those curves, she wouldn't. Although he'd heard stories of women who did just that, either to gain somethin' they were denied by society—and usually for good reason—or to protect themselves from molestation.

Surely that wasn't her plan. Everybody in town knew her. She couldn't hide in plain sight simply by wearin' pants.

He froze. Perhaps she meant to move. Where nobody knew her true identity. He heard tales of women Pony Express riders, women saloon keepers, women doctors who dressed as men. Even one woman who was romantically involved with a murderer and took on the role as his teenage son so the two could escape capture.

If this was the kind of person Becky Campbell was, she'd certainly fooled him. And if she'd deceived him in this manner, in what other ways had she misled him?

He spun on his heel and headed toward his horse.

He was done here for the day.

Maybe for good.

Because despite his resolution to protect his heart from this woman, the ache in his chest just confirmed what he already suspected.

He was fallin' in love with a woman he didn't really know.

Becky gritted her teeth. If this kept up, she'd need to visit the dentist in Silver Valley.

Drat that Zeke Graumann.

She swiped at the sweat running down her face at ten o'clock in the morning. So early, and already so hot. What was it with the weather—and the men—of this country? One as hot as Hades, the other as cold as the North Pole.

For the life of her, she couldn't figure him—or any of the male species, for that matter—out worth a hoot. Just when she'd thought they were getting along fine, he up and snubbed her for the past two days.

This time, he walked past the shack, talking and joking with the two diggers, not even sending a glance in her direction. As though she wasn't standing there in the doorway, plain as the nose on his face.

And a very cute nose it was too. Upturned on the tip, kind of broad. Flared just so when she talked to him, like a nervous pony ready to bolt. But it wasn't his nose she focused on. It was his eyes. Those hazel-green orbs, as deep as a well, dark, inviting her to simply succumb and slip in.

She shook her head. Apparently, he wasn't as enthralled with *her* nose. Or *her* eyes. Or any part of her. Judging by the way he'd acted over the past few days. As if she didn't even exist ….

Well, she'd show him.

She followed the three men to the mouth of the mine, the cuffs of her dungarees kicking up tiny puffs of dust on the dry ground. The diggers picked up a shovel and pickaxe each and headed inside, while Zeke lingered near his makeshift desk—a board slung over a couple of sawhorses—checking the prior day's sluice-work, picking up a tiny bit here, examining it, before tossing it in the tailings pile or the assay box.

She slowed, took a deep breath, and exhaled. Then pasted on a smile. No point in ruining his day this early. And if she had her way, she'd not spoil his apparent good mood at all. "Morning."

He turned and nodded in her direction, then resumed his study of the muddy combination of rock, soil, silver, mulch, the odd small-animal bone, and whatever else the men had removed from the tunnel the day before.

She waited, but when it became apparent he wouldn't speak, she tried again. "Cat got your tongue?"

"Nope."

"Good day yesterday?"

"Fair to middlin'."

"Need anything from town?"

He shifted his weight to the other leg. "If I do, I'll get it."

"No more trouble in the tunnel?"

He crossed his arms over his chest. That very broad chest. "I'll be sure to let you know if we need your help."

The tiny emphasis on the *your* didn't escape her notice. "Did I do something to offend you?"

He stared at her, blinking slowly, his Adam's apple moving up and down as if he was having trouble swallowing. "If you think you did, then perhaps you did."

She took a step back, his words stinging like an open-handed slap across the face. "I didn't think I had, but if so, I'd like the opportunity to apologize." She peered at him. "The important thing is, do *you* think I did?"

There. Now she'd turned it back on him. He'd have to respond or leave the implication hanging between them.

He scanned her from top to bottom, then back up, his gaze lingering on her legs and waist. Heat rose in her neck and face.

Her initial reaction to the dungarees had been correct—the material clung in all the wrong places, revealing far more than was proper. What had she been thinking? Had her desire for comfort overridden her obligation not to titillate the men in her employ? Had her concern for being able to work hard been more important than their feelings?

She waited until his eyes fastened on hers. "It's the pants, isn't it?"

Once again, his gaze flicked to below her waist. She smoothed the pants down over her abdomen and thighs, wiping sweaty palms on the sturdy cotton material, wishing for a plain day dress and long-sleeved over-jacket to cover her exposed skin and shape.

Yes, her mother would be horrified.

And apparently, too, was Zeke Graumann.

When he remained still as a statue, she continued. "After the episode in the tunnel, I decided that if I was going to work like a man, perhaps I should dress like one. It seems you are more agile, quicker to respond, and less likely to trip in your clothing than I was in a long skirt." The uncomfortable manner in which he averted his gaze prompted her to get to the point. "And since cutting my skirt shorter wasn't an option, dungarees seemed appropriate."

As soon as the words were out of her mouth, she wished she could snatch them back. His face turned a deep shade of red reminiscent of any of the dozens of times her mother had reacted in a similar manner to one of her escapades or pronouncements.

When would she ever learn?

She drew another deep breath. "But if my attire makes you or the other men uncomfortable, I shall return to my prior clothing. At least, when you are present or likely to be."

"Does wearing those pants make you feel like a man?"

"Goodness, no. In fact, dungarees remind me with every step that I'm not. Perhaps, in time, I'll become accustomed to them, but right now, they feel foreign."

He nodded. "So if we're here, you won't wear them?"

"If you don't want me to."

"My sister-in-law wears a contraption that's like a skirt sewed up the middle. She says it's more comfortable when she's out ridin'."

That seemed a reasonable compromise. "Perhaps I'll try that with my oldest day skirt, the one I was going to tear up for rags."

He gave a single, brief nod. "Sounds fine."

She stepped toward him and touched his forearm. "Good. Well, back to work, I guess. The kitchen garden needs weeding, and I have some sewing to do."

She turned and headed for the shack, her fingers still tingling from their touch.

At least he hadn't pulled away. Either physically when she approached, or emotionally when they talked.

Maybe there was hope for them.

CHAPTER 7

Zeke whistled a nameless tune as he strode down the road leadin' to the Becky Mae Mine. Although it was Saturday—and technically one of his two days off—he decided to pop in and see Becky. After their close call two-and-a-half weeks ago, and the pell-mell pace of the work ever since as they strove to catch up for lost time, might be nice to observe her in a less stressful atmosphere.

He chuckled as he rounded the last turn. He had a sneaky suspicion that life with Becky Campbell would never be slow and peaceful. She'd always find somethin' to buck off, rub off, or just plain roll off. Like an unbroke filly, she never seemed to stay still very long. Or trust him more than about four heartbeats either.

Take the cave-in, for example. Despite the fact Miguel could have died, and she got herself a beauty of a bruise on her leg when that rock fell on her, she'd worked as hard the next day—and ever since—as though nothin' happened.

He shook his head, doubtin' there was any such thing as relaxin' with her around.

He tapped on the door of the shack and waited for her reply. After spyin' her through the window in her dungarees, and the ensuin' tension until she'd explained, he didn't want to tangle with anythin' like that again. She might use the shack as her office-cum-restaurant, but it was still her home.

When she called out, he entered. She sat—as expected—at the table, ledgers spread around, while she tapped the end of her pen against her front teeth.

She smiled, and he resisted the urge to turn around. Dumb. But the fact her expression was only for him warmed him from inside, sendin' an uncomfortable glow up his chest and into his face. Likely his ears were red as embers and his neck as flushed as though he'd worked all day in the hot sun.

He removed his hat and hooked a chair from under the table with one foot before sittin'. "G'mornin'."

"Good morning to you." She quirked her chin toward the stove and the coffeepot sittin' on the back burner. "Want some coffee?"

He shook his head. "Had my limit already." He nodded to the books. "What'cha doin'?"

She sighed. "Checking numbers. I'm hoping I made a mistake somewhere and that I actually have more than the books currently show."

If she knew what he'd done—no, better she didn't. She'd kill him. Or worse. "Find anythin'?"

"No. And I'm almost at the end. It's not as if I have years of records."

"Price of silver is droppin'."

"But I should still make a profit." She glanced out the window. "I don't have any debt to pay or interest to keep current. I don't take a salary myself. There's only you and the two diggers to pay."

He winced at her words. Yep, she'd kill him for certain. "You goin' to work all day?"

She peered at him, her head tilted to one side. "Did I sense a gigantic ninety-degree change of subject?"

"Nope. Just wonderin' what your plans were."

"Laundry. Baking. Cleaning. I've got to wash the hem of my Sunday dress so I can go to church tomorrow and not be ashamed to be seen in public. And after that—" She paused, and now it was her turn to flush.

Curiosity overcame his tactfulness. "And after that?"

She shook her head, tendrils of that rich-earth-brown hair ticklin' her shoulders. And her ears. And curlin' around her jawline just so—he pulled himself back to the present. "Never mind. That was rude of me to pry."

One side of her mouth lifted in a smile. "Let's say I have a full and busy day ahead. And what about you? Don't you have cattle to shift, or hay to bale, or steer to—well, whatever you do with them?"

He chuckled. "You've been listenin' to me talkin' with Dakota."

"With a name like that, I expect he has some ranching experience."

Zeke slapped his knee. "Him? Not likely. The closest he ever came to a cow was drinkin' milk or eatin' steak." He waved off her words. "Nah, it's a name he decided on to get folks to stop askin' about his past." He leaned closer. "I 'spect it's a mite shady."

Her eyes widened. "Do you think he's a wanted man?" Her hand played with her collar. "Or maybe he's dangerous."

"I don't think so. I've known him a few years now and never seen nothin' to give me cause for alarm. Had him to dinner at my ma's place more times'n I can count."

"I'll trust your judgment when it comes to things like that. His dark eyes rather scare me, and I'm glad there's no reason for us to be here alone."

Her concern tugged at his heart. If Dakota—or any man, for that matter—so much as laid a hand on her or hurt her in any way, why he'd—he'd—he didn't want to think what he'd do. And hopefully, he'd never need to find out either.

Then again, he suspected Becky could give any man a run for his money. She practically wore him out with work from Monday to Friday, so much that his brothers teased him about the Boss Woman who could teach Zeke Graumann a lesson or two. The waggle of their eyebrows, the winks, nudges, and nods all led him to believe they meant somethin' more than diggin' for silver, but if they ever voiced those thoughts, he'd—well, that would be downright disrespectful, and he'd silence their insults for sure.

Not that his own mind hadn't wandered in that direction more than once, but like the preacher said, just because the pump spout dripped didn't mean it had to turn into a flood. No, siree. He nipped those thoughts in the bud, just like the sermon last week talked about. And he wouldn't let any other man have thoughts like that about Miss Becky Campbell neither.

He stood. "Well, I'd best be off. You got lots to do, and I got—"

"Beeves to round, and steers to—well, you know."

Yes, he knew. And he loved the way that even thinkin' about castratin' a bull calf was enough to bring a blush to her cheeks. Why, that was just plain sweet. And innocent. Just the kind of girl he was lookin' for. One he never expected to find in a rough-and-tumble town like Silver Valley.

An hour later, however, he started havin' second thoughts about Becky's suitability as a wife for him. His sisters-in-law, raised on local ranches, rode like men alongside their husbands as the family worked their combined herds. Sue, his oldest brother Ted's wife and expectin' their first child in the fall, whooped and hollered at a balkin' range cow and calf while Ted tried to get a rope around its neck.

And over there in the brush, Nan, strong as an ox and with a face to match—but not the personality, thankfully—hog-tied a calf near the brandin' fire while his other brother Joe did the hot work.

Ma was back at the ranch house gettin' the midday meal for twelve ready and plannin' dinner for eight. All the while runnin' out back to supervise his two younger sisters, Viola and Lucy, doin' the laundry.

Becky had a lot of strengths. She was good with numbers. She could read and write. She sure looked good in a skirt or in pants. And in a pinch, she could come up with a solution to a problem.

But that didn't make her rancher woman material.

And if she wasn't, would it be cruel to pursue a romantic relationship, only for her to learn—perhaps too late—that she wasn't cut out for cattle and cowboys?

Judgin' by the knot in the center of his chest where his heart should be, he suspected he didn't want to find out the answer to his question was *no* either.

To be fair to both of them, he should just stop thinkin' about her that way.

He sighed.

Might as well ask him to stop breathin'.

Long after Zeke left, Becky opened the trinket box on the corner of the table and took out the lapel pin and watch. All that was left of her father's earthly life.

No, that wasn't quite true. She flipped open the watch case and stared at her family's faces, frozen in time. A happier time, to be sure. A time when Papa was home and Mother acted more like a girl than her eight-year-old daughter often did. And the lapel pin, a dainty basket waiting to accept a sprig of baby's breath from a bouquet, or a wilted dandelion from his daughter.

But what about his ring? Had he truly sold it? She thought not. If not, then where was it? Did her father's killer sport that item as a trophy? A reminder of the man he'd killed.

A sob caught in her throat, but this time, she gave in to it. Monday through Friday and Sundays were enough days of the week to be strong, to keep going. Today—right now—she'd have a good old cry. She laid her head on her arms, the watch gripped in one hand, the lapel pin in the other, inhaling the scent of paper, sunshine, and lye soap. She closed her eyes and pretended she was wrapped in her papa's arms, comforted by his strong presence, knowing everything would be all right because he was there.

CHAPTER 8

The next Saturday, Becky took a final glance at her reflection in the blade of the table knife. The metal arched her forehead to one side and her cheeks to the other, but she could at least determine that no stray tendrils of hair hung askew and that her bonnet was on straight.

At the sound of wagon wheels in the yard, she headed for the door, grabbing her carpetbag and drawstring purse along the way.

She looked ahead to spending the weekend at Zeke's ranch.

Correction. She would spend the day with Zeke, the night at his parents' home, and then she'd ride into town with them and attend church as usual tomorrow.

No matter the specifics, this was the most excitement she'd had in weeks. Months, maybe. Except, of course, for her recent home invader.

She paused on the stoop outside the door and made sure the latch securely engaged. Just Wednesday, when she'd left to walk to town, apparently the door hadn't closed properly. A skunk had gotten into the shack and—well, done what skunks do. Despite her pulling out everything not made of metal and dousing it with boiling water and lye soap, the place still smelled like the rascal was in residence.

She smiled at the still-unpleasant memory. At her screams, Zeke and the diggers had come running, each with a weapon of some sort in hand. Zeke with a gun, and the two diggers with shovels. When they'd seen the black-and-white creature, the three had backed up as if they faced the devil himself.

Zeke had shaken his head. "Not goin' in there. Leave the door open, and it'll come out when it's ready. Satan's spawn, that's what we call them 'round here."

She'd understood their reluctance to take on such a creature, but really, it wasn't much bigger than a rat. Smellier, yes, but no more vicious, surely.

But the men would not be moved, and so she'd waited. And waited. Round about sundown, the skunk had saunter-waddled out into the dusk, arching its tail and glancing over its shoulder at her from time to time before disappearing into the underbrush.

Sleeping in the wagon bed for two nights as she waited for the odor to dissipate hadn't been much fun either. Which was why she now headed for the Graumann ranch for the weekend. Apparently, Zeke had told his parents of her unwelcome visitor, and his mother had insisted she stay with them.

Not that this changed anything between her and Zeke. This was about a day away from camp so she could breathe through her nose again. And surely his mother's cooking, the open range, and even Zeke himself had to smell better than her burnt potatoes, the dirt and dust of the mine, and that old skunk.

Satisfied with the security of the door, Becky stepped into the early morning sunshine. Delivered earlier in the week, her most recent acquisition—two mules named Belle and Stubby—grazed in her newly built corral. They were on loan, really, since she hadn't the funds to pay for them, but she hoped they'd ease the workload for the diggers by hauling the wagons of ore and debris out of the mine. With food and water topped up, they'd do fine until she returned tomorrow after church.

Zeke hopped down from the wagon and met her partway, offering his arm. Not that she really needed it. Not yet, anyway. But she returned his smile and tucked her arm through his, relishing the feel of sinewy muscles through his long-sleeved cotton shirt, the solidness of him walking alongside her, and the way his jaw clenched as he led her to the wagon.

Not accustomed to traveling in such a conveyance, she listened intently to his instructions about placing one foot on the hub, the other near the brake handle, and with his hands clasped around her waist, she hoisted herself as decorously as possible up the four feet or so to the floor of the wagon. Exhaling when she reached the top, she flopped—or so it seemed—onto the seat, then scooted over to make room for him.

Two deft steps and he sat beside her, his hip touching hers, though through layers of skirts and petticoats. Oh yes, no dungarees or skirt pants today. She shifted a mite to break the contact, then fanned herself with her hand. Goodness, so hot so early in the day.

The ride to his ranch went quickly. Too fast, if she had a say in it. The pair of chestnuts—she asked, and he explained the minute differences in shades of brown when it came to horses—pulling the wagon seemed anxious to get back home, but she wished they weren't quite so enthusiastic. Perhaps if they carried on an actual conversation unrelated to the mine, she could make the most of the time.

She pointed to a large bird hovering over a field. "What kind of bird is that?"

"Turkey vulture."

"Do they eat turkeys or just look like turkeys?"

He turned to look at her. "Dunno. That's what they're called."

Great. Some conversationalist. She tried again. "Things seemed to go better at the mine this week."

A smile tickled his mouth, easing the lines around his eyes. "Apart from the skunk."

"Yes." She sighed. "Apart from the skunk." She smoothed her skirt. "I bet you didn't have to come to my father's rescue all the time."

"True."

"Did you know him well?"

He shrugged. "A neighbor I saw from time to time."

"Not like me."

He scanned her up and down. "No, not like you."

Heat rushed to her cheeks. "Did you worry about him?"

Another lift of the shoulders. "Seemed like a man who knew his way around just about any situation."

"Unlike me."

"Right."

She nudged her shoulder against his. His fingers, encased in leather gloves, flexed several times. "You seem a lot more relaxed today."

"Don't have to wonder what you're gettin' up to when you're in plain sight."

She gnawed on that a while, not sure if she liked the idea that he worried about her. How could she ever prove herself if he felt he had to keep her close?

More importantly, why did her desire to be an independent woman fade in the light of his concern?

As they headed down toward a small bridge, the trees grew thick on the river banks. A long-legged, white bird waded in the water, dipping its head under the surface and coming up with a wriggling fish in its beak.

She pointed. "Oh, it's beautiful."

He nodded. "A white heron. They come through in the summer. Nest here, have their young. That's the first one I've seen this year."

"It would be nice to catch fish that easily."

He glanced at her before returning his eyes to the road ahead. "You like to fish?"

"Don't know. Never done it."

This time he fastened his eyes on her, the hazel tinged with flecks of green. "Now why doesn't that surprise me?"

"The closest I've come to fishing is picking my lobster from a tank at a restaurant." She laughed. "Or digging clams on the beach in Cape Cod."

His mouth screwed up in a grimace. "Now, that's just plain wrong. That's as bad as namin' your steers, knowin' you'll be eatin' one of 'em come winter."

"I could have gone my entire life without having that picture in my head."

"Well, where do you think your beef comes from?"

She twisted the ribbon ties on her hat together. "I know where it comes from. I just don't want to think about it."

He chuckled. "I 'spose you don't want to talk about where eggs come from neither?"

Heat raced up her neck. Seemed as if every topic of conversation with men came down to procreation in some way. "No, I don't."

"Sorry." Zeke focused on the reins looping through his fingers. "I forget sometimes you're not used to our rough ways."

She laid a hand on his forearm. "It isn't that you're rough. Perhaps … more open to the natural world. Such things are not discussed in—"

"I know. In the *city*."

"Don't say it as if it's a bad word. It's actually a beautiful place. Tall buildings—"

"That block out the sun."

She refused to look at him. He could be so obstinate. "Shops with everything a body could want."

"Except fresh air, a good night's sleep, and a clear conscience."

Her strong desire to make him understand her passion for her hometown took her by surprise. "Music and theater and plays and orchestras—"

"All makin' such a racket a man can't think."

"I see you've already made up your mind to dislike a place you've never seen."

"And ain't likely to neither, no matter how much you talk like their self-appointed ambassador."

She gritted her teeth to bite back a sharp retort that could spoil their day before it hardly started. Instead, she surveyed the open pastures on either side of the road, dotted with reddish-brown and white cattle with short horns, and larger, darker beasts with long, pointed horns.

While longing to know the difference between the two and the reason for mixing them together, she held her tongue. After his rude words, she wasn't ready to strike up a conversation yet. Let him wonder why she wasn't talking. Maybe he would consider his behavior and apologize.

They turned the bend where the pastures ended at a barbed-wire fence, and a large yard continued with a two-story house as its focal point. Scattered around in no apparent order were two large barns, paddock areas—called corrals here in the West—and a number of smaller buildings. Three or four young horses—yearlings, perhaps?—trotted over to the fence and nickered for attention, while a dog jumped from its resting spot on the veranda and raced toward them, tail wagging while it barked a greeting.

Zeke pulled up in front of the house, set the brake, then jumped down. He patted the dog and spoke a few low words, and the black-and-white animal returned to its place and lay down.

He tipped his hat back on his head and extended his hands toward her. "You get down in the reverse order of how you got up there."

"You don't say." The nerve of the man. Insulting her home, then her intelligence by stating the obvious. "I can get down myself, thank you."

His smile slipped away, then returned. He stepped back and held his hands shoulder high in surrender. "Fine. I'll stand by in case you need help."

She didn't need his help. Now, how did this go? One hand on the brake, she eased her foot down, searching for the hub. It should be right there. No. Maybe over here. No. Her other foot slipped out from beneath her, and before she knew it, she landed in the dust on her derriere. As she sat there trying to regain her breath and her composure, laughter rang across the yard. She turned to ascertain its source.

Zeke bent over, hands on his knees, hat in hand, guffawing like a mule at her predicament. The front door of the house opened, and an older woman exited, wiping her hands in her apron. Oh no! Zeke's mother. What a way to make a first impression.

Now Becky truly understood her mother's definition of mortified.

She was, well and truly.

A pang of guilt pierced her at the angst she caused her own mother. The emotion sat heavy on her heart and sour in her mouth.

Mrs. Graumann hurried toward her. "Zeke Graumann, shame on you. Embarrassin' our guest like that. You help her up right now." As she neared, she swatted at him with a dish towel. "Get on with you. What will she be thinkin' about our rough ways?"

He straightened, his laugh caught in his throat, and he seemed to choke on it.

Served him right.

His gaze dropped to the ground, and he swatted his leg with his hat. "Sorry, Ma." He stepped forward and offered his hand. "Sorry, Becky. It was just such a sight, seein' you droppin' like a rock. And all because you were too proud to accept help."

She stared at him. Is that what he thought? She never credited herself with that particular shortcoming, but perhaps her words—and her behavior—communicated a haughty spirit. What had the sermon been about last Sunday? About pride going before a fall.

She offered him a half smile and held out her hand. "If that was an apology, it was a pitiful one, but I will accept it in the spirit it was given. Now, be a gentleman and help me to my feet."

He grinned and grasped her hand, yanking her upright with such force that she collided with him as he let go. She planted her hands against his chest to steady herself and looked up at his face. The strong chin with the cleft. The nostrils flaring like a runaway horse. His lashes, so long and dark, the envy of many, no doubt. And those eyes. Laughing, but not *at* her now.

Laughing *with* her.

Her heart thundered, deafening her. After about an hour—seconds, more likely, much too quickly—she stepped back, putting some distance between them. She struggled to regain her thoughts, her speech, her breathing. Surely a simple fall from a wagon shouldn't leave her gasping for air like this.

Mrs. Graumann stepped closer. "Forgive my son's lack of manners, Miss Campbell." She held out a hand. "I'm Zeke's ma. You can call me 'Ma' too. Ever'body does."

Ma. Not Mother. Not Mrs. Graumann. The word rolled off the woman's lips in a familiar, loving tone. She didn't mind being everybody's ma. Becky returned the handshake. "And you can call me Becky."

Mrs. Graumann took her by the hand. "Come on in. Breakfast is on the table."

Becky's stomach grumbled, reminding her she'd done as Zeke suggested and hadn't eaten at home. "Sounds good. I am hungry."

The older woman smiled. "It's a wonder that boy didn't turn you off your food for the day, the way he drives and the way he natters on without thinkin'." She paused and peered at her. "That's why you're angry at him, right? He went and said somethin'. I raised him better'n that. I'll talk to him."

"He's fine. Nothing inappropriate. We're just getting to know each other is all."

Mrs. Graumann—Ma—nodded. "I remember when me and the mister was courtin'. All the time gettin' on each other's nerves. Folks was certain we'd kill each other before we ever got to the altar."

"Oh, Zeke and I aren't—"

Ma patted her arm and leaned closer, fresh air and sweet biscuits her cologne. "It's fine, honey. Don't worry. I can see you have feelin's for him. Your secret is safe with me."

Zeke trailed Becky nearly within earshot. Whatever those two were talkin' about sure seemed serious. And what secret was his mother thinkin' Becky was keepin'?

What wasn't Becky tellin' him? Was it about the mine? Unlikely Becky would share somethin' with his mother she hadn't told him. Was it about her life? Her *other* life? The one she'd no doubt return to some day in New York, leavin' all memories of Colorado—and him—far behind like a bad dream?

Or—no! Was she courtin' another?

Whatever it was, this secret concerned him, and he'd find out. Get her to let her guard down, and she'd spit it out like a piece of moldy bread.

But right now, breakfast. He was so hungry his stomach was gettin' to thinkin' his throat had been cut. He entered the house and went straight for the kitchen and sat. Becky hovered near his mother, bringin' platters of food to the table accordin' to the order his mother hauled them from the warmin' oven. His gift to his parents for their anniversary, along with the new table. His father had been delighted—lookin' forward to more pies and cakes, perhaps—while his mother had smiled and joked that perhaps he'd take the old oven and put it in his own house when he built it. Keep it in the family, so to speak.

Just thinkin' about buildin' him a house tied his guts into knots with shivers of joy and panic. He had no call to build unless he was fixin' to marry. Which he wasn't. At least, not anytime soon. And if Becky's secret had to do with another beau, not for a very long time.

He reached for the flapjacks in front of him, but his mother batted his questin' fingers away with a wooden spoon. "Did you wash your hands first?"

"No, ma'am."

"Then get to it. You know the rules."

Feelin' like a six-year-old, he ducked his head and went to the basin outside the back door, applied soap, and washed, then dried his hands before returnin' to his seat. By this time, the rest of the family crowded into their usual spots like milk cows in a barn, leavin' his mother and Becky standin'.

He cleared his throat and quirked his chin toward his brothers, then stood. They followed suit, with Joe pullin' over the extra chair to make room for Becky. He gritted his teeth. He should have been the one to do that, not his married brother. What would she think of him and his manners?

Nothin', that's what.

Because she had a secret. Well, he'd uncover it before the day was out.

After breakfast, Zeke waited around the house while Becky and the girls did the dishes and cleaned up the kitchen under his mother's supervision. There was a lot of lighthearted laughter and teasin' goin' on, and he wished he was included.

But men were strictly ushered out from underfoot, as his ma always said, while the girls talked about the midday meal, babies, curtains, and such women-talk. He exhaled, thinkin' about the hours wastin' while he could be off doin' more productive work. But he wanted to include Becky in his day, so he waited.

And paced. And sat. Just when he thought he'd burst, she stepped through the back door and tossed him a smile.

He'd have waited all day just for that.

"Sorry to keep you sitting around."

He waved off her words. "No worries. I was just contemplatin' what needs doin' today, linin' it up in my mind."

"Contemplating?"

"Yeah, contemplatin'. I know some fancy words too."

"I never doubted you did." She sighed. "It's so lovely here." She breathed deeply. "A curious mix of smells. Grass. Something—" She wrinkled her nose. "Something nasty?"

"Chicken coop across the way. Needs cleanin'. That's Viola's job, and she hates it."

She nodded. "And another smell."

"Manure. We pile it up over there behind the barn to put on the kitchen garden. Sun bakes it up real good, and sometimes it gets to stinkin'."

She gestured to the bench he sat on. "Will we sit, or will we get to work?"

He stood. "I'm gonna get to work. But I didn't bring you out here to get yourself dirty. If'n you want to stay here in the house with Ma, that'd be fine." With his mother, perhaps. But not with him. He wanted her beside him as much as possible. "Or you can come with me. If you want."

She tipped her head to one side. "What you really mean is I don't know enough to help. Don't worry. I'll go with you and watch."

"Thought we could take a ride out and check the fence lines. I can go out later and do any repairs needed."

"That will work fine. I promised your mother I'd come back to help her with dinner." She slowed her step. "I've only ridden sidesaddle. In Central Park. And not very often. Horses tend to smell, and they leave … droppings behind."

He chuckled. "Everythin' alive leaves droppin's, as you call them."

"I know, but it's so embarrassing."

"Yeah, but it's part of nature. How God created us. And everythin' else too." He smiled and hesitated, unsure how she would respond if he gave in to the urge to tease her. "Kind of like … skunks."

She stared at him for about five heartbeats, and he was certain she would screw her face up in a disgusted expression and maybe change her mind about passin' the afternoon with him. But she didn't. Instead, although she worked that pretty mouth hard not to, she smiled.

Then she giggled.

He joined in. The fact that she could laugh at herself moved her up a notch in his estimation.

If a person couldn't laugh at themselves, well, they shouldn't laugh at anybody else.

He stopped beside a stall. "I'm actually kinda glad Mr. Skunk did his thing in your shack. Got you away from workin' all weekend."

"I'm glad to meet your mother. Spend time with your family. Get to know them."

And what about him? Was he just a diversion? And what was her secret? Did she have a beau back East? Simply needed a way to make the time pass more quickly?

Better to know the truth now before he wasted any more time—or heartache—on this woman. "I know comin' here is an inconvenience."

"No, it's a treat for me."

He petted the flank of the pinto that nuzzled his hand for a treat. "I know you have lots to do on the weekends. Cleanin'. Bookkeepin'."

She leaned against the wall. "Ever since you asked me yesterday, I've looked forward to today. Getting away from the humdrum. Away from the mine." She chuckled, her face relaxin' into peacefulness. "Away from the smell."

"Yes, the rascal." It was all he could think to say. Zeke shifted his weight. She sounded genuine enough. Maybe this weekend would show him one way or the other. "This here's your pony for the day."

She turned and faced the pinto he indicated. "Seems bigger than the ponies I'm used to." She held a hand about three feet from the ground. "In New York, ponies are about this high."

"Out here, we call anythin' we can see over a pony." He coaxed the paint toward him, then slipped a bit into its mouth and a halter over its head. "He's got a soft mouth, so you shouldn't have any trouble."

"Soft mouth?"

"He'll respond to a touch on the reins. Won't fight you."

"Hopefully he's got a soft saddle too."

He chuckled at her wit. "We'll get you fitted up. We don't have a sidesaddle, but you should be fine with all them skirts and such." His cheeks burned. "Promise not to stare at your ankles."

"If I knew I was going to ride today, I'd have worn my dungarees."

His eyes widened as he set the blanket in place, tugging it snug at the corners. "We might seem like a rough lot, but my ma would be horrified to see a woman in men's clothes." He set the saddle into place. "Pass that girth under, will you?"

"Girth?"

He pressed his forehead into the horse's side. Didn't she know anythin'? He raised his head and met her gaze over the pinto's withers. "The strap that holds the saddle on."

"Oh." She bent and did as he asked. "Sorry. When I went riding, the horses were ready to go."

He nudged a knee into the horse's belly so it would exhale as he tightened the leather strap and fastened the buckle. Then he tested the saddle for firmness by graspin' the horn and the cantle and givin' it a good tug. "Good. I'll help you up, and you can walk him around the barn, gettin' used to him, while I saddle my horse."

She joined him on the left side and tucked her foot into his cupped hands. He hoisted her up, grinnin' when she gasped as she settled into the saddle. She squirmed in place and tugged her skirts as much below the knee as possible. Then she gathered the reins, one in each hand, and clicked her tongue.

The pony turned its head to look back at her.

She clicked her tongue again.

Still nothin'.

She looked down at Zeke, a frown marrin' her otherwise perfect face. "It won't move."

"What are you doin' with the reins?"

"Holding them."

"That's not the way we do it around here."

"And why doesn't that surprise me? I'm accustomed to riding English. No—" She jabbed at the horn. "Nothing sticks up this much." She waggled her foot. "And these stirrups are huge."

"That's to protect your feet when you go through brush or

cactus."

Her eyes widened, and her eyebrows rose almost to her hairline. "Next you'll be saying I need to learn how to ride all over again."

"Maybe you do." He pried the reins from her fingers, bundled them together, and placed them into her right hand. "To make him turn right, you lay the reins across his neck like this." He moved her hand to the right. "Left, the opposite." He used his hand wrapped around hers to illustrate, enjoyin' the warmth of her skin through her kid gloves, so soft and delicate against his calluses. "To stop him, pull back on the reins and say 'whoa.'"

"How do I get him to go?"

"Squeeze your legs together and tap his sides with your heels. You can say 'giddup,' but he really doesn't need it."

She did as he said, and the pony walked forward. At the far end of the barn, she laid the reins across its neck, and it turned left, then returned to where he watched.

He nodded. "You've got the hang of it. Keep practicin' while I get my horse ready."

The steady clip-clop of hooves as he saddled his own mount indicated her willingness to accept instruction. This was a good sign. Perhaps she wasn't as proud as he first thought.

Maybe there was hope for her yet.

For both of them.

The morning passed quickly, and before she knew it, Zeke turned them back to the house for the midday meal.

Feeling much more comfortable in the saddle, Becky urged her pony into a faster walk. "Truth be told, I'm glad we're heading back. I could use some time on solid ground."

"Are you holdin' up okay?"

"Oh yes. Although the saddle isn't as comfortable as the flatter English version I'm accustomed to."

"Thought you didn't ride much."

A man who paid attention. Nice. "Well, I don't. But it seems the leather was softer, and the—" she gestured to the rise at the rear of the saddle—"whatever that is called—was a lot smaller."

"Cantle. Helps you stay in the saddle when you're goin' up a steep bank."

"Cantle." She shifted, digging her heels deeper into the stirrups. "And this thing sticking up here."

He chuckled. "Not much use for a saddle horn, I 'spect, in the city."

"No." She stared off at the horizon. Would the farmhouse never appear? "Of course, I didn't usually ride for three hours straight either."

As they headed over a low rise, she marveled at how comfortable he looked. Almost as though born in the saddle, he rode with a loose posture, using his strong legs to lessen the impact when they urged their mounts into a canter—or a lope, as he called it.

She sighed. Would she ever keep all this straight? The saying was true, apparently. She could take Becky out of New York, but she couldn't take New York out of Becky.

Her hair, now flowing down her back and around her face from the breeze, blew into her eyes, and she pushed the tendrils behind an ear. "I must look a mess."

"I think you look right fetchin'."

His easy compliment rested on her like a warm blanket. But he was just saying that to be nice. Wasn't he? "Surely we've ridden at least a hundred miles. Are you sure the owner won't mind?"

"Mind? This is all my land."

"Your land? But I thought—" She paused, flustered. What had she thought? That he was one of those hardscrabble farmers she'd read about trying to make a living on twenty acres? "How much land do you own?"

He shrugged. "My pa and brothers and me own about twenty-five thousand acres. If we rode the perimeter, it would take us about two days."

"My goodness. How many cows do you have?"

"About five thousand cattle. We're just a small spread." He adjusted the brim of his hat, his eyes on the path before them. "But every one of them is important."

"So do you mean all those cows—cattle—we passed belong to you and your family?"

"Yep."

"So why did we spend so much time looking for that one missing cow?" Earlier, he'd led the way down into a rocky ravine where he suspected they might locate the animal in question. They'd found her standing guard over twin calves, which according to Zeke wasn't unusual but was a sure blessing. "With that many, isn't it just a waste of time? You could be doing that every day and get nothing else done."

He chuckled. "When it's your livelihood, you tend to keep track of things like that." He shifted in the saddle. "Besides which, findin' a lost cow with a calf or two is a little like findin' gold and silver in the same vein."

The reference to the mine reminded her that this was not her life, although for a few hours she was happy to imagine herself here. Riding the fence line was easy work. Then again, living as a rancher's wife wouldn't be. She wasn't so naïve as to think she could simply wile away her hours while her husband did all the work. Zeke's sisters-in-law and sisters pitched in where needed. An operation this size, one that could support four families, required everybody's labors.

And she simply wasn't cut out for this kind of life. She didn't know one end of a horse from the other—well, she did know that. She didn't know a calf from a heifer from a range cow, though, and although she noted the physical differences between cows and bulls, she wasn't certain she would ever know one cow from another.

She slowed her pony as they made their way down a steep hill, giving it its head as Zeke instructed. The sure-footed mount picked its path amongst the rocks, dead tree limbs, and even a couple of holes that Zeke said were prairie dog tunnels. When he spoke to her of this land, his face lit up, and he appeared more relaxed than she ever saw him at the mine.

He loved this place, loved his life.

Needed this life.

She wanted to but knew herself well enough to understand that what she felt wasn't a passion for raising cattle. She longed for something permanent, even more permanent than the mine. Or a ranch. Something where years down the road, people would say her presence made a difference. That something she said or did changed them.

Not like that was about to happen. Not in a big land like this.

Sure, a woman miner might be an oddity, but she wasn't the only woman running such an operation. And others were far more successful than she'd ever be.

No, she was simply a socialite from the East chasing down her father.

A father who was as dead to her now in actuality as he'd seemed most of her life.

Sittin' at the table, Zeke studied Becky, feelin' a little as though he were tryin' to cram for a final examination in a subject he had no clue about, one where he hadn't attended a single class. He searched her face, lookin' for hints of what she was really thinkin', diggin' past the words and the laughter for the real her.

Because without a doubt, somethin' had changed since this mornin'. Not that she said anythin' to him. And not that anythin' happened he could put his finger on. A subtle shift in the way she wouldn't meet his gaze, maybe. Or the way she looked when she thought nobody was watchin' her, like somethin' troubled her.

Like she'd come to a difficult decision.

His mother kicked him under the table. "Zeke, your turn to say grace."

He reached his left hand to hold hers, then raised his right to grip Becky's. "Family custom."

She bent her head, closed her eyes, and rewarded him with a tiny smile.

He asked a blessin' over their food, and before the last syllable of the "amen" faded, his brothers were already dishin' food onto their plates. His mother cleared her throat and narrowed her eyes at them, but they took no notice.

Or seemed not to.

More likely they were doin' this to embarrass him in front of Becky.

At the other end of the table, his father cut the roast beef into paper-thin slices, as he always did. And his sisters chattered on about flowers and gardens while his sisters-in-law discussed the new milk calf born the previous evenin'.

His mother turned to Becky. "Did you notice the new range and table in the kitchen?'

"I did. Lovely."

Ma quirked her chin in his direction. "That son of ours bought them for us for a weddin' anniversary present." She sipped her coffee. "Thoughtful boy."

His father handed around the bowl of potatoes. "Could be spendin' his money on gamblin' and other vices, but he doesn't."

Zeke stared first at his father, then his mother. What were they up to? If he didn't know better, he'd say they were matchmakin' him and Becky. But that couldn't be. They hardly knew her.

His mother nodded. "I told Zeke he should save the old range to put into his house when he builds it." She smiled at Becky. "Doesn't that make sense?"

Becky's cheeks colored. "It does."

His father cleared his throat. "For when he gets himself a wife and all."

Now it was Zeke's turn to be embarrassed.

Time to change the subject.

He glanced at Becky's plate. The girl had about three green peas, a teaspoon of mashed potato, and a piece of meat that wouldn't fill an eye tooth. He nudged her with an elbow. "Don't be shy. There's plenty."

Her mouth lifted at the corners. "Looks like it."

But she still didn't add more to her plate.

His sister Lucy paused, her fork midway to her mouth. "So, Becky, tell us about yourself."

"Not much to tell." She sipped her water. "Born and bred in New York City. Came here to be with my father."

Zeke's mother set her fork down, a sure sign somethin' was botherin' her. "We were sorry to hear of his passin'."

His pa grunted. "Seems minin' brings out the worst in some people."

Viola, her chestnut hair shinin', reached across the table. "If you ever need someone to talk to, well, I'm here."

His other brother Ted laughed. "And even if you don't need someone to talk to, Viola'll chew your ear off with her silliness."

Viola punched her older brother, a frown erasin' her previous smile. "Don't mind him, Becky. He don't know nothin'." She sniffed. "Like most men."

Becky turned her attention to the speck of food on her plate and continued pushin' it around, not hardly eatin' anythin'.

Like she was already full of somethin' else.

A secret, perhaps?

Well, that was fine, because he finally made up his mind about somethin' too.

While he hoped stoppin' his wages was only temporary, now he knew the truth.

He had to protect her.

Even though she wasn't his—and likely never would be—he wouldn't add to her troubles.

They could both have their little secrets.

CHAPTER 9

Matilda Campbell looked up from her needlepoint when the maid entered the parlor. "Yes, Welsh?"

"The morning mail just arrived, ma'am."

Matilda returned her attention to her cushion cover. "Set the tray there."

Welsh cleared her throat softly. "There is a letter from Colorado, ma'am. It's on the top."

Matilda's heart quickened like that of a wallflower asked to dance her first polka. "Thank you."

She waited until the girl set the tray on the table and left the room before snatching at the envelope. News from her husband. Or her daughter. Either would be a tonic to the ache in her chest that had remained since Rebecca had left to follow in her father's steps. She glanced at the postmark. Silver Valley. Using the letter opener kept handy in her project bag, she slit the paper at the seam, removed the single page inside, and smoothed the cheap drugstore linen on her lap.

A ten-dollar bill fell onto the floor. Why would Rebecca send her money? Did she think her mother needed her support? Was this a guilt payment? But for what? Matilda retrieved the bill and turned it over and over, looking for a secret message. A clue, perhaps. Or had her daughter contracted a fever and lost her mind?

Perhaps the letter would enlighten her.

Dear Ma,

She paused and scanned the writing. Despite the substandard paper, this was her daughter's penmanship. She'd recognize it anywhere. But Ma? Always Mother.

She shrugged and continued reading about her daughter's exploits in this far-off place. The words were articulate, the sentences well-structured. Surely no brain fever had robbed her child of her senses.

The job she held—in a mercantile! She shuddered. If her friends knew—why wouldn't the foolish child put off her daydream and accept help? And living behind the shop like a—like a common clerk. Even the girls at Bloomingdale's were paid a living wage. Why, Rebecca should return home this instant and—what was that? Attending church? She'd not been able to drag her daughter inside the Presbyterian church the family attended—and had a pew marker with their name on it—since she was twelve.

Matilda settled back, fanning herself with the page until her heart slowed enough so she could breathe through her nose comfortably, then she returned to the letter. Met a man, become great friends.

She laid her head back on the wing chair, closed her eyes, and moaned. What kind of man was her daughter tied up with? Hopefully, she wouldn't do anything foolish like—

She continued reading, then gasped. No! Her worst fears realized. Her only daughter marrying. A man she'd met just a month or so ago in a nondescript town in the middle of Indian Territory. Did the girl not have a grain of sense? There was no future for her there. Her rightful place was here in New York, with her mother, her friends, the society she'd been groomed to enter. How much opportunity for promotion would there be in a small town? Why, it could be years before she'd be counted amongst the upper echelon of even this tiny pond.

She checked the date on the letter. May seventeenth. But that was more than a month before. And Rebecca planned to wed on—the P.S. at the bottom said—oh no! July eighteenth.

She must travel to Silver Valley and stop this farce before her only child made a huge mistake.

Matilda folded the letter and shoved it into her shirtwaist pocket.

"Welsh! Get me the cross-country train schedules to Colorado. And pack my bags for an extended trip."

But first, a letter to her daughter.

A very difficult letter.

She pondered the words and phrases, laboring over each as though birthing them. Perspiration beaded on her upper lip, and she paused several times to blot the dampness with her handkerchief. Her chest ached with the exertion, and once she set the pen aside and opened her bottle of smelling salts. She must do this. She must write to her daughter and convince her to wait for her arrival.

Dear Rebecca, I received your letter with joy but your news with dismay. Please, please promise me you won't do anything drastic until I arrive. Child, your entire future hangs in the balance, and marriage to an assistant postmaster isn't in your best interest. I will travel on the fastest train possible, risking my health to save you. I pray this is all a misunderstanding which we will one day laugh about. Give my love to your father. I cannot wait until we are all together again.

The maid entered the room and handed her a stack of brochures. "Had to send a boy down to the train station. Seems there's a straight-through that will get you there in about three weeks. Twenty days, to be exact. I took the liberty of booking a sleeper." She turned to leave, then stopped. "Will you be needing my services on your travels, ma'am?"

Matilda considered Welsh's question. While she was not accustomed to doing for herself, her needs would be minimal on the train, and surely there were porters and the like who could assist if needed. And once there, she wasn't certain what the accommodations would be. Perhaps this small town had no hotel, and she'd be forced to sleep with her daughter.

An extra person might well be one too many.

She shook her head. "No, Welsh, thank you. In my absence, you may take a month's paid holiday. And then prepare the house for our return in about six weeks."

Welsh smiled. "Thank you, ma'am. Miss Rebecca will return

with you, ma'am?"

A single nod. "Yes, she will."

Matilda hoped her powers of persuasion equaled her resolve.

Polly Matheson stared at her second-youngest daughter. Seemed that with every passin' day, the girl reminded her more and more of what she'd lost.

And now this letter.

Unable to read herself, she'd hidden the envelope and its contents from her husband. He was still so angry at Sally for refusin' to marry the man he chose for her. A groundskeeper, with a steady job and some hope for advancement. A slight rise in social status, which was the real reason for the arrangement. Her husband hoped he could get in good with the master of the house by marrying into service. Still, not much money, and Sally likely would end up like she had, supportin' the family by workin' three jobs. Keepin' a ne'er-do-well husband in beer and four kids in shoes seemed never-endin'. 'Specially when he wouldn't work. Too caught up in his grand ideas to get rich quick to be bothered showin' up for a paycheck.

No, she wanted better'n that for her children.

Now her husband snored in bed, drunk again. He'd come home singin' loud and staggerin' from side to side, bangin' on doors and trippin' as he made his way to their cold-water flat on the third floor. After scarfin' down his dinner, he'd collapsed on the saggin' mattress and fallen asleep in minutes.

Dorcas, two years younger than Sally, scanned the page. "I'm tellin' you, Ma, that's what it says. 'Dearest Mother.'"

While Polly didn't blame Sally for not mentionin' her father in the openin', not callin' her *Ma* was almost as bad. Had her daughter gone all hoity-toity on her? Maybe she had no room in her life for the likes of her family.

Sally gestured to Dorcas. "Keep readin'. Might as well find out what she's sayin'."

Her daughter continued, sharin' the news that Sally had arrived safe and sound in some place in Colorado called Silver Valley. Owned a business. Lived in a shack—what kind of business would have her livin' in a shack? Would replace the curtains. Well, that would be nice. Sally always was a good hand with a needle and thread. Met some nice people. Hoped her mother was well. Would write again.

That all sounded fine.

It just didn't sound like her daughter.

More like a stranger.

Polly shook her head. "Is that all?"

"Yep."

"She didn't mention you young'uns?"

"Nope."

"Nor her pa?"

Dorcas snorted. "Only somethin' which made no sense about him buildin' a shack. But I wouldn't have blamed her if she didn't say nothin' 'bout him. He riled her so much. That's why she left."

Polly glanced toward her husband. "Shush, keep your voice down."

"What you goin' to do, Ma?"

"The only thing I can do. Go to her. She's tryin' to send me some kind of message. Tellin' me she's in danger or somethin'. Wonder how much it costs to go to this Silver Valley, Colorado?"

Dorcas's eyes widened. "A lot, I 'spect. Like a hundred dollars or somethin'."

"I hope it's not that much. I have a few dollars put aside. I'll go down to the station and see what's what. Pack me a bag. I'll leave tonight if there's a seat."

Her husband snorted and turned over. While she hated leavin' her other four children in his care, she had no choice. If Sally was in danger, it was her duty to rescue her.

And for that, she'd travel to the moon if need be.

CHAPTER 10

Becky smiled at Zeke as he pulled his wagon up in front of her house. "Thanks for the lift home."

He picked up the reins and nodded. "You're masterin' the skill of gettin' out without landin' on—well, you know."

As she recalled the first time two weekends before when she'd tried to disembark without assistance—and all because of her pride—her hand went to her backside, sore again from their ride today. "Thanks for the compliment. I sure enjoyed this weekend. But your mother shouldn't think she has to invite me every week." She raised her nose and gave an exaggerated sniff. "No more skunk smell here."

He chuckled. "She knows. I think she likes teachin' you how to cook and such."

"And I've enjoyed learning." She gathered her skirts and navigated out of the vehicle with deft movements. "See you tomorrow morning."

She waved as he pulled away, and he returned the gesture. She turned toward the shack, then froze. Something was off. The place was too quiet. Where were the—

She whirled around. "Zeke. Wait!"

He stopped the wagon and twisted in the seat. "What is it? Another skunk?"

"I don't see Belle and Stubby."

He cocked his head. "You're right. They might have gotten out." He turned the wagon around and put the brake on in front of the shack. "Get the horses a bucket of water, and I'll take a look around." He dismounted and grabbed the rifle he kept beneath the seat. "Stay here."

He trotted around the corner of the shack toward the corral and lean-to where Becky housed the animals. Belle, a pretty little jenny, and Stubby, short for stubborn, which he certainly was, worked hard and asked for little. But they should have been braying and calling for a late breakfast right about now.

She chastised herself for thinking more about her weekend reprieve from the mine than the safety of her property. Despite mentally acknowledging that she had no place on a ranch, she still gladly accepted Zeke's invitations to spend time with his family. While she grew to love them the better she got to know them, she knew, deep in her heart, the real reason she accepted.

And it had nothing to do with staving off loneliness. Or incorporating herself into her new community. Or even getting a delicious meal she neither prepared herself nor burned. She might try to fool herself into thinking she could learn to cook and bake by spending time with Zeke's mother, but that wasn't the whole truth.

No, she wanted to spend time with him. In spite of herself.

She knew there was no future for them, yet her heart longed for his touch on her hand, his shoulder to brush against hers, a smile just for her. This morning, at breakfast, while he'd licked cinnamon from his mouth after eating one of his mother's cinnamon rolls fresh from the oven, she'd imagined how his lips would taste right then. Sweet. Spicy. Soft.

Her cheeks burned at her racy thoughts. What would her mother say if she knew her daughter's mind? Mortified, to be sure.

And what would Zeke say? Would he think her forward? Or would he welcome such imaginings? She could hardly guess. He pulled her close one moment, then stepped out of reach the next.

As though he kept something from her.

A conundrum, to be certain.

She drew two buckets of water from the well and set them in front of the wagon team, marveling as they plunged in their velvety noses and slurped the contents to the bottom. She patted the near one on the shoulder. "You boys were thirsty."

She glanced across the yard to the shack where the men stayed during the week. It squatted near the path leading to the mine. Maybe Zeke was right, and the mules had gotten out and made their way over there. She headed in that direction, pausing when she rounded the small building so she didn't startle them.

But despite the cool shade and deeper grass in this area, no mules.

She looked toward her cabin. Where was Zeke? He should have been back by now whether the mules were there or not. Perhaps Miguel or Dakota had come by and seen them, thought to move them somewhere else. She checked the door. No note. Silly her. Neither could read or write.

Unable to wait a moment longer, she followed in the direction Zeke had headed. Maybe he was in trouble. Not that she could help much. Although she possessed a loud scream, nobody would hear. Even the next claim belonging to Arthur Wilson lay too far away for her voice to carry there.

When she rounded the corner, she spied Zeke walking, his gaze fixed on the ground. A check of the corral confirmed her fears. The mules were gone, and the crossbar that usually blocked the entry rested at least ten feet away. Even if the mules had knocked it down, the log wouldn't have landed there.

She called out as she walked toward him. "What is it?"

He held up a hand, and she quieted. "I'm checking for tracks."

Tracks? The yard was covered in tracks. Hers, his, the diggers', the mules'. How could he possibly hope to find anything of relevance?

She hugged the perimeter of the shack, keeping to the grass near the foundation. When she ran out of places to step, she paused, waiting for his next instruction.

Finally, he looked up and beckoned her over. When she joined him, he pointed to the ground. "See there?"

"No."

He knelt and outlined an indentation in the soil with one finger. "This here is a mule track. No shoe."

"I see it."

"And here is my horse's print." He pointed to another, this one deeper and more pronounced. "Heavier animal, so it leaves more of a mark. I walked him out here Friday and put him in the corral." He gestured to another. "See that?"

"Same print, but deeper."

He nodded. "You're gettin' it. I rode him out of the corral when I left at the end of the day."

She swept an arm over the other tracks. "So what does the rest of it reveal?"

"You tell me."

She lifted the hem of her skirts so she didn't brush out the marks, then followed a line of prints heading toward the edge of the woods. "Looks as if you rode over here."

He joined her. "Not me. *My* horse has a chip in his right rear shoe." He led her back to the original tracks and pointed out the difference. "See?"

She spread her hand over the print, and holding her measurement in place, went back and studied the marks. "I see that now. And these prints are a little smaller. No shoes." Becky cocked her head and studied him. "Who doesn't shoe their horses?"

"The local Indians, the Southern Ute, don't."

Alarm jangled through her as her gaze darted to the woods, thick with massive pines and tangled hedges near the river. "When?"

"Yesterday or early this mornin'."

"How can you tell?"

"Wind came up around sunset, and there's debris in some of the tracks. Bits of leaves. Cottonwood seed."

"You think they stole my mules? Why?"

"They relish mule meat, so I'm told."

The hair on the back of her neck tingled. Were they out there right now? Watching them? She'd not heard of any reports of run-ins with the natives, but she'd read enough penny dreadfuls to know that these things happened. "You mean they—they would eat them?"

He shrugged. "Don't know." He glanced around, rubbing his jaw. "Not convinced."

"Why?"

"The Indians around here are shorter. Not so heavy as white folk. And these marks seem too deep for an Indian pony with a brave on board." He knelt beside another print. "Then there's these small marks here."

"What do you think it is?"

Adjusting his hat, he squinted up at her. "Could be nail holes in the hoof. Where somebody took the shoes off his pony to make it look like it was Utes."

"That's plain mean."

She rubbed the shiver from her arms. What would have happened if that person had come when she'd been home alone?

"Yep." He stood and brushed off the knees of his pants. "Could start another range war."

"How will we know for sure?"

"Don't know if we ever will. I'll tell the sheriff when I go through town on my way home." He fixed his gaze on her, eyes narrowed and mouth turned down. "I don't like the idea of leavin' you here alone."

She glanced toward the empty corral and sighed. "They got what they came for, didn't they?"

"If it was somebody fixin' to lay the blame on the Utes, yes. If not—"

"If not, what?" Would the man never finish a sentence? Always stopping at the most important part. "Tell me."

"If it was natives, they might have hoped to catch you here alone. Took the mules as second best."

She waved off his suggestion. "And what would they want me for? I can't cook. I can barely sew. I'm more cantankerous than those mules. If they—"

Now it was her turn to stop. She'd read the stories about what Indians did to white people.

To white *women* in particular.

And while she generally accepted that those stories in the pulp fiction books were highly exaggerated, she never was certain. And this was no time to wonder.

He slapped his hat against his thigh. "You should come stay at my parents' place for a few days. 'Til we know what's what."

But she had a business to run. A home—such as it was—to keep up. Chores to attend to.

Running and hiding wasn't an option.

When she didn't answer, he sighed. "Or me or one of the boys could stay here on the weekends."

The three already stayed Sunday night through Friday, going to their own homes on the weekends. If Zeke or any man stayed here without the others the other two nights, tongues would soon wag. Not that she cared much for all of that. But she did care about the men's reputations. Particularly Miguel, who was married and had children. And Zeke, who—well, was Zeke. Honorable. Marriageable. A man of valor and integrity.

Plus, there was no way she was staying here alone with Dakota. As she'd confided to Zeke, that man pure scared her.

No, the real problem was, if she spent more time with Zeke, her heart might override her head.

And that would never do, for either of them.

What in tarnation was wrong with that woman? Zeke stared at Becky the next mornin'. Sure, she was still sore about losin' her mules. And maybe a mite scared that braves were even now watchin' them from the woods. And perhaps she was a bit flustered because she didn't get everythin' done yesterday she'd planned on doin'. Wasn't his fault he'd had to take her back to town to spend the night with Sally until they figured out somethin' else. He couldn't leave her out here by herself, could he?

His mother would kill him.

And now there she stood—well, sat, actually—bold as brass at the kitchen table while he and the diggers wolfed down their food, and told them they'd have to work Saturdays to make up the difference for the missin' mules? If they wanted them replaced, she needed to make enough money to pay for the stole ones. And the only way she saw was workin' an extra day.

Miguel glanced across the table at him, wagglin' his biscuit toward him, encouragin' him to respond. Miguel had a family to take care of on a tiny spread half a day's ride from here. He couldn't stay away six days in a row. And what of the safety of the man's wife and children? Did she pay no mind to that?

Apparently not, because she went on with some other changes. Fewer breaks. Get right to work when they got there. A production incentive for diggin' more ore.

He thought slavery was abolished in the war. But it appeared she hadn't gotten the news.

He set his coffee cup down and held up a hand, waitin' until she stopped speakin'. "Workin' Saturdays wasn't part of the deal. For any of us."

"That was before." Her face flushed. "We don't have a choice."

"Maybe you don't. But we do."

She froze him with a hard look. "I guess you could always look for another job. Not that there's much hiring going on. I suspect if anybody would hire any of you, you'd already be gone. Working for a woman is bad luck, isn't it? At least, that's the gossip I hear down at the mercantile when you all think nobody's listening."

His ears burned. He'd been part of one or two of those conversations. Not exactly agreein' with what was said, but not speakin' up to defend her either. "That's not the point. We work for *you*. You can't make a decision like that without discussin' it with us."

Her sweet smile oozed with insincerity. So unlike her. "I thought that's what we were doing."

He shook his head. "You're not discussin'. You're tellin'."

She rolled her eyes. "Same thing."

"No, it's not. And you're not listenin'." He glanced around the table and garnered a tiny nod from each man. "We won't work Saturdays. We can't."

Tears brimmed in her eyes. His gut felt filled with rocks. He made her cry. If even a single drop of water dripped down her cheek, he'd cave in and work Saturdays, Sundays, twenty-four hours a day if she said so.

Instead, she blinked rapidly, then nodded. "Could you give me Saturday mornings?"

Miguel set his biscuit on his plate. "Only until harvest. Then I must take care of my family."

Dakota nodded. "I could do that."

Zeke considered her words. A few hours on a Saturday wouldn't hurt. Until hayin' time came around. Like Miguel, he needed to care for his family. "Same here."

"Fine." She stood. "It will take at least twice as long to save enough money to pay for the missing mules, but if you're willing to work with me, I'll work with you."

He blinked a couple of times. Whatever he was expectin', that wasn't it. She never gave in so easily.

She must be truly burdened down with worries.

He was right to keep his little secret to himself.

On Tuesday, Becky sighed, then shifted the pot of stew to a cooler spot on the stove. She lifted the lid, releasing steam and heat, and stirred the contents. Yep, just as she suspected. Stuck to the bottom again.

Hoping against hope that the burnt taste wouldn't permeate the entire pot, she resisted scraping at the blackened bits of meat.

Maybe she could cover the taste with something else. She scanned the shelf over the stove. It didn't need more salt. Maybe a little more pepper—oh no! A tablespoon or more of the spice fell into the stew, sinking below the surface before she could lift the spoon to retrieve it.

When would she ever learn? She watched Mrs. Graumann cook, and the woman always shook her seasonings into her palm, measuring by some mysterious standard only she understood. A pinch. A touch. Half a teaspoon. All governed by the way the volume sat in the curve of her hand.

All she needed was to push them into quitting with more horrible cooking. Which they'd come pretty close to doing the previous day when she'd broached the subject of working Saturdays. Heavens, had she riled up a hornet's nest. It wasn't as if she asked them to pledge their firstborn son or something. Although to hear Miguel talk about his, she might not mind having the boy live with her. At least then she wouldn't be alone at night.

Speaking of which, the sheriff hadn't seemed any more interested in finding who'd stolen her borrowed mules—red man or white—than he had in finding her father's killer. Not that she'd had much time herself to look into either matter. Maybe once she paid for Belle and Stubby, she could use her extra time to hunt down the murderer—and the mule thief, for surely they weren't one and the same—and bring those criminals to justice.

She snorted. Extra time indeed. She didn't have any extra time before she had the mules or after. Maybe they hadn't been such a good idea. When she'd told the owner, her neighbor Arthur Wilson, of their loss, he hadn't seemed concerned. Simply shrugged and said those things happened. Told her not to worry about repaying him for them. But that's not how she operated. She'd pay back every penny if she died trying.

Maybe instead, she should think about hiring on another digger. Or a laborer. She leaned against the kitchen table as she thought. Four dollars for a mule would only pay a man for a week. So she could have another man for two weeks, or—

She sniffed. Now what was burning?

She yanked open the oven door and grabbed at the biscuit pan with a bare hand, searing her fingers in the process. She dropped the pan, which fell to the floor with a clatter. Golden bottoms up. Great. She hadn't burned the biscuits, but now she'd ruined them by—she glanced out the window, then quickly scooped the biscuits back onto the pan, brushing a bit of dust off a couple of them. What the men didn't know wouldn't hurt them.

She arranged them on a plate which she set on the table before returning her attention to the oven. Something still smelled. Not the stew. Not the biscuits. Oh no, the coffee pot. Using the edge of her apron to protect her stinging fingers, she lifted the lid. Boiled dry again. And that was the last of her coffee until she went into town.

She set the pot in the pan with the other dirty dishes. They'd have to drink water. Again. She couldn't abide the smirks and knowing glances they'd pass around and across the table as if she wasn't watching. If just one more thing happened, she'd scream.

A shout from the yard drew her attention, and she peered through the still-raggedy curtains—when would she have enough time and energy and money to buy the yardage to replace them?—toward the mine opening. Smoke or dust poured out. Not another cave-in!

With a final glance at the stove to make sure nothing would catch fire and burn the shack down, she untied her apron, tossed it on a chair, and raced toward the mine, grabbing two buckets Zeke insisted she keep filled in case of fire. Miguel staggered out of the tunnel, his kerchief covering his face as he coughed and heaved. As she neared, the buckets sloshing around her ankles, she noted black smudges covered his olive-skinned face. He looked as though he'd been painted with coal dust.

She skidded to a stop and set the buckets down, afraid to ask the question but afraid not to. "What is it?"

The digger leaned over, hands on his knees, coughing and spitting. "Fire. In a rafter."

"Where are Dakota and Zeke?"

He pointed. "Dakota's still in there. Zeke went to get him out. I couldn't breathe."

She patted his back. Having burned enough meals lately to fill the shack with smoke several times over, she understood completely. "When you catch your breath, dump the water from these buckets on the flames and fill them again. Then fill every container you can find and bring them here. Understand?"

He nodded, and she tore the hem off her petticoat, glad for once she hadn't gotten her dungarees washed on Sunday. After ripping the material into three pieces, she dipped the rags into the water and wrung them out, then clasped one to her face and plunged into the tunnel.

Instant darkness surely blacker than Hades engulfed her, and she hesitated, unsure which way to go. She moved to the side of the tunnel, feeling for the wall, and tripped over something—a rock, a tool?—twisting her almost-healed ankle. She bit back a groan and pressed on, breathing through the wet rag, stopping every few feet to get her bearings.

When she came to the first intersection, she cursed her stupidity. She should have asked Miguel more questions. No time to go back now. She listened. Muffled voices came from ahead, and she continued on.

About twenty feet away, Zeke and Dakota emerged from the smoke as though conjured by a magician. She hurried to Dakota's side and slipped her shoulder into his armpit. She handed her two extra rags to Zeke. "Breathe through these."

He nodded. "Can you hold him up while I tie this around his face?"

She shifted her stance. "Go ahead."

Zeke released his grip on the digger, and she gritted her teeth beneath Dakota's weight while Zeke covered the man's face with the bigger of the two pieces of cloth. Then he slipped an arm around Dakota's waist, held the final rag to his own nose and mouth, and they half walked, half carried the injured man toward the opening.

Miguel met them there, dropping his buckets and hurrying to take her place. She followed in their wake, then knelt beside the almost-unconscious Dakota. She dabbed at his forehead with her rag, easing him upright when he coughed. Miguel ran for the dipper, and soon the injured digger slurped thirstily at the water.

A knot appeared on Dakota's forehead, and she rinsed the rag and laid it across the injury. "Lie back and rest."

He pointed in the general direction of the tunnel. "The fire."

"We'll look after that. You have a nasty bump on your forehead."

"Rafter came down on me. We didn't know nothin' until we smelled smoke. Miguel tried to put the fire out, but we didn't have enough water. So we headed for the opening." A twisted grin lifted his mouth. "I wasn't as fast as him."

She pressed him back down when he tried to raise himself up again. "Rest here. You'll do nobody any good—least of all yourself—in the shape you're in."

He nodded and relaxed, breathing deeply. She studied his face, wondering if she should ride for the doctor. Or help with putting the fire out. Torn between concern for Dakota and her mine, she hesitated.

Within seconds, she had her answer. Zeke and Miguel staggered from the tunnel, empty buckets in their hands. She hurried to meet them.

Zeke lowered the rag. "I think we put it out."

"What was it?"

"Like they said, a fire in a rafter. Might have been smolderin' there for days. Or weeks. Good thing it didn't burn completely through. Could'a brought the whole roof down with it."

Miguel shook his head. "Not burning for days or weeks."

She turned to him. "How do you know? Zeke said—"

"Dakota and me replaced that rafter last thing yesterday. Was fine then."

She stared at him. She heard his words. She understood his words. But they simply made no sense to her. If they'd put that rafter up new not much more than eighteen hours ago, then that meant—no, it was simply too horrible to contemplate.

And too terrifying to voice aloud.

But speak it she must. "Then that means somebody set the fire after you stopped working yesterday."

Zeke shook his head. "Could be some other explanation."

She stared at him. "Such as?"

"Such as—" He paused as though trying to gather his thoughts. Finally, he hung his head. "I don't know any other way." He looked at each of them in turn. "But like I said before, I know all the men in this area. I can't think of a one who would want to hurt Dakota or Miguel. Or me."

She nodded, hands on her hips. "That leaves me. Somebody is out to ruin me. Or scare me off." She gazed out over her claim. "If they think they can do either, they've got another thing coming."

She turned back to Zeke and her diggers. Her next words pained her to even think, let alone speak, but they had to be said. "If you want to quit, I understand completely. You, Miguel, have a family depending on you. Zeke, you have a ranch to run. And Dakota—well, Dakota will land on his feet. He always does. But I can't hold you to your word to keep working for me. Not after all that's happened." When they didn't answer, she figured she had her answer. "Fine. If you'll come to the shack, I'll give you your wages. As for me, I have a burned stew to dump somewhere." She sighed. "Wish I had hogs. Or a dog."

She returned to the shack and pulled out her ledger book and her cash box, then sat to figure out what she owed each man. Placing each amount in a pile on the table, she tallied the remaining coins. Six dollars and a few pennies. Not much for two months' hard work. Not enough for a train ticket back to New York and her mother. Maybe she could find work in town to supplement her funds.

Footsteps at the back door drew her attention. Miguel and Zeke propped Dakota against the door jamb, washed their hands and the injured man's, then walked him to the table. Miguel brought the stew and biscuits to the table, returning to the stove as though missing something.

She could stand it no longer. "What are you looking for?"

"Coffee."

"I burned it. Again."

He chuckled. "Either you need to learn to cook, or somebody else needs to take over."

She sighed. "You're right. Know anybody wants to buy a claim?"

His brow drew down. "I don't mean take over the claim. Take over the cooking."

"Does this mean you're willing to take your chances on the food one last time, so you don't have to leave on an empty stomach?"

Dakota shook his head, then wrapped his hands around his temples. "Oh, I gotta remember not to do that."

Zeke chuckled. "No, we were more concerned you might kill a tree if you chucked the stew in the woods, so we figured we'd eat it up for you." He waited until each man nodded. "Then we reckon we'll go back to work. Nothin' else to do on a fine Tuesday afternoon."

She blinked back tears again. What was it about these rough-and-tumble Coloradans that melted her heart every time they did something nice for her?

She'd have to find something nice to do for them. "The biscuits—"

Zeke bit into one and moaned in pleasure. "Best ones yet."

Dakota nodded. "Agreed. What did you do different?"

"Nothing."

Well, maybe she was getting the hang of at least one thing in this new life. She could start small.

CHAPTER 11

"You can't do this to me!" Becky stomped a foot, raising a cloud of dust that drifted off on the breeze. If only her troubles would disappear so easily. "We had an agreement."

Miguel hung his head and studied his boots. "Sorry, Miss Becky, but it's getting too dangerous to work for you."

Dakota nodded. "We're not doin' you any favors. All we're doing is takin' your money. We ain't findin' any new veins."

Since the fire on Tuesday—just four days before—tensions had run high at the mine. Becky had sensed the men's reluctance to enter the tunnel. She'd caught Miguel's final glances at the sky before he went in, as though he thought he'd not see it again for a long time—or ever.

Well, all that was expected, wasn't it? The men were doing dangerous work. And they toiled long hours. Adding four more hours to their workweek might not have seemed like such a huge thing originally, but she found the extra commitment wore her down too. She had an extra breakfast and midday meal each week to prepare. Less time for her own chores as she made certain the men had what they needed. Less opportunities to spend time with Zeke at his ranch.

Didn't they realize she was part of the team, not just the boss? She'd even pitched in and helped move the ore to the sluicer since the disappearance of the mules.

As expected, the sheriff didn't add that particular criminal activity to the top of his list. If he even had a list, in priority order or otherwise. In fact, she doubted he'd done anything to find her animals.

Just yesterday, she'd asked around town about Indian activity in the area, and nobody confessed to knowing anything about it. Perhaps Zeke was right, and a local man had disguised his horse to blame it on the natives.

The bigger question was whether everything that had happened in recent weeks—the cave-in, the explosion, the missing mules, and, most recently, the fire—were all unfortunate accidents. Or the work of one person intent on scaring her away.

Or maybe Dakota was right.

She hadn't let on, but she'd overheard him muttering under his breath to Miguel about how "women in a mine was bad luck." She'd stifled a snort at that comment. Bad luck, indeed. Men were injured or killed almost every week in these parts in mines where a woman never set foot. The fact she had more than her fair share of troubles wasn't because she was a woman.

She had no time for superstition or for the ignorance that bred and populated such beliefs. No, her own hard work and the hard work of others was all that mattered. And somebody worked overly hard to send her skedaddling, as the locals would say.

Well, she wasn't leaving. This claim was hers, and she meant to keep it that way.

Zeke stepped forward. "Miguel, Dakota, please. I'm willin' to keep workin' if you will."

Miguel shook his head. "My missus sent word that I need to come home."

Dakota shuffled his feet in the dust. "And I can't do the work on my own." He studied the westward mountains whose peaks still bore snow as though wishing he was there instead of here. "Think I'll move on. Got a hankerin' to see more of the country."

Zeke studied her, his brow furrowed. With concern? Disgust? Then he looked back to the men. "If I bring in a couple of my own wagon horses to haul the ore, will you stay?"

She glared at him. What was he thinking? Offering his own animals as if he owned the place. Through narrowed eyes, she peered at him. What did she really know about him? Other than what he told her, that is. Maybe this was his idea all along. Come in, make himself indispensable. Treat the place as if it were his. Set up all these accidents. After all, he was here every time something happened. He was the one who didn't want to name names. Well, no wonder if he was behind the events.

Was she turning into a paranoid woman? Great. If the men learned that, she'd confirm their beliefs about an emotional female trying to run a business. She took a couple of calming breaths. Clearing the cobwebs from her head, she considered her next step. Without the diggers, she couldn't work the mine. Without the mules, *they* wouldn't work. And even with them, they might not.

She counted to ten until her racing heart slowed. "Would you at least work today? And if nothing happens, come back on Monday?" When they didn't answer, she continued. "And starting next week, no more Saturday work."

Dakota and Miguel exchanged glances while she prayed a prayer of sorts. Even though she hadn't talked to God in years, maybe He was still listening.

Please, let them say yes. Don't let my father's dream die here.

She blinked while she waited for their decision. Her father's dream? Is that what she was doing? Trying to fulfill his wishes?

What about her own?

At what point would this mine become hers and not her father's?

At what point would the dream be something more than a desire to prove herself to her father?

Could she really build a life on what her father had or hadn't wanted? No more than she could build her character on her mother's assessment of right and wrong.

She needed to make choices that were best for her, not for them.

"Okay."

She pulled back to the present. Had she heard correctly? "Okay?"

Miguel nodded. "If nothing bad happens today, I come back Monday."

Dakota held out his hand. "If he's in, I'm in. But Saturdays off."

She looked to Zeke for his input. "What about you?"

"I'll ride hard for the wagon horses. Got no mules, but the chestnuts should do fine so long as they don't spook in the mine. Back in twenty minutes."

The diggers picked up their tools and headed for the mine opening, Zeke trotted to his horse in the corral, and she returned to the shack. She had breakfast and a midday meal to cook.

Hopefully, without burning either.

And if she did, maybe Miguel wouldn't consider her culinary mistakes under his preface of nothing bad happening.

Two hours later, Becky straightened from the laundry tub over the fire outside the shack. Was that a shout? She listened, glancing around to determine its source. Miguel burst from the mine opening, one hand over his mouth, the other fumbling at his waistband.

What in the world?

He raced around the rear of the chicken coop to the privy, flung the door open, then slammed the door.

Unmistakable retching noises and moans followed.

Next Dakota appeared. When he skidded to a stop at the outhouse, he smacked the door with an open palm, cursed, and hurried into the brush at the rear of the shack.

Good heavens.

Zeke sauntered out of the mine. He glanced at the privy before heading in the opposite direction, picking up speed as he disappeared around a small rise.

Miguel staggered into the mid-morning sunlight, wiping his mouth and holding his stomach. "Oh, Miss Becky. I made a mess in the—in the—"

But his words were apparently choked by what rose in his throat because he turned away and vomited into the dirt. She wrinkled her nose at the sour mess at his feet. He faced her again, opened his mouth to speak, then beelined for the outhouse.

Dakota emerged from the brush, his face pale yet mottled as moldy buttermilk.

She stepped forward. "Can I get you some water?"

"Not unless it's in a tub. I need to get down to the stream and wash up."

He sidled away from her, walking sideways. When he got near the stream and stripped off his dungarees, she saw why.

The back of his pants was wet and dark.

Compassion for her diggers pulled at her. And what about Zeke? Was he suffering the same malady? Had they contracted influenza? She'd heard about entire towns decimated because of the illness. Perhaps she should go to town for the doctor. She could probably manage Zeke's horse that far. Under his excellent tutelage over the past weekends, she'd become comfortable if not adept in the saddle.

As she considered her course of action, her insides gurgled. She looked down, surprised to hear her body make such a rude noise. Then her stomach lurched, roiling and threatening to erupt.

The outhouse, still occupied by Miguel, was out of the question. She had no choice. She raced into the underbrush as quickly as her wobbly knees and long skirts would allow.

How mortifying!

"Food poisoning."

Thud. Thud.

With those two words, the final nails in her coffin. Or rather, in her mine's coffin.

But right now, more like her own.

Becky stared up into the kindly face of the town's doctor. How

Zeke had managed to find the strength to summon him, she didn't know. But she was glad he had.

The afternoon sun cast long shadows through the small window onto her bunk. Miguel and Dakota, stretched out on the benches at the kitchen table, snored. Dakota mumbled something in his sleep about a horse and a saddle he'd lost in a card game. Zeke lounged in the only chair in the shack, his legs stretched out in front of him.

Becky turned back to Doc Raymond. "Are you sure?" She licked her parched lips. Would this thirst never be sated? "I was afraid it was influenza."

"Positive." He straightened and tucked his tools into his black bag. "Came on suddenly. No other influenza symptoms such as lethargy, dizziness, aches, pain. Symptoms are subsidin' quickly. No temperature." He glanced around the shack. "What all did you eat for breakfast?"

Zeke chuckled. "How many times have I told you your cookin' would kill us?"

Oh, that man! "Never saw you offering to take over."

He held his hands in surrender. "That's women's work."

"Lots of men cook on trail drives. In logging camps."

"Only three men here, and they're all miners. You're the cook. Even if you do burn everythin'."

She sighed. Not only were his words true, but they stung to the core. It wasn't her fault her mother had failed to train her in *women's work*. "Breakfast wasn't burned."

He tossed her a smile. "You're right. Wasn't cooked enough. Eggs were runny. Bacon was raw. And those biscuits."

She glared at him. "What about them? You ate three."

"Had to fill the hole in my gut with somethin'."

The medical man cleared his throat. "Children, children, stop arguin'. Sounds like the problem was either the eggs or the bacon. How old were they?"

She squeezed her eyes tight as she thought. "Bacon came fresh out of the larder. Bought it at the mercantile this week. Wanted to treat the men." Tears threatened to overflow, and she chewed her bottom lip to quell them. "I collected the eggs this morning. But I hadn't used eggs in a few days, so they might have been three or four days old."

The doctor nodded. "And maybe older if you happened to miss some the last time."

She could hold back the deluge no longer. A sob threatened to choke her, so she let it out. What was the use of putting on a good face when she'd almost killed her employees with her cooking?

The doc patted her arm. "Not your fault. I had an old teacher in medical school who talked about poultry and hogs carryin' all kinds of filth in their blood that can make people sick. Could be the eggs or the bacon. Next time, make sure you cook it completely. And wash your hands in between handlin' them, 'specially if you're cookin' other food at the same meal. Scour the washin' area and the plates." He glanced at the kitchen, where breakfast dishes still lay piled high. "No leavin' dirty plates and pots around either."

She nodded, the movement causing the room to spin. She closed her eyes and waited for the sensation to subside. "We've been so busy. I was going to clean up but decided to do laundry first and—"

"You need to work less and clean more."

Miguel moaned and struggled to rise. The doctor hurried over and handed him the water dipper, and the digger drank greedily before lying down again.

Doc Raymond checked on Dakota and nodded. "They're both doing well. When they wake fully, they can head home and take it easy for the rest of the day."

This news lifted Becky's spirits some. "That's great. Tomorrow is the Fourth of July. We can relax and spend time in town for the celebrations."

The doctor smiled. "I hear they're havin' a pie-eatin' contest. And a pig roast."

Dakota groaned and held his stomach, and the doc laughed.

"Sorry. Forgot. You won't be eatin' much tomorrow, I 'spect. But you can come back to work fresh on Monday."

Miguel raised his head. "Not me. I quit."

Becky sighed. Not this again. "Miguel—"

"We had a deal. Work today and if nothing bad happens, work Monday." He opened one eye and stared at her. "This is bad. I think Dakota will agree. Sorry."

The doctor stepped in. "It could happen to anybody."

Miguel stared hard at the older man for a long moment. "I dunno."

Zeke stood, holding to the back of his chair. She knew exactly how he felt. Then his legs wobbled, and he sprawled in the chair. "I'll be here on Monday. What about you, Dakota?"

Dakota shrugged, one arm dangling over the side of the bench as though reaching for the floor. "Guess explorin' can wait a while. What do you say, Miguel?"

"If you can talk my wife into letting me come, I guess I can try once more."

He laid his head down, turned his back to her, balancing on the narrow bench, and soon snored.

She glanced at Zeke, who shrugged, then dropped his chin to his chest, closed his eyes, and joined Miguel in sleep land.

Just when it looked as if she was out of the mining business—again—she was back in just as quick.

But how long would the reprieve last this time?

This much bad luck shouldn't happen to anybody.

Later that night, after Miguel and Dakota left, Zeke stepped out of the shadow cast by the full moon on the shack and headed for the mine openin'.

None of what had happened here today—or any other time, for that matter—was Becky's fault. And as much as he didn't want to accept that somebody he knew would purposely set out to hurt

Becky or derail her minin' operation, he couldn't argue this was more bad luck than ever the number thirteen attracted.

Well, he'd keep guard here tonight—and every night if need be—until he learned the truth.

He froze in his tracks as his thoughts took another direction.

Could Becky herself be behind all these accidents? The previous incidents had involved only the men, even though she'd helped rescue the diggers from the cave-in. Was that her motive? A heroine complex of some sort? Trying to prove herself smarter and more resourceful than the men? He didn't think so. But then again, what did he really know about her, other than what she told him?

Nothin'.

Nothin', that is, apart from what he saw in her. She worked hard. She invested her own money into the business. She had good manners and treated his family with respect. She acknowledged her ineptitude when it came to preparin' food, and she graciously accepted cookin' lessons from his mother.

She tried hard when it came to learnin' to ride a horse and likely suffered through many hours of sore muscles as a result.

She never backed down from a situation, and, as he'd seen when she dove into the hole and pushed Miguel out, she didn't consider her own safety when it came to people she cared about.

All in all, she seemed a good sort. The kind of woman who would stick by her man through thick and thin.

Of course, appearances could be deceivin'. His mother often said that. But as a fine judge of character, Ma'd never even hinted that somethin' might not be right about Becky. And if Ma thought she was okay, then she likely was. He could sure do worse in pickin' a woman.

He doubted Becky was the source of these troubles.

But if not her, then who?

He was fairly certain not the diggers. He spent enough time around them to know they would never purposely put the other man's life in danger.

Which meant it had to be somebody from town. Or another miner. Or a lunatic drifter intent on creatin' trouble.

His mind cast back through his own list of acquaintances. Was somebody out to get him? Was he attractin' this bad luck? If so, he'd quit in a heartbeat. No way he'd put Miss Becky in any kind of danger. No, there was no doubt in his mind these were the intentional actions of another, meant to accomplish one thing, to drive Becky away.

But why? Why would anybody want her to leave?

Did somebody have a vendetta against miners? When he'd asked around town, nobody had admitted to havin' her kind of troubles on their claims. He'd checked with Wilkerson at the land office, but the man had denied knowing anythin' about somebody harassin' miners.

Could one of the long-time residents—a rancher or farmer, perhaps—want the land? No, it wasn't worth grazin' or plowin'. Too rocky.

The stream burbled over the rocks, reflectin' the moonlight across its expanse. Water. Water rights. Maybe a local wanted the water. Just as he needed water for his own herds, perhaps somebody was lookin' for a cheaper way to acquire those rights.

He considered the property owners in the area. Most of these hills were divided and sub-divided into mine claims. More than a dozen men—and one woman—eked out a subsistence livin', diggin' deeper into the hillsides in search of that ever-elusive silver, the new gold.

None of them owned more than a few head of stock, and none would be interested in water rights. They all had access to the stream and took what they needed for free.

He stepped carefully across the yard toward the corral and called for his gelding usin' their secret code—two snaps of his fingers, originally intended as a signal to call the animal back if it ran loose. He'd had to use it only a couple of times. Once, he'd twisted an ankle and needed the horse to come to him so he could mount and ride home, and the other to impress a girl.

His horse whinnied softly and loped toward him. He dug in his pocket for a sugar cube, which the animal ate from his palm, and when it snickered for more, he rubbed its nose to quiet it. No point in rousin' Becky. If she heard him out here, she might get scared. Maybe the next thing he needed to teach her was how to use a gun, although if she came out with one in a panic, shootin' at anythin' that moved, he'd best be out of range.

He smiled at the picture of her, shotgun cocked against one hip, the moonlight behind her, her nightgown flappin' at her ankles, then brought himself up short. If she knew he thought of her in her bedclothes—well, it simply wasn't proper.

Mayhaps he'd leave the shootin' lessons for a while yet.

His horse's ears pricked in the direction of the mine, and Zeke stiffened as he listened. A rock skittered across the dry ground. The sound of a boot against the dirt. A five-heartbeat silence, then a hush and a sigh like somebody copied him and paused until convinced nobody else lurked in the area before continuin' on their way.

He covered his horse's nostrils with a hand. Well-trained, the gelding stood stock still. Footsteps faded in the distance. Either the man—for who else would be out at this hour?—left or he went into the mine.

Either way, Zeke would find out.

He released his horse, pattin' the chestnut's shoulder and pushin' it toward the lean-to. "Hush."

He waited until the animal obeyed and moseyed away before turnin' toward the mine. Takin' care not to make the same mistakes the intruder had, he crossed the open space, pausin' at the mouth of the tunnel. From inside came the unmistakable sounds of metal against rock—diggin'.

Was the man settin' another trap? Or was he stealin' Becky's silver?

He'd know soon enough.

He stepped into the mine, wishin' he'd thought to strap on his pistol before beginnin' his night rounds. He would—tomorrow. And he'd carry a few matches next time too. The mine, dark enough during the day, was almost impenetrable once the sun went down.

He inched his way inside, listenin' before steppin', feelin' for the side of the tunnel to keep his bearin's. Givin' the ore wagons wide berth. Balancin' on one foot when he bumped the water bucket, prayin' the dipper wouldn't tip over, givin' him away.

Then he turned a corner, and a lantern cast a flickerin' glow on the walls and ceilin'. His breaths quickened, and he cast caution to the wind. There was only one way in and out of this tunnel, and to escape, the intruder would have to go through him.

In his haste, Zeke grasped the wall, sendin' a small avalanche of dirt and rubble cascadin' to the floor. The diggin' noises ceased as abruptly and completely as though they'd been a figment of his imagination. He paused again, glancin' around for a weapon. Within reach, against the wall, rested a shovel. From past experience, he was well aware that one of those to the back of the head took the wind out of the biggest man's sails.

He gripped the rough wooden handle in one hand, the metal spade in the other, then stepped into the circle of light.

Nothin' except a pickaxe layin' against a pile of dirt.

Nobody.

He turned to look behind him where he sensed rather than saw movement.

Too late.

A length of wood raced toward his head. He ducked, raisin' the shovel in defense. Wood glanced off wood, slidin' toward his hand, where it connected with his knuckles. Pain shot through his hand and arm. He dropped the shovel and raised his arm to deflect the next blow.

Too slow.

The feeble light glinted off somethin' shiny in the man's hand—

or on a finger. A ring, perhaps?

Then the board connected with the side of his head, and the lights went out.

Zeke groaned and opened his eyes. His mouth felt like it was stuffed with cotton.

He worked his tongue around. Wait a minute—it *was* stuffed with cotton. His kerchief, previously around his neck, now prevented him from speakin' or callin' for help.

What had happened?

His head throbbed like he'd been held upside down for two days. Some kind of Indian torture? He breathed deep through his nose. No, not natives. No bear grease. No musky scent from their wild tobacco or peculiar oils.

And Indians didn't dig in mines.

Metal rang on rock, then shufflin' sounds indicated activity. He wriggled his hands tied in back. Bound almost as tight as his feet. Unable to move or call, he lay prone, trussed up like a hog-tied calf waitin' for the brandin' iron.

Or the slaughterhouse.

He grunted when a hand appeared out of the circle of light and gripped him by the neck of his shirt. When he twisted to release the hold, an open palm across his cheek reeled him onto his backside again.

"Behave yourself." The voice hissed like a bullsnake. "Or else."

Unable to see the face of his captor, Zeke struggled to identify the man by voice alone. No such luck. He needed to be smarter than this if he wanted to get out of this alive.

Which he did.

Although why the man hadn't killed him already was beyond him. Would have been much easier.

The man loomed over Zeke, a knife in hand, his face covered in a kerchief. Zeke's breath caught in his throat. Was this the end?

He closed his eyes. *Lord, if this is it, please protect Becky from this man.*

The man bent over and slashed the rope bindin' Zeke's feet before he stepped back and gripped the knife in his hand, serrated edge up. "Stand up."

With no other choice apparent at the moment, Zeke did as he was told.

"Turn around."

This was it, then. For some perverse reason, the man chose to stab him or slit his throat from behind.

God, help me.

But instead, his captor tied a rope around his waist, then prodded him at the base of his neck with the blade. "Walk. And don't do anythin' sudden-like. And no turnin' around."

When he stepped forward, the rope went taut. He paused, uncertain what to do next. The kerchief in his mouth felt as big as a ham, threatenin' to choke him. His nose ran, mucous drippin' down over his lip.

"I said, walk forward."

Another poke with the blade and Zeke stepped forward, strainin' like a cart horse into his makeshift traces. Somethin' tied to the other end of the rope dragged across the ground.

A bag of ore, based on the weight and the man's previous activities.

He leaned into the load and hauled it a few feet before pausin' to catch his breath. His captor prodded him after a brief respite, and he continued, pullin', pausin'. Pullin'. Pausin'.

Finally, he reached the mouth of the cave and rested against a boulder.

The man pointed upstream with the knife. "Thataway."

Zeke glanced over his shoulder, a movement that garnered him another jab with the knife. This time, blood trickled down the back of his neck, warm and sticky on his skin.

"I said, no turning around. Walk."

The moon cast a glow over the path ahead, and Zeke trod carefully to avoid missteps. Twistin' an ankle out here would likely be the death of him. Grippin' his hands together, he pulled where the man directed. His gelding, silhouetted against the light, pressed against the corral rail.

He wriggled his fingers to get the circulation goin' again, then snapped his fingers twice. The sound, almost drowned out by his breathin', seemed as faint as the rustle of a butterfly's wings.

He kept his eyes glued to his horse. After about six heartbeats, the gelding's ears pricked.

His captor pushed Zeke forward. "Keep movin'."

As he lost sight of the gelding, his fingers touched a cuff button. He twisted the disk and dropped it on the ground. Kind of like leavin' a trail of breadcrumbs.

He hoped he wasn't headed to the oven in the fairy tale.

CHAPTER 12

Becky woke with a start, sitting up in bed and staring through the darkness, trying to discern what awakened her. The hoot of an owl? The yip of a coyote or the howl of a wolf?

Her ears strained to pierce the darkness, and her eyes, wide but unseeing, scanned the room. A moonbeam poked its way through a tear in the curtain, puddling on the floor near the kitchen table like spilled milk.

Still nothing.

Wait. There it was again. A horse's nicker. She settled back on her pillow. Nothing to worry about. Just Zeke's horse talking to—to whom? Or what? Zeke was long gone.

Except if he was, his horse would be with him.

Heart racing, she slid her feet into her boots, forgoing the laces. No time. She yanked her wrapper around her, struggling to force a hand through a sleeve turned wrong way out.

Easing the back door open, she stepped out into the yard. The full moon lit the yard barely enough for her to make out shapes. The lean-to. The corral rails. The horse, staring toward her.

Wishing she had some sort of weapon, she inched forward. The gelding mince-stepped from the far side of the small enclosure, tossing its head and looking back over its shoulder as though trying to communicate an important message.

Horses. She knew little about their behavior apart from the fact they liked sugar cubes—and if Zeke thought she didn't notice her dwindling supply each day, he had another thing coming—and, if others were like this one, thought nothing of waking a body in the middle of the night.

She glanced around. Everything seemed quiet. Maybe she was overreacting. Perhaps Zeke had decided he didn't want to leave her out here by herself. How sweet.

She headed past the mine toward the shack where the men slept, Zeke on one side of a dividing wall, Miguel and Dakota on the other. She tapped on his door. "Zeke. Your horse needs you."

When she received no answer, she lifted the latch and peered inside. The small area, not much larger than the cot itself, was empty. Perhaps he was in the privy. Heat flooded her cheeks at the thought of finding him coming back from a late-night trip to the necessary—or worse yet, encountering him still inside.

She paced the area in front of the shack, trying to decide what to do. But nothing came to mind. Watching her step, she froze, one foot still lifted. What was that?

About twenty feet away, just outside the mouth of the mine, a small, white disk glinted in the moonlight.

She hurried over and picked it up. A button. Strange place to lose a—she studied the ground ahead of her. Something was dragged here recently, by the looks of it. Maybe earlier today. A sack of tailings, perhaps? She followed the trail. No, if it was rocks and gravel that passed through the sluicer, the diggers would have dumped that down the bank toward the stream.

These marks led upstream.

And—another button.

But who would lose two buttons so close together? She surely didn't feed the men well enough that they were bursting through their clothes.

No, this was more like—like someone wanted to leave a trail for another to find.

Like breadcrumbs in the fairytale.

Thirty feet ahead, another button, but this one went to the left at a fork in the path. A broken twig confirmed her conclusion. Somebody had passed by here recently. Somebody who had wanted to alert those behind as to their direction.

The drag marks appeared as a deep rut in the gravelly path, although in reality, in daylight, would have been barely visible. She continued around a turn—and then the marks veered off the path and down toward the stream.

She followed, bending a twig here, piling a couple of stones there, as she traveled through the underbrush. Her own personal breadcrumbs.

At the water's edge, a canvas sack lay on the river bank, the tow rope tossed aside.

She scanned up and down the stream. Nothing. No movement. No buildings. Apart from the bag, no evidence anybody had been here.

Following her markers, she returned to her path and continued uphill. Another button. And another. That made five. Hopefully, she'd find the wearer of the shirt before he ran out of clues for her.

Another hundred feet and fifteen minutes later, when she despaired that she'd lost the trail entirely, a grunt from the woods to her right stopped her dead in her tracks. Although she'd never seen a wild pig, she'd heard plenty of stories—some vastly exaggerated but perhaps some true—and encounters with the beasts never ended well. Particularly for an unarmed woman, alone in the woods at night.

And if not a wild pig—for surely those stories were about the Arizona Territory, not about Colorado?—perhaps a bear? Meeting a she-bear separated from her cubs was not an encounter Becky relished.

How she wished she'd paid more attention to these stories, particularly the part about how the person got out of the situation to live to tell the tale. She racked her brain. Make a noise to scare a bear, or not? She couldn't recall.

Another grunt. About the same distance away. Thrashing in the underbrush. Grunt. *Thunk*. Scratching. She turned her back and wrapped her arms around her head. There was no way she could outrun a bear—that much she recalled. Perhaps if she pretended not to see it …

Grunt. Thrash. Grunt-grunt. Grunt.

Almost as if somebody sought to signal her.

She lowered her hands and peered into the woods. "Is somebody there?"

The trees swallowed up her words.

She tried again. "Who is it?"

Grunt. Grunt. Thrash.

She stepped toward the aspen and spruce that wove together into an almost impenetrable wall. "Where are you?" For surely nobody would make such a racket unless they needed help. The wearer of the shirt, perhaps. "I can't see you."

Following the series of grunts and thrashing, she pushed aside tree branches and stepped over a boulder and a fallen log into a small clearing. About ten feet away, the whites of a man's eyes shone in the dark. She peered at him. "I have a gun. Don't try anything."

Her words were braver than she felt, to be certain, but if he thought she was armed, perhaps he'd behave himself. His feet, tied together, thumped on the forest floor, and a rag shoved into his mouth prevented him from calling out. Ropes around his upper body pinned him to the trunk of a decades-old spruce. He didn't look very dangerous.

She hurried across the clearing, and as she neared, his features came into focus.

"Zeke!"

He whipped his head from side to side in response.

She knelt beside him and, with fumbling fingers, untied the kerchief filling his mouth.

He leaned over and spat and gagged a couple of times before looking up at her. "You didn't bring any water, did you?"

"Do I look like I'm hiding a canteen?"

He eyed her up and down, no doubt taking in her diaphanous wrapper and thin nightgown, the incongruent boots, and hair which cascaded over her shoulders. She flicked the offending tresses back and pulled her clothing tighter around her.

A tiny smile lifted his countenance. "No. I can't see a single place where you might."

She huffed and stood. "Fine. I'll leave you here to your own devices if you think you're so clever."

He lifted one brow and pulled the other down. "No, don't do that. Please. I've been here all night it seems."

She knelt again. "Speaking of which, what *are* you doing?"

"I was keepin' guard on your place, and I saw someone go in the mine. When I went in, he knocked me out and—"

She laid a hand on his arm—his finely muscled arm—noting that his shirt hung open to the waist, revealing an equally finely muscled chest with a smattering of blond hairs. She was certain her face flamed red in the darkness. "Wait a minute. What were you doing guarding the mine?"

"Not the mine, although that was part of it." He exhaled. "Okay, I'll 'fess up. I was worried whoever is behind all these accidents might come back again. I didn't want to see you get hurt, so I thought to stand guard and catch the varmint in action."

"You could have been killed."

"But I wasn't."

"Or badly injured."

He smiled up at her. "You care. I'm touched."

She shook her head. "Touched is right. In the head for coming out here to find you." The man was so conceited. "It's not that I care about you. I care about the mine. And I love your mother and wouldn't want to be the one to tell her that her son was killed in some hare-brained scheme—"

"Not hare-brained. It was a good plan. I did catch him."

She looked around. "Really. The only person I see tied to a tree is you."

Zeke had to agree with her on that point. He *was* the only person tied to a tree. The knowledge—and the admission—did nothin' to help his ego.

If his father was here, he'd say Zeke's pride was more tender than a sore tooth.

And that would surely be the truth of the matter.

Where just a few hours ago he'd set out to be the knight in shinin' armor for his damsel in distress, now same fair damsel was savin' his hide. Because truth be known, just as his captor had intended, if he'd spent much more time out here tied to this tree in the middle of nowhere, he'd have died. Dehydration or wild animals or even the weather would soon have done him in.

Once again, he owed his life to this woman, who was, in reality, the furthest thing from needin' his help than almost anybody he knew.

But he'd never tell her that.

He squirmed, wrigglin' his hands to the side. "Can you untie my wrists so we can get out of here?"

She fumbled with the knots, then shook her head and sat back on her feet. "Too tight. Do you have a knife?"

He nodded. "Down my left bootleg."

She slid her fingers between the leather and his dungarees—now why did that feel like a lightnin' bolt tickled him?—and pulled out the Bowie huntin' knife in its sheath before cuttin' the ropes, nickin' his wrist only once. For which she apologized several times.

He pulled the last of the rope apart and held his hands in front of him, flexin' his fingers and arms to get the blood flowin' again, then he held out his hand.

She stared at him, the knife restin' in her lap. "What?"

"The knife."

One corner of her mouth lifted in a half-smile. "I can cut the ropes on your legs."

He shook his head and reached for the blade. "I'll do that myself, thank you very much."

"Sounds as if you don't trust me." She handed over the weapon. "But if you insist."

He neatly slit the bonds, then stood, usin' the tree for support, until feelin' returned to his feet and his head stopped spinnin'. A quick check of the back of his skull confirmed he had a knot the size of a goose egg, but no blood where his captor had hit him. After several deep breaths, he was ready to go.

Becky headed back the way she came, but he hesitated. It would be difficult to follow the man's trail in the dark, but he wanted to go after the scoundrel who'd caused all this trouble. He didn't want his captor to gain any more ground.

Unless, of course, the man wasn't goin' anywhere fast. He knew the woods and trails pretty well. Made Zeke drag the ore to a spot on the stream where a small canoe could pick it up and take it somewhere else for processin'. As though he intended to stick around.

Definitely seemed the man was a local.

A fact which stuck like a stone in his craw.

He'd already attested to the integrity of the men in this area to Becky more than once. But somebody seemed intent on provin' him wrong.

Well, fine. He'd reveal this bad apple.

Sooner or later.

Laughter and music greeted Becky as she neared the large tent at the end of town. Zeke had driven her in to church first thing this morning, and then to the Fourth of July celebration that began with food at noon and would end tonight with a dance and perhaps some sparklers.

The early afternoon sun beat down, and she swept her hair back from her forehead. Clothed in her pale-brown Sunday dress and best hat—both of which she'd trimmed with a three-cent length of ribbon that nearly matched the chocolate-brown of her eyes—she loved the way the fuller chambray skirt swished around her ankles, making her feel dainty and elegant. Dungarees might be practical, and the skirt thing sure made working in the mine easier, but there was nothing like a pretty dress to make a woman feel beautiful.

Nearby, a woman stood behind a table bearing tin mugs of lemonade, and Becky's mouth watered at the thought of the sweet, tart, and cold beverage.

She shook her drawstring bag. Just a few pennies scraped from her meager savings.

Water would have to do for now.

Miguel tipped his wide-brimmed hat as he strolled toward her, his arm looped around a very pregnant woman with four toddlers in tow. Goodness, she hadn't given much thought to his family situation. She understood now why he was anxious to return home each weekend. And the serious impact of sickness or injury on his part.

Dakota strolled over. "He's sure got his hands full."

Zeke smiled at the man and his family. "That he does."

"Well, I'm headin' off." Dakota cleared his throat, and his eyes fixed on the saloon. "Time to wash the dust from my throat." He tipped his hat to Becky. "See you later."

Zeke clapped him on the back. "Don't forget tomorrow's a work day, and you were hoverin' close to the pearly gates yesterday."

One corner of Dakota's mouth lifted. "But today I'm as alive as I ever was or ever will be again, so it's a day to celebrate."

When he trotted across the street, dodging a man on horseback, then pushed through the swinging doors of the saloon, Becky sighed. "That's likely the last we'll see of him today."

Zeke pushed his hat back on his head. "Prob'ly."

"Well, thanks for the ride. I'm sure you have people to see." She quirked her chin toward Dakota's destination. "Or places to go ..."

"I work much too hard to waste my time and money on that stuff. By the end of the day, he'll be drunker'n a skunk and broker'n a church mouse." He shook his head. "Seems a darn fool way to spend life."

"In that case, I'm heading toward the plant table. I want to ask for tips on raising a good kitchen garden next year. My beans don't seem to be doing too well."

He chuckled. "And even if they were, you'd burn them until they weren't recognizable."

She mock-punched his arm. "Any time you want to step up and take over, just let me know." She leaned closer and lowered her voice. "I'll haul on my dungarees and supervise the men, and you can cook."

He backed up, hands held at shoulder height in surrender. "Not me. We'd all starve."

"If she depended on you to cook, that's for sure the truth."

Becky turned at the voice behind her. Mrs. Graumann and her girls crowded around, their gaily decorated hats in red, white, and blue proclaiming their patriotism and love of this celebration. She smiled at Zeke's mother, who pulled her into a hug. "Hello. It's so good to see you again."

His mother released her to allow her daughters and daughters-in-law to embrace her as well. "You need to come out to the farm again real soon."

As the onslaught of hugs continued, Becky peered out from between an assortment of the girls' hats, almost smothered by the lace and ribbons. "I'd like that."

Zeke pulled his mouth down. "What? No hug for me?"

Mrs. Graumann pushed him away. "You've already had your share." Then she laughed and pulled him close. "But I guess one more will never hurt."

Sisters Viola and Lucy joined their mother as all three wrapped their arms around him. Sisters-in-law Sue and Nan stood to one side, their heads close together as they whispered and glanced at

Becky.

Uh-oh. Those two were up to something, she was certain.

Then Zeke's mother linked her arm through Becky's. "You simply must come along. We saw the most amazing booth over here. Hats galore."

Becky resisted. "Oh, I don't need another hat."

Nan stepped forward. "We're not here to buy. Just to try them on. To daydream. Come with us?"

"I don't think—" Becky turned to Zeke. "We had plans, didn't we?"

Zeke held up his hands in surrender. "There is no stoppin' the Graumann women when they have somethin' up their sleeve. I'm stayin' out of it."

Seeing no way to bow out graciously, Becky allowed herself to be steered along the street, glancing back at Zeke once or twice, pleading with her eyes for him to rescue her.

Instead, he shrugged and strolled in the opposite direction.

She'd get him.

Although Zeke didn't see Becky for at least two hours, she was never far from his thoughts. Every time he spied a pretty piece of material or a length of hair ribbon bein' hawked by the many tinkers in town for the Fourth, he wondered if a dress in that pattern would look nice on her, or if that shade of ribbon would set off her hair just so.

Even last night—or was it early this mornin'?—when he was trussed up like a Thanksgiving turkey, he'd thought of her. Faced with the possibility of dyin' in the woods alone, even though nothin' was declared between them, he'd passed the time and tried to ease his fears by wonderin' if she'd cry when they found his body come spring. If she'd miss him. He had no cause to even go down that path, but he couldn't help himself. Might she feel a responsibility to honor his memory and never wed, choosin' instead a solitary life of minin' and livin' in that shack?

That particular thought brought him no joy at the time, and it didn't now either. A woman as alive and full of vitality as Becky Campbell deserved a man her equal.

A man like him.

The truth of what his heart was tryin' to tell him all along hit him like a lightnin' bolt. He'd been a fool to deny his feelings for her. An idiot to think there was any sensible reason he shouldn't pursue her. A numbskull of the highest proportion to believe he could simply walk away and forget her.

Finally, he needed no more convincin'.

When he finally spotted her draggin' her tail behind her just before the pie-eatin' competition got underway, it was like breathin' a fresh lungful of spring air. He stepped toward her and held out his arm. "Care for a cold lemonade?"

She hesitated, then slipped her arm through his, whispering from behind her hand. "Your mother and the girls have worn me to a frazzle."

He gestured to a table beneath a tree. "Let's sit over there in the shade. And I'll get you a special treat." He peered at her, brow furrowed, mouth drawn flat with concern. "You haven't eaten, have you?"

She dabbed at her upper lip with a handkerchief. "No. But don't dare enter me in the pie-eating contest."

He chuckled. "Hadn't thought of that. Might have been interestin', though. Be right back."

He trotted to a booth next to the one selling baked goods and placed his order, buyin' two doughnuts to go along with his surprise. Then he returned to their table and set his purchases in front of her. "Didn't know whether you wanted cherry or lime, so I got one of each."

Her eyes widened. "Oh my. What is it?"

"A snow cone. Latest new thing, apparently. Made from shaved ice and fruit. And this—" he pointed at the bag containin' his other treat—"is a doughnut. Correction, two doughnuts. The same, so no need to choose."

She fumbled in her drawstring purse. "Allow me to reimburse—"

He held up a hand and placed it on his chest. "Do not insult me, fair maiden."

She smiled and chose the lime snow cone. "In that case, I'll take this one." She bit into it, savorin' the cold and sweet before coverin' her mouth with her hand and gigglin'. "Oh my. That's wonderful. Thank you."

He tucked into the treat also, and before he knew it, both the paper cones and the bakery sack were empty. He crumpled all three together into a ball. "They're roastin' a calf over hot coals, and later on, for dinner, there'll be corn, green beans, garden greens, and lots of pie for dessert."

"Sounds wonderful. What shall we do until then?"

He gazed around the park area. Couples strolled hand in hand along the pathways. Children played ball or hoops. Over yonder, men played horseshoes, and under the next tree, several older women rocked and knitted. Seemed most of the town turned out for the Fourth.

"Maybe we can do a little investigatin' into these accidents."

She tilted her head in question. "How do you propose we proceed?"

"Thought we could wander around, listen in on conversations, ask a few well-placed questions."

"Won't we appear suspicious? Simply walking the area, sitting in uninvited?"

He chuckled. "You don't know these people very well."

"I haven't been here long enough to get to know them."

He stretched his hands over his head, then clasped them together behind his neck. "They love to talk. They'll welcome you quicker'n a hen welcomes orphan chicks."

"If you say so."

He stood and offered her his hand. "I do say so. And if they think you're with me—" He left the rest of the sentence unsaid. Hopefully, he didn't have to spell out everythin' for her. "Shall we?"

She studied his hand for a moment, then looked around. Color rose to her cheeks. "You mean, they'll think we're—oh, dear, I don't—I wouldn't want to—oh."

He wasn't certain which upset her more—that somebody might think they were a couple, or that she thought perhaps if they did, that would somehow be wrong.

He persisted. "We don't have to say anythin' that isn't true. Just ask a few questions."

"Such as?"

"Anybody new in town. Anybody lose stock. Accidents. Mischievous children on the loose."

Her brow drew down. "You don't really think the cave-in and explosion are accidents, do you? Or young hooligans with too much time on their hands and too little supervision stole my mules or started the fire? Or poisoned our food?"

"No. But if we allow folks to think that's what we think, maybe they'll let their guard down."

"Well, that's fine, then." She accepted his hand and stood. "So long as we don't give them the wrong impression about us."

His pleasure at her touch overrode the burnin' question in his mind. What was so wrong about folks thinkin' they were a couple?

Or maybe she wasn't worried about others.

Perhaps she was more concerned about how *he* viewed their relationship.

On the ride home that night, just before midnight, Becky groaned as she eased her boots from her feet and sank back onto her seat. "Hope you don't mind, but my feet feel like they're on fire."

Zeke, next to her on the wagon bench, clicked the reins. "Not at all." He leaned forward, elbows on his knees. "Pick 'er up, boys. Let's get the lady home."

She swatted at a moth that hovered too close. "What a day. Long and hot, for sure." Her stomach gurgled, and heat rushed to her cheeks. "Oh my. You don't think I ate something that didn't agree with me, do you?"

He grinned. "What? Like the doughnuts? Or the shaved ice? Maybe the fried chicken or the lemonade Mrs. D made? Or the ham sandwiches or potato salad Ma brought?" He shook his head a couple of times. "I declare, I don't think I've ever seen a woman eat so much."

She giggled. "I might have overdone the celebrating a little, but really, I was so glad to be upright today, I threw caution to the winds."

He kept his eyes on the road, his tone deepening with sincerity. "I think this was the best Fourth of July ever."

His words warmed her several degrees beyond what the evening air already had. "Me too."

"So where did Ma and the girls take you?"

She rolled her eyes. "Just about everywhere. I'm sure I talked to everybody in town. And that was before I managed to escape and then you and I made the rounds."

Becky closed her eyes and relaxed in her seat. The best day ever. Had the company had anything to do with the quality of the day? Probably. After his sisters returned her, Zeke had stuck to her side like a tick to a hound dog, as Mr. Graumann was fond of saying. Every time she turned around, there he was. For which she had no complaints.

Something her mother often said came to mind: "Sometimes I sense your father near even I can't see him."

Is that what it meant to really care for somebody?

She needed to keep her mind clear. If she wanted to make her place here, she had life-altering business to conduct. Today had marked a serious beginning to her investigation into her father's death, even though it hadn't yielded the results for which she'd hoped. "Too bad we didn't discover anything directly related to the accidents or my father's death."

"Well, I didn't 'spect we would particularly. Just hoped to narrow down the field some."

"I think the best part was talking to people who knew him."

"Yeah, that Mr. D can talk the leg off a chair."

She smiled, thinking back to the kindly older man's words—and the pleasant surprise of how willing the townsfolk had been to share memories with her. "He said my father always paid his bill on time." A man of integrity, as the shopkeeper had phrased it. "And then Sally's George shared how Papa helped him finish his deliveries when the wheel fell off his wagon one day."

He chuckled. "I liked the story the widow told about how Robbie Campbell could chop a cord of wood faster than anybody she knew, and how he proved it by keeping her supplied during the winter."

"Yes. She said she'd sorely miss him.'"

The older woman's tale enabled Becky to see another side to her father. Had she failed to see these attributes in him before? Or had his life here changed him—for the better?

Zeke rubbed his jaw and frowned. "Your father sure went out of his way to validate his claim, sendin' telegrams to the state capitol to check land records and livin' in a tent for a month even after the searches came back negative."

"He didn't want to steal another man's work." Becky slipped her boots back on, her toes sufficiently cooled. "And after all that, he still waited before he came down and filed the claim and paid the fee to build his shack and start digging."

Zeke switched the reins to his right hand and laid his left along the back of the seat. Touching her shoulder. Sending a tingling sensation down her spine. Warming her insides. Somehow, talking about her father with Zeke seemed natural. Comforting.

Intimate.

She shifted slightly to prolong that feeling.

In response, Zeke tilted his face toward her. "I think he was concerned."

The thought of her father realizing something was amiss with somebody in his new community unsettled her, loosing a wave of twirlings in her tummy. "I agree. George said Papa saw signs of digging at the mine opening."

Zeke nodded, his eyes bright in the darkness. "But the fact that your father never had any trouble after filin' his claim is what made his death so dad-gum surprisin'." He shook his head. "It's like one minute he was there, and then,"—he snapped his fingers—"the next, he was gone."

Becky shivered. Zeke's words highlighted how suddenly her life—and her mother's—had changed. And honestly, she'd been so wrapped up in her own pain and trying to figure out how to tell her mother of his death, she hadn't considered the impact of her father's death on those around him. For her, he'd been gone for so many years that, in some ways, it was as if he were already dead. Still, knowing she'd never see him again—at least, as the preacher said, not this side of heaven—was a shock and a fact she was still getting used to.

As they turned the final bend in the road to her place, questions rose about Zeke's association with the final group of people they'd visited that day—natives who had huddled around a campfire at the far end of the park, cooking something in a pot over the flames. Questions she wanted to get in before they said goodnight. "How did you get to know the local Utes?"

He shrugged. "Dunno. Went to school with some of them. Sold them beef. They may not believe like we do, but the locals are a good sort. They've never made any trouble."

"Not everybody thinks so, do they?"

"No matter where you go, you'll find somebody who hates somebody else. Just because of the color of their skin, their job, their religion."

"They make me nervous." She swallowed hard. "The big knives. The bows and arrows. They always seem ready to fight."

He patted the pistol on his hip. "No different than me, really. I always wear this. No tellin' when I'll come across a rattlesnake that needs dispatchin'." He chuckled. "Besides, you likely scare them more than they scare you."

"I saw how they looked at us when you asked about buying mules from them." She wrapped her arms around herself. "Murderous, I thought."

Holding the reins in one hand again, he twisted in his seat to face her. "Just because they're not white doesn't mean they're 'thievin' Injuns,' like lots of folks call them. They were here long before my family or anybody else in town ever lived here."

She dropped her gaze before his penetrating stare. "Sorry. I don't have much experience with natives."

"That's okay. They think all white people are liars and thieves too."

In fact, the two families had been very nice. Reserved but polite. When Zeke had mentioned that Becky needed a couple of mules, they hadn't seemed to know anybody who might have a pair for sale, which was the usual habit after natives stole stock. Hunting was good right now, so thieves would have no reason to eat what they took.

Wanting to change the subject—since this one seemed a sore spot for him—she grasped for something to say. "Your horse woke me last night. Did you teach him to do that?"

He nodded. "Originally, I trained him to come when I called. If I was hurt and couldn't get to him. Or needed a rope but couldn't let go of the calf. Times like that. I used sugar cubes as a reward. But he likes sugar cubes so much—"

"I noticed."

"He likes sugar so much, I thought I'd take advantage and teach him more. Sometimes a whistle can alert others when you don't want them knowin' you're there, so I use snaps of my fingers. One snap, come here. Two, neigh. Three is the signal to dump the rider. In case somebody tried to steal him." He chuckled. "He was prob'ly confused when you didn't give him sugar."

"As far as I'm concerned, he can have sugar every day. He saved your life."

And perhaps hers too.

CHAPTER 13

Matilda Campbell stared through the partially fogged window of the dining car at the trees streaking past. Using her linen napkin, she swiped at the vapor clinging to the glass—and indeed, to every surface, although she suspected that was simply how it appeared. She turned her head toward the front of the train and then the rear, hoping to see something more interesting than the present scenery.

She sighed and sat back into her seat. Nothing but more of the same. Would they never get through Kansas? However did the migrants in the wagon trains bear it? No wonder so many halted in their tracks and homesteaded here—they couldn't bear another day of the monotony. Why anybody would choose to live in such a harsh climate, one devoid of so many of the necessary comforts such as cities, street lamps, and good help was beyond her.

Her morning coffee service appeared before her, delivered by the same woman who had served her yesterday. Slight, pale, and perhaps her own age—maybe even younger. Difficult to tell since the years hadn't been kind to the server. Matilda glanced up and offered a nod and a half smile. As this was her first long-distance train journey, she still wasn't sure about the social customs expected with the help. So far, she hadn't met another female passenger of her own class and thus had no example to follow.

The shadows under the server's eyes seemed darker this morning, however, and despite the differences in their social standing, Matilda's heart—as a woman and a mother—ached for her. Apart from a couple of men deep in conversation at the far end of the car, who were attended to by a colored server, she was the only other diner. Surely a kind word couldn't be wrong. "Thank you for your prompt and efficient service."

The woman, whose name tag read Polly, dipped her head, never raising her eyes from her hands. Her worn cuffs and the scuffed tail of her dark skirt bespoke hardship. And the silver threads in her reddish-brown hair bespoke worry. "Thank you, ma'am."

Matilda leaned closer, her taffeta traveling dress rustling. The colored female steward had done a fine job washing, starching, and ironing the bouffant sleeves, high, rolled collar, and pleated skirt last evening. "Polly, I sense something is bothering you. Can I help?"

Even as the words left her lips, she wished she could snatch them back. For surely the woman had problems that required money. Didn't most? Perhaps now she'd have to listen through a long and drawn out—and quite possibly exaggerated and untrue—story of a sick husband, a dying mother, a lame child, or all three.

Instead, Polly lifted her head and stared at her, tears welling in her eyes. "Thank you, ma'am, for askin'. I'm on my way to Colorado to see to my daughter. I think she might be in some kind of trouble."

Relief washed over Matilda like a tidal wave. "What a coincidence. I'm traveling to Colorado as well. My daughter is getting married." She gestured to the seat across from her. "Please, sit. I've been most lonely on this train. The people don't seem inclined to talk, and, frankly, apart from cowboys and gamblers, there are few worth speaking with."

Polly glanced around. "Well, I don't know …"

Matilda waved off her words. "If anybody harasses you, I'll tell them you're comforting me." She fanned her face with the napkin. "I fear my daughter is about to make a huge mistake, and I'm simply overcome with worry and apprehension."

When Polly sat, Matilda pushed her coffee cup toward her. "There now, drink." While Polly did as instructed, Matilda considered where to begin. Perhaps at the beginning. Well, maybe not quite that far back. "My husband is an adventurer. He travels the world, seeking out all sorts of excitement."

Polly's eyes widened as she sipped her coffee.

Breakfast can wait. This is far more important.

Using her hands, as was her habit, to embellish her story, Matilda continued. "He went to Africa. All over the United States. Canada. Mexico. South America. Bringing home the most fantastic stories you could imagine." She paused and savored the memories, like a tasty marzipan or a bit of the chocolate he brought her from one of his travels. "Our home in New York City is filled to the rafters." She raised her arms and created a half circle to demonstrate the extent of his extravagance. "Bursting, you might say, with mementos of his travels."

"Oh dear. Is he never home?"

Matilda chuckled. "Occasionally. And his homecomings are always—um—exciting and entertaining." She winked at her companion. How often she'd joked with the ladies in her bridge club about happy reunions with Robbie. "I'm sure you understand, being a married woman and all."

Polly stared at her for several heartbeats, then a flush raced up her neck and cheeks. She set her coffee cup on its saucer, her hands trembling so much the china rattled. "Oh dear."

Matilda saw at once that despite this woman's rougher exterior, she was an innocent on the inside. She must watch her tongue. She lowered her voice. "But this time I fear something has happened. My daughter decided to follow him to a hamlet in Colorado, and when she wrote me, letting me know she arrived safely, she made no mention of him."

"Nothin'? Never mentioned her pa?"

"Not a word." Matilda crossed her arms over her ample bosom. "If he wasn't there, I think she'd have said so. Don't you?"

Polly sat forward. "Was she on good terms with him?"

"Absolutely. Adored him. Called him 'Papa.' Me, I was only ever 'Mother.' 'Papa's Little Girl,' I called her."

"Did you have just the one?" Her gaze dropped and her cheeks flushed. "I'm sorry. That was rude of me."

"Yes, just the one, but it wasn't for—" Matilda bit the words back. She was going to say "for lack of trying" but feared Polly might be too shocked at that. She tried again. "It wasn't because we didn't want more. It simply didn't happen. Which is why I think he spoiled her all the more. Bringing her gifts. Sending letters and telegrams filled with tales of the people and places. Sometimes I wonder if he isn't half gypsy."

"So your daughter is gettin' married?"

"She is. I'm excited, of course, but also worried. He's the assistant postmaster—of a very small town, for goodness' sake. I mean, what opportunities are there for advancement? And she completely neglected to tell me about anybody else other than the shopkeeper who gives her room and board and a small salary. She lives in a room behind the shop, can you imagine that?"

Polly chewed on her bottom lip. "I'd be mighty proud if that was my daughter you was talkin' about."

Matilda hesitated. Of course, this poor woman listened to her going on and on, complaining about her own lot in life when she was the one with dark shadows under her eyes. Probably hadn't had a decent night's sleep since boarding the train in—where did she say she was from? Goodness, she hadn't even given Polly time to say three words about herself. "Why don't you fetch us a double order of toast with jelly and another coffee cup, and we'll settle in here for a grand old chat?"

"Well, I don't know."

"Don't you worry one minute. If need be, I'll pay your ticket to wherever you're going. I think we're going to be fast friends."

Polly hurried off to get their food, and Matilda stared out the window once again. Suddenly, the trip wasn't so boring. She'd met another woman—not of her class, of course, and one she'd never likely talk to in the city—and already liked her.

Perhaps Robbie was right, and social standing wasn't as

important as she thought.

She gritted her teeth. He was so often right and she so often wrong, especially when it came to people.

She hoped she was wrong this time about her suspicions that Becky didn't mention her father because he was dead.

Not that her lifestyle would change—she was the one with the money—but she surely did enjoy his homecomings. Even at her age—middle-age by some accounts—she still found absence made the heart grow fonder.

As trees blurred past, she sighed. "Oh, Robbie, my love, where are you?"

As Polly exited the kitchen and headed back to Mrs. Campbell's table, she pondered her situation. Sure, the woman was nice enough to ask what was troublin' her, but then she went on and on about herself. The fact they both had daughters who had gone to Colorado gave them somethin' in common, she supposed, but that's where any similarities ended.

For one thing, Mrs. Campbell had class. That was apparent in her lovely dark-blue travelin' dress, the gold locket nestled in her bosom, and the fact she ate every meal in the dinin' car, never buyin' food at the train stations as she herself did if there weren't leftovers from the kitchen.

For another thing, she had money. Travelin' first class, with a sleeper car, not to mention her pale white skin, manicured nails, and at least four suitcases—goodness, this was at least the fifth outfit change in the ten days they'd been on the train. Polly rinsed her apron and underthings in the kitchen sink each evenin', her single faded-green day dress twice since leavin' New York.

Plus Mrs. Campbell had a husband who worked. Or at least, did somethin'. Traveled the world. Brought home gifts. She paused when her hands shook so much the silver on the tray rattled. Had sweet homecomin's.

Unlike her husband, who had nothin', drank up what little she earned, and did little else except beat her and the kids and get her with another to care for. A husband she wished would walk out one mornin' and never come back. She'd be better off without him. At least then she'd qualify for widow's benefits from the parish.

But he never did her any favors before. There was no reason to think he'd start now.

She returned to the table and set the tray down. "I told the cook that this was all you wanted, and he said after I served you, I was free until the midday meal." She slid the extra cup and saucer toward Mrs. Campbell. "Shall I pour?"

"Oh, do. And yourself another, as well." The woman lifted the lid on the jelly and marmalade jars. "Orange marmalade. Seville, do you think?"

"Not sure, ma'am. But they do say it's very good."

"Then marmalade it is." She slathered the sweet concoction on a toast triangle. "And please, no 'ma'am.' My Christian name is Matilda."

"Well, perhaps when it's just us, ma'am. Matilda, I mean." The name served to emphasize the difference in their stations, a gap as wide as the ocean, and one not bridged by simply callin' each other by first names. "How is your coffee?"

"Hot and strong, just the way I like it." She took a bite of toast. "I've done enough talking. Tell me about yourself."

Polly shrugged. "Not much to tell. Married. Five children. My oldest, Sally—well, her pa wanted her to marry the son of this fella he knows, and she wasn't havin' any of it."

Matilda smiled, and it wasn't one of those fake smiles neither. Polly saw right into the woman's heart, it seemed. Maybe she was wrong about her. Judgin' her based on her clothes and such. Much as she'd been judged by others all her life.

Matilda sipped her coffee, her little finger stickin' out like she was royalty or somethin'. "My Rebecca didn't seem to have any interest at all in getting married. Of course, she was in the debutante class of last season. Oh, the boys swarmed around her like honeybees around a flower. But one by one, they all drifted away when she wouldn't give them the time of day." Matilda's fingers flittered again. "There I go, doing all the talking. Tell me about your Sally. And your other children."

And so for the next half hour, Polly shared stories about Sally, Dorcas, and the others. But especially Sally. What a hard worker she was. Took care of the young'uns. Wanted to be a wife and mother someday, but not just yet. Wanted to see the world.

Here Polly paused. "She would love to talk to your husband, I'm sure. She'd hang on his every word. She looks at pictures in books all the time. All the time she isn't workin', that is. Books from the library about Africa, Australia, and—and—" For the life of her, she couldn't recall any other countries. "And the like. Makin' up stories about what the pictures showed. Savin' her pennies to buy a travel book or two." Polly closed her eyes, the memories overwhelmin' her and increasin' the ache in her chest caused by Sally's abrupt departure. "Well, like I said, she's a good girl."

"Sounds like my Rebecca and your Sally would get along famously."

"That would sure cheer this mother's heart, knowin' she had someone like your daughter watchin' out for her."

Matilda's hand went to her chest, and she groaned like she was chokin' on a crumb. Polly pushed a glass of water toward her, but the woman shook her head. Instead, she dug into her purse which rested on the seat beside her, extractin' a small bottle. After removin' the cork stopper and droppin' a small white tablet into her hand, she placed it under her tongue, then sat back and closed her eyes.

Uncertain what to do, Polly turned to her faith for both direction and strength. She prayed, askin' God to sustain Matilda until she at least saw her daughter married. That's what she'd want if the situation was reversed and she the one needin' help.

After several minutes, Matilda opened her eyes and offered a tiny smile. "My apologies. My heart, you know. I get these pains, and I can't breathe. The doctor said not to worry." She blew air through her lips. "He obviously doesn't know me very well. I worry about everything. Whether to take a parasol because it's going to be sunny or rainy. Whether to pack extra shoes in case my feet swell. Whether my daughter is marrying the right man or not." She drew a couple of deep breaths. "I am feeling much better now."

Polly allowed the tension to slip from her shoulders. Goodness, travelin' with a bad heart. Matilda was very brave. "Maybe I should leave you be."

Matilda reached across the table and touched her hand. "Please, don't go. This has been such fun. Tell me more."

"Well, there's not much more to say. Sally wrote me. Well, she must'a had a friend write to me since she can't read nor write. Said she arrived safely. Has some kind of business and lives in a shack."

Matilda chuckled. "Well, at least my Rebecca lives in a building. That's some comfort, I guess."

The woman's words stung, but she wouldn't let on. Matilda had enough of her own worries. "Hopes to save enough money to buy more equipment. Oh yes, and she talked about sewin' up new curtains for the shack. All that sounds like my Sally."

"But something alarmed you?"

"Kind of like your girl, she hardly mentioned her pa … or the little ones. Dorcas said probably she was still mad at her pa for tryin' to marry her off like that, but even so, I think she would have mentioned the young'uns. And she opened the letter with 'Mother.' She never called me that in her life. Always 'Ma.'"

Matilda straightened. "What did you just say?"

Was she hard of hearin'? Or maybe she'd dozed off. "I said she always called me—"

"Never mind. I heard that part. What does she call you?"

"'Ma.' When she didn't, I wondered if she was in some kind of trouble. You know, like somebody forced her to write the letter or somethin'." Her daughter, so pretty and so smart, could still have fallen victim to some crazy person or scheme. "So I had to see for myself. Didn't have money for the train, so I talked them into lettin' me ride for free if I worked every day of the trip. So that's how come I'm here. And right pleased I am to be too. I sleep in my own bed without a man pesterin' me. No babies wakin' in the night to be fed or held. And I eat pretty regular."

Matilda's mouth turned up in a half smile. "I think we have more in common than we know."

"How's that?"

"I think I received your letter and you mine."

"What?" Her hand flew to her chest. "How could that be?"

"Envelopes got mixed up." Matilda sat forward. "My letter opened with 'Ma.' Not 'Mother,' like yours did." She tapped the table to enforce her point. "My letter contained a ten-dollar bill—for train fare, one can only assume."

Polly couldn't stop herself from blinkin' several times at the woman's disdainful tone. "And what's wrong with that? If I'd gotten money like that, I wouldn't have to work my way to Colorado."

Matilda sighed. "Forgive me. I meant no offense. It is just that my daughter knows well that I have no need of pocket money."

"Makes sense." She offered a conciliatory nod. "Where did your daughter settle?"

"Silver Valley."

"That's where my letter came from."

Polly's regal companion finished her tea and relaxed against the cushioned seat. "This evening, perhaps you can fetch your letter for a comparison. I have no doubt both will be written in Rebecca's hand."

"I will do that." Polly clasped her hands to her chest. "If the girls know each other, it sure does my heart good to know they're together."

Matilda nodded. "I'm feeling better than I have in months."

"Well, sure. You're goin' to see your daughter soon."

"Better still, she isn't marrying the assistant postmaster. Your daughter is."

Matilda's world tumbled and twisted around inside Polly's head as she struggled to make sense of them. Sally. Marryin'? Oh, what joy if that were true. And to a nice man who worked. For the government. A future. Provision for her eldest daughter and the family she'd eventually have.

But that meant … "Oh, you thought you were goin' to see your Becky married off."

"That's not my greatest concern right now."

"Then what is?"

"I'm concerned that Rebecca didn't mention her father because he's dead."

CHAPTER 14

"Please, Mr. Wilson. I need to get back to work." On this, the second Friday in July, Becky gritted her teeth to keep from screaming. Her ledgers called to her. Her unfinished chores mocked her. And this man was irritating her simply by refusing to leave. "I'll let you know if I decide to accept your offer."

Standing in her front yard, the man who owned the claim just upriver bristled. "You won't find anybody else to offer you as much, you know."

She sighed. "Yes, you already told me."

"I'm only trying to do you a favor. On account of your father."

"And owning two claims so close together would make it easier for you, too, I'm sure." His smarmy manner and the way he leered at her were getting on her nerves. "Thank you. I'll keep it in mind."

"Well, as I said—"

"Good day, Mr. Wilson."

"Well, you just remember this: mining is dangerous business. And even more so for a woman."

His words chilled her to the bone, and she turned and headed for her cabin, certain he wouldn't follow her inside uninvited. Already, he'd been there over two hours, inspecting the mine and asking questions about the sluicer and veins and yield.

Questions she had no desire to answer.

And while his purchase offer was more than she'd paid for the claim, she tired of his subterfuge. Coming here pretending to be concerned about her, when all along, he really wanted to see if the place was worth making an offer on.

Thankfully, the man headed down the road. Something about

going to town.

Well, she hoped he did—and kept right on walking.

She entered her cabin, closed the door, and leaned back against it, trying to shut out the competing voices in her head. One said to take the money and head back to New York, while the other mocked her for giving up on her dream and her father's dream.

Unable to decide which to listen to, she shut out the world around her.

Which was why the knock on the door startled her so much.

Had that man come back?

"Go away."

"Becky? It's Zeke."

Zeke? Oh, thank heavens.

She eased open the door and peered past him. "Is he gone?"

"Wilson?"

"Yes." She stepped back from the door and let him in. "Is he?"

"Yeah. I passed him on the road." He eyed her up and down. "You got your dungarees on."

She exhaled. "I had to clean the chicken house this morning. Do you mind?"

His eyebrows raised. "No, no." He peered at her, his brow furrowed in concern. "What's goin' on?"

"Nothing." She headed for the kitchen. "Coffee?"

"That stuff you keep burnin' in that pot?"

"No. Fresh."

"Sure." He sat at the table. "What did Wilson want?"

"Nothing important."

"Looks like he wore you to a frazzle."

"It's nothing, really." She pulled out a couple of mugs and a plate of not-too-badly-burned biscuits. It would have to do. She filled the mugs and carried the meager offerings to the table. "What brings you out here?"

"Just got back from town. Here's the receipt for the blastin' caps." He set the paper on the table. "And here's the mail. Looks like you got yourself a letter."

She nodded. "Thank you. I expect it's from my mother. I forget how long it takes for things to move out here."

"Doesn't take long at all once it's here. But New York City sure must feel like the other side of the world."

She set the coffee and biscuits on top of the ledgers spread all over the table. Payroll. Accounts to pay. Ledgers to update. Seemed the work involved with running a business never ended. She nudged the envelope to one side. "It certainly does."

Zeke placed the envelope and receipt beside her cup. "I'll leave you if you want to read it in private."

Becky tucked the letter into her pocket. "No hurry." She sipped her coffee. "Let me see, I mailed my letter almost two months ago. It won't hurt to read it later. Whatever is in it is all history now, anyway."

He smiled, breaking a biscuit in half and holding up one side for inspection. "Like them newspapers ever'body seems to fuss over. Weeks old already."

Becky sighed. "Not like in the city. A fresh newspaper and mail delivery every morning and evening but Sunday."

"For heaven's sake, what would you do with that much readin'? A body'd do nothin' but sit." Zeke smeared some butter on his biscuit and took a bite, chewing with apparent appreciation. "When would a man get any work done?"

She chuckled. "The evenings seem longer in the city. There are lanterns, and I even hear some houses are equipped with gas lamps."

"Sounds dangerous to me. And stayin' up later means a body is tired in the mornin's. Can't get up at dawn if you've been up past eight o'clock the night before."

Becky just shook her head. Why keep arguing with the stubborn man?

Signaling a change of topic—or rather, a return to the previous topic—Zeke quirked his chin toward the door. "I don't like that fellow hangin' around here."

"He's not hanging around, as you put it."

"Well, I don't like it."

"It's none of your concern."

"He's got a bad reputation, and I don't want you talkin' to him alone again, you hear?"

"I can take care of myself. I doubt he'd kill me in broad daylight."

At that, Zeke paused and leaned across the table until their noses almost touched. "Your father was gunned down not ten feet from where we're sittin'."

His words stole her breath. Or maybe it was his proximity. Rejecting the vivid picture created by his words, she stared at the freckles across the bridge of his nose. His nostrils flared like a racehorse in the gate, ready to bolt. Was he really that afraid for her—that his concern would turn to anger when he felt she wasn't taking him seriously enough? What else did he expect her to do?

Becky's vision blurred, and she chewed on her bottom lip. Then she did the only thing she could.

She surrendered to the tears burning at the back of her eyes and the sobs clawing their way up from her heart. Humiliated at her show of weakness, she jumped up and ran out of the shack and into the outhouse, slamming the door behind her, leaning against it as though she could keep him out if he really wanted in.

Which apparently, he didn't.

No huge surprise there. Why should he want to get tied up with an emotional female? One who didn't know one end of a pickaxe from a frying pan, at that? Who burned most everything she cooked or left it so raw it bled on the plate?

Selling out might be easier.

Not that she was of a mind to avoid the difficult.

If so, she wasn't her father's daughter.

The envelope in her pocket mocked her, taunting her silent declarations that she was strong enough to survive in this country. She wasn't even willing to open her mother's letter for fear of what the woman would say. Even from two thousand miles away, Matilda Applewhite Campbell wielded control like an iron fist over her only child.

After a good cry—and long enough that Zeke gave up on her and left—she returned to the empty cabin and the accounts she was working on before Mr. Wilson arrived. She set her pen in the crease of the ledger and closed the book. Enough of figures today.

She straightened her shoulders and drew a deep breath. She'd deal with her mother's response. Perhaps the woman had turned over a new leaf, realizing that her efforts to control her husband's life had failed, so she should relinquish attempts to control Becky's. Perhaps her letter included relief expressed over her safe arrival, congratulations on owning a business, and hopes for a visit at Christmas.

And perhaps three little kittens would learn to knit mittens.

Using a table knife left over from breakfast, she slit the envelope and removed the letter. Just another social *faux pas* her mother would frown upon. She checked the signature. *Mother.*

Oh, dear. Not *Your Loving Mother* or *Love, Mother* or anything even resembling.

Mother.

Translation: a permanent frown. Mortification. A lecture at the least, remonstrations at best.

Another sigh.

Dear Rebecca. Received your letter of May last. Pleased to hear you arrived safely and found time to write.

Translation: You finally took time from your busy day to write to your poor, worried mother who envisioned you dead in a ditch along the railway in some unnamed place.

While encouraged to learn of your employment, am concerned about your future plans.

Employment? A funny choice of words, to be sure. And future plans? About the only thing she'd mentioned in the letter was her desire to change out the curtains in the shack. Seemed a strange way to view something as inconsequential as that.

I beg of you, don't do anything so rash as marriage.

Marriage? What was she talking about?

And to an assistant postmaster.

Becky sat back. Had her mother lost her—oh no! Had she gotten the letters mixed up when she put them in their envelopes? If so, Sally's mother had no idea her daughter was planning to marry in less than ten days. And her own mother was under the mistaken impression she was wedding George.

However much I pray you will wait, if you choose not to, I will endeavor to be happy for you.

Becky read that last line again. *Happy for you.* That didn't sound like her mother. Maybe she *had* changed.

Since you left, I've had bad news from the doctor. My heart has weakened with the strain of first your father's long absence and then yours, and he advises me to not suffer stress or shock. I spent several weeks in hospital in June because of the same, and the good man said I may not survive the next. But I cannot see my only child married without being present, so am leaving tomorrow morning—

Becky checked the postmark again. June 24th. Her mother was already *en route*.

—and plan to arrive in time to assist you with your wedding plans.

She gasped. Not only could her mother die at any moment from her heart condition, but she was traveling to Silver Valley. The arduous journey alone might kill her.

Thinking ahead to future grandchildren who will comfort me in my ailing years has given me a new lease on life.

If she told her mother there was no wedding, that news—or disappointment—could finish her off. But not only was there no wedding, there was no potential groom.

Despite how much her mother sometimes grieved her, Becky had no desire to send the woman to an early grave.

She'd figure out something, even if it was only a pretense.

∞

Zeke strode to the mouth of the tunnel. That Becky Campbell was one ornery female. Tryin' to put on an act, when underneath she was as delicate as a butterfly. Like after Wilson's visit. Somethin' sure upset her. And when Zeke had tried to find out what, she up and burst into tears, runnin' to hide in the privy.

Women. He'd never figure them out.

And stupid him, givin' her that envelope. Already up to her ears in papers, she didn't need anythin' else on her plate. He could have held off and delivered it later today. Closer to quittin' time. Or even tomorrow. But he'd seen the return address. Mrs. Robert Campbell. Her mother. Becky needed to hear from her mother.

But she'd treated the letter like an unwanted account from a supplier. Or an announcement from an attorney with bad news.

He sighed. Well, back to work. The diggers would soon come out, hot and sweaty. He'd check the water bucket, maybe rustle up some cold beans and a biscuit or two from breakfast, and—the unmistakable, heart-stoppin', bone-shatterin' boom of dynamite, followed by a cloud of dust, rock, and gravel, spewed from the tunnel. His feet refused to move—seemingly frozen to the ground—even though his brain screamed at him to do somethin'.

Fifty feet away, the shack door crashed back on its leather hinges, slammin' against the front boards, and Becky emerged, her face white and mouth in a tight line. "What's going on? Not another cave-in?"

He shook his head. "Not this time. Heard the dynamite first."

She trotted toward him. "They're not scheduled to blow today, are they?"

"Nope. And if they were, they'd be outside the tunnel, not inside."

She whirled to face the openin'. "They—they're still in there?"

"Yep." He grabbed a couple of buckets and handed them to her. "Let's get goin'."

Near the table he called his desk, he grabbed a couple of shovels, then held up a hand to stop her from runnin' into the mine. Dust still swirled in the openin', so he dipped his kerchief in water before tyin' it around his nose and mouth. "Go back and get a kerchief for yourself."

She shook her head. "No time."

He gripped her arm. "No point in you gettin' overcome. I need you in good form."

She stared at him before noddin' and turnin' toward the shack. "I'll be right back."

He lit a lantern kept handy for such an event, adjusted the wick, then stepped inside. The glow of the light barely pierced the darkness. *Must be what hell is like.* He took a few tentative steps. At a sound behind him, he turned and squinted through the gloom. Somebody stood not three feet away, and while he couldn't make out her features, he knew it was Becky in that crazy skirt thing.

While he waited for her to close the distance between them, bits of rock and dirt dripped from the roof of the tunnel like meltin' snow, some snakin' down his back underneath his shirt, some peltin' his head, one even ploppin' on his cheek near his eye.

She pressed a hand to the kerchief obscurin' her face. "Now what?"

"Give me a minute to see how bad the damage is."

When she nodded, he turned away and continued down the tunnel. About fifty feet in, two smaller lines branched off the main one. Everythin' to the left looked clear, but rocks and debris littered the right-hand branch. He picked his way over and around, duckin' his head where a couple of timbers seemed cracked and threatenin' to collapse any minute.

Another twenty or so feet, and a wall of collapsed rock and timbers prevented him from goin' farther. Memories of the previous collapse played across his mind. With enough time, he and Becky could get the men out.

He stepped up to the blockage. "Miguel. Dakota. Can you hear me?"

Muffled voices filtered through the debris. "Boss man, it's Dakota. We hear you."

"Good man. Are you hurt? Is Miguel with you?"

"Not hurt. Just a few cuts and scratches. We're both here, and we'll live."

"Okay. I'll get Miss Becky, and we'll start diggin'. If you can safely help from the other side, do so. Should have you out in about four hours or so."

He'd turned to leave when a shout came from behind. He paused. "What did you say?"

"We don't have four hours. Water is comin' in. Blast must have opened up a spring."

Zeke's heart pounded in his ears like a stampedin' herd of cattle. "How deep is the water?"

"Right now it's about two inches, but this is a small tunnel. Won't take it much more'n an hour to fill."

An hour. Not enough time to get through this mass of dirt and rocks. *Oh God, we need Your help here.* "We'll get you out. Hold on. Start diggin'. Down low. That way, once we break through, the water will drain out this way."

"No such luck, boss man. The tunnel is slanted upward in our direction."

Zeke groaned. Would nothin' go right? He dropped the shovels and raced toward the tunnel openin', trippin' over rocks, almost turnin' an ankle when he emerged into the main shaft. His breath, hampered by the kerchief, labored in his chest. He yanked off the square of cotton, riskin' inhalin' dust in favor of drawin' more air.

When he burst out of the tunnel, Becky jumped up from the rock where she perched. "Are they safe?"

He set the lantern down and bent over, hands on his knees, to catch his breath. He nodded, and she offered him a cupful of water, which he accepted and downed. "They're trapped. In the west tunnel. And water is risin' in the shaft. We might have an hour."

She glanced around as though seekin' the solution, then turned back to him. "I'll ride to town and get help. We'll need three or four strong men to move rock and to dig. I'll be back in a flash."

"Good idea." He dipped his kerchief again. "In the meantime, I'll go back in. Start removin' what I can. Keep them calm. They're goin' to dig from their side."

She ran to his horse in the corral. No saddle. He glanced back to the tunnel. No time.

He called to her. "Ride 'im bareback. Grip with your knees like I taught you. Head toward town. He knows the way."

She nodded, led the gelding to the fence rails, and, usin' the bottom rail as a stirrup, mounted. She twined her fingers into the horse's mane, and in a flash, the pair headed for help.

He picked up the lantern and a pickaxe and returned into the darkness.

If he had anythin' to say about it, Miguel and Dakota would sleep in their own beds tonight.

Becky raced into the mine yard, half a dozen riders close behind her. Before her mount came to a full stop, she alighted, almost tripping in her skirt pants. Zeke was nowhere in sight, and almost thirty precious minutes had elapsed since she'd left.

She pointed to the tunnel while lighting a couple of lanterns to illuminate their way. "In there. Hurry. The first tunnel on the right."

The men dismounted and followed her directions, while she gathered the reins of their horses and tied them to a tree, the animals' sides heaving from the race.

Then she tied a dampened kerchief around her face and followed them. The two trapped men worked for her, and she couldn't stand idly by—not even to prepare bandages or boil water for coffee—while others rescued them.

For the next thirty minutes, she worked feverishly beside Zeke and the others, including the sheriff and Mr. Dixon, while Dakota kept them updated on the water level. When the first shovel finally pushed through to the other side, a cheer went up. When the hole was large enough, they pulled first Miguel, the smaller of the two, and then Dakota, through. The half soaked pair collapsed at their feet, breathing heavily.

Becky thanked each rescuer in turn, barely discerning one from the other because of the kerchiefs, dirt, and gloom. If not for the whites of their eyes, she'd hardly know where they stood.

Two men each grasped a miner beneath the arms and half walked, half carried him from the tunnel. Within minutes, they all stood in the waning sunlight, breathing deep and spitting out dust and dirt. Becky hurried to offer water, while Zeke did a cursory inspection for injuries. Pronouncing both workers in fine shape, he saw the men assisted to their bunks then dismissed the rescuers, thanking each for a job well done.

After they left, the area seemed hauntingly quiet. Becky stood, hands on hips, and surveyed her claim. Almost like a cemetery. But not today.

Today, they overcame the odds.

Today, they won.

Zeke hunkered down next to the campfire outside his shed, a cup of coffee clutched between his hands.

Somethin' didn't set right with him about this entire thing.

About a hundred times, he'd questioned his memory, but as hard as he tried to convince himself otherwise, he knew what he'd heard—the roar of dynamite right before the blow-out. And since the miners hadn't been blastin' today—he held custody of the caps, and his inventory was spot on—somebody else had set the charge.

Which meant someone had tried to kill his men.

He set his cup down and headed for the shack. Despite the late hour, he couldn't let this go. He knocked on the door, and Becky opened it.

"Good evening, Zeke."

"Sorry to bother you, but somethin's on my mind."

She stepped outside and gestured to the two chairs on the porch. "If it's bothering you, it must be important."

He sat and waited while she settled herself. "We weren't blastin' today."

"You said that earlier." She swiped a hand across her forehead, still smudged with dust and dirt, then focused on her filthy fingers and frowned. "Heavens, I've been too tired to even wash my face."

He resisted the urge to wipe a smudge from her cheek. "Somebody set that charge."

She turned to face him, her eyes wide. "You think someone wanted to hurt our men?"

"Or scare us away."

She stood, her mouth and brow turned down. "Well, that's not going to happen. What next?"

"We need to take a look at the shaft. See if there's any evidence of who did this. Should be safe enough now."

"You're not going in alone. I'm coming with you."

He opened his mouth to protest, then snapped it shut. She was one stubborn woman. She'd do what she wanted, never givin' a thought to the danger to herself. Headstrong as a wild filly. Still, when gentle-broke, a wild filly made the best cow pony. He glanced at her, heat rushin' to his cheeks. She wasn't any horse.

And she wasn't his to break.

He nodded. "Grab another lantern."

With Zeke leadin' the way, they picked a path through the debris until they reached the branch in the main tunnel. She touched his arm. "We'll cover more ground if we split up."

He considered her words. One part of him agreed, but the other screamed at him not to let her out of his sight. He sighed. It was late, and his bedroll called to him. They could stand here and argue—discuss—the matter until she wore him down, or he could simply agree right now. "Fine. But don't touch any rafters or beams. Don't move any rocks. And if you find anythin' at all, come back here and wait for me." Usin' his hands to draw a map in the air, he outlined the shafts. "About twenty feet ahead, there's a fork. If you come to that before findin' anythin', turn around and come back."

"But I want to—"

"I know. You want to march in there and find the bad guy bendin' over a keg of powder. Or see his monogrammed hankie he dropped. But you need to promise to do as I say. Okay?"

She blinked a couple of times, and he stifled a smile. She needed reinin' in when tempted with takin' off on her own. And he was just the man to do that.

Strong, but gentle. Get her to come alongside like it was her idea all along.

He shone his lantern down the left tunnel. "I'll light your way as far as I can, then I'll go over to this leg of the mine and see what I can see."

Holdin' her lantern in front of her, she tossed him a smile. "Be careful."

"You too. Shouldn't take you even five minutes to get to that first fork, and five minutes back. So let's meet back here in about ten minutes. If we don't find anythin' by then, we'll leave it for mornin'."

She headed away from him, weavin' down the yawnin' maw of the earth like a drunk on a midnight stroll. Her shadow, elongated and scarecrow-thin, danced along the roof. Then she turned a corner and disappeared from sight. He listened for several more minutes as her footsteps distanced her from him until he couldn't hear her at all.

Still, he waited. Ten heartbeats. Twenty. Finally, he sighed and made his way along the tunnel that had almost claimed Miguel's and Dakota's lives today. He studied every nook and cranny, pokin' his finger into a few cracks in the rocks.

And there, just before the rubble that delineated the earlier fall, he found what he sought.

A blastin' cap, crushed in a boot print. He knelt and ran a finger around the perimeter of the indentation. To the unobservant, just another mark in a scuffle of dust, dirt, and rocks. But to him, confirmation of what he already suspected.

Somebody was out to stop them from minin' in this area.

Why, he wasn't certain.

But one thing was as sure as the nose on his face: he'd find who. And why. And they'd pay for what they'd done.

He stood and brushed off his hands, then picked up the blastin' cap and tucked it into his pants pocket. Time to get out of this place and get some rest. He headed back to the branch and waited. He judged there was only a minute or two left in their allotted time. He'd sent her down the tunnel where he was pretty certain she'd find nothin'. Made sense, since the blast had occurred in the right-hand tunnel.

He stifled another smile. She'd be none too happy to learn of his find when she came back empty-handed. At least, he hoped she came back with nothin'. If she did find somethin', that meant the entire mine was in jeopardy. Which just didn't make sense. If somebody wanted to buy the claim, why would they dynamite the tunnels? A collapsed mine wasn't worth anythin'.

More and more, it felt like he was missin' somethin'. But what, he wasn't certain.

He shone his lantern down the tunnel. She should be here by now. He held his breath and listened for her footsteps. Nothin'. Had she lost track of time? Had she found somethin'? He shook his head. Now he'd have to go after her.

Lantern held aloft, Zeke strode in the direction she'd headed. The deeper he went, the chillier the air became. He should have thought of that and insisted she take an overcoat. He'd lend her his when he found her.

Around the corner, he studied the floor of the tunnel. Her smaller footprints, faint here, a little clearer over there, led him along until he came to another fork. She shouldn't have come this far in half the time given for their search. Five minutes out, five back. That's how most folks would do it.

But not Becky Campbell, apparently. Not only had she lost track of time, it appeared she'd lost her mind too. He gritted his teeth. The woman wasn't cut out for minin', or for livin' in the mountains, or for bein' a cowboy's wife.

He froze in his tracks. Now, where had that come from? She had never given any indication of wantin' to be a cowboy's wife—or anybody's wife, for that matter. He exhaled loudly, his breath carried off on an unseen breeze.

Where was she?

He called her name, the syllables echoin' down the damp tunnel. To his right, water dripped from the ceilin'. To his left, silence. Which way? He walked a few steps to the right, watchin' for her telltale footprints. Nothin'. He turned around and retraced his steps to the fork, then covered about twenty feet past. Was that stone moved out of position? He scooted down. Yep, looked like it.

He straightened and called her name again. Still nothin'. He considered his options. He could wait here and hope she made her way back. He could follow her and hope to find her tracks. He could leave her and let her spend the night in the tunnel. That would serve her right for not doin' as he said.

He shook his head. He couldn't do it. He'd stay until he found her, or he'd die tryin'.

Becky resisted the urge to scream. Or kick a rock. Or run blindly back the way she'd come.

Which might prove difficult. Because in truth, she wasn't exactly certain of the direction needed to retrace her steps.

Oh, why hadn't she paid more attention to her path? And why hadn't she listened to Zeke's warning about not going past the fork? Then again, when she'd come to what looked like a cross-shaft, she hadn't really considered it a fork. So when she'd come to the next one, she'd turned around. But apparently, her eyes had been glued to the floor of the mine, and at the crossroads, all paths looked the same.

No worries. She simply had to follow her footprints out.

Holding the lantern aloft, she scanned the path behind her. And groaned.

Dozens—perhaps hundreds—of boot marks marred the dusty surface.

Why, oh why, hadn't she paid more attention when Zeke was showing her how to distinguish tracks?

She clenched her fists. This wasn't a Sunday stroll under a clear blue sky. She stood at least a hundred feet below the surface of the earth. She could scream until her voice went hoarse, and still, nobody would hear her.

She should have been more careful.

She checked her lantern. The oil was getting dangerously low, and soon she'd be left in the dark.

Maybe if she sat and waited, Zeke would find her. How embarrassing. Getting lost in a mine. In her own mine. How inept. How amateurish. If she perished here, the shock would kill her mother for certain. No, if for no other reason, she must survive.

Whom was she trying to fool? She didn't want to live only for her mother. She wanted to live for herself. For the years and experiences she hadn't had yet. First love. Marriage. Children. Hopefully, someday, grandchildren. Success in the mine. Proving all the wagging tongues wrong. She could make it in this country. A woman could run a mine.

Not to mention to prove herself to her father.

She would get out.

But how to accomplish that?

Wandering around in the gloom would result only in getting more lost. What did those survivalist manuals say? "When lost, sit and wait for rescue."

She could do that.

She found a relatively clear spot and sat, then tucked her skirt pants around her rapidly chilling feet. She lowered the lantern's wick to conserve the oil and waited.

At a chirping and skittering nearby, she raised her lantern. Several silver-brown creatures with long whiskers and longer tails, their eyes shining red in the dark, noses twitching, stared back at her. She gasped, her hand shaking so badly the light bounced crazily back at her. She set the lantern on the ground beside her, crossed her arms over her chest, and tried to console herself with the thought that the rodents were more afraid of her than she was of them. Although, if that were the case, why did they stare so?

She scooted to turn her back to them. If they attacked, she didn't want to see them coming. Better not to know the end was near.

Hunched over, she rocked and sang to herself. Lullabies. Songs from her childhood. Every hymn—or part of a hymn—she could recall. Anything to stave off the silence and the dark.

Head dropping with exhaustion—strange how a body could be so afraid and so weary at the same time—she almost missed the foreign sound of one rock hitting another.

Almost.

Her head snapped up, and she held her breath, listening, straining her ears. Her brain screamed for a repeat. A single sound. Almost as a prayer to the mine, she promised she wouldn't miss the next, no matter how faint.

And there, again. Like somebody trudging down a path who'd lost their energy to lift their feet.

She scrambled upright, the lantern bouncing and casting its light on the walls and ceiling like something from a horror house. "Zeke? Is that you?"

A muffled shout answered. "—ky?"

"Yes, it's me. I'm here."

Within something less than three heartbeats, he emerged from the mouth of the tunnel like a knight in shining armor. She rushed into his arms and wrapped her own around his waist. His heart raced in her ear, and the earthy smell from him seemed like heavenly incense. Only after her knees stopped shaking did she release him.

She stared up at him. "You are a sight for sore eyes."

His mouth lifted in a half smile. "You too."

She stepped back, aware for the first time how close they stood. How flushed his cheeks seemed. How suddenly the temperature in the shaft had risen at least twenty degrees.

Or was it just her?

She lowered her gaze. He must think her forward. Or brazen. And yet, how right it had felt, nestled against him.

He gripped her by the forearms as he surveyed her. "Are you hurt?"

She shook her head. "Nothing but my pride. I can't believe I got lost."

He shrugged. "Happens to the best of us once in a while."

"I should have kept better track of time. And direction."

"Yes, that too." He peered down at her. "How many turns did you take?"

"I'm not certain. I guess I expected more of an angle. And then when I got in there, and everything looked the same … well, I kind of panicked."

"Mines hide lots of secrets, including ways to get lost, and things that can hurt you."

She tossed him a half smile. "If I never come down here again, neither of us will complain."

"Agreed." He offered her his arm. "Let's get out of here."

She nodded and looped her arm through. "Did you find anything?"

He dug into a pocket and pulled out what looked like a wire

attached to a burned-out, braided thread. "It's a blastin' cap. Found it in the other tunnel. It isn't the type of cap we use. It has a longer fuse."

She held the cap up to the lantern. "Are you certain?"

"Positive." Concern etched creases around his eyes and mouth. "I knew I'd heard an explosion."

"Someone is out to ruin me. It's the only thing that makes sense."

"I know all the men around here. I don't want to believe one of them would do somethin' like that on purpose."

Becky sighed and rolled her eyes. "As you keep telling me. But you did tell me not to trust Arthur Wilson."

He held up a hand. "Whoa, there, little lady. It's a long stretch from not trustin' to tryin' to kill somebody."

She balled her hands into fists and glared at him. Why did he have to be so insistent nobody he knew would do such a thing? Unless— "Maybe the guilty person is a little too close to home."

He frowned. "What do you mean by that?"

She stepped back out of his reach. "I know you don't like working for me. For a woman. Maybe you're trying to get me to leave so you can take over the claim for yourself."

"Do you really believe that?" He flung out a hand, and the lantern swayed, casting shadows like dancing demons on the walls. "If I were, why would I come lookin' for you?"

She swiped her arm across her forehead. "I'm sorry. I didn't really mean that. I'm just so tired of always struggling. To make this mine pay for itself. To make friends of the townspeople." She gulped back the lump in her throat. "Having to keep looking over my shoulder for danger."

As they finally emerged into the fresh, cool night, Zeke quirked his chin back toward the tunnel. "To prove yourself to your father?"

She drew deep breaths of fresh air. "That, too, I guess. And my mother. Prove I can manage on my own."

He wrapped an arm around her shoulders. "Things will look

better in the mornin'."

She allowed him to assist her to her shack, his touch convincing her heart that everything would be okay. When he eased her into a chair, she wanted to pull him into the vortex of peace she longed for even while her every bone and ligament screamed in protest. Things would look different in the morning—that was certain.

First and foremost, she would be safe in her home again. Not lost in a mine. Eaten by rats.

On the other hand, her mother would be one day closer to Silver Valley.

CHAPTER 15

A half hour later, Becky lifted the coffee pot toward Zeke. "More?"

He laid a hand over the mouth of his cup. "Thanks, but my back teeth feel like they're floatin'. Plus, I want to sleep tonight. Or rather, this mornin'."

She'd toyed with the idea of asking for his help with the personal quandary in which she found herself but still hadn't worked up the courage. Perhaps tomorrow …

No, this was a plan best hatched in the dark. By sunrise, she'd either have talked herself out of it, or something else would come along and keep her from broaching the topic.

She drew a deep breath, hoping her racing heart would slow enough that her words didn't catch in her throat. "There's something I need to tell you." She shoved her hands into her pockets. "My mother is on her way here. She thinks I'm getting married."

He chuckled. "And how did she get that idea?"

"Seems I mixed up my letter and Sally's." She rolled her eyes. "And Sally's mother will think her daughter owns a business."

Zeke peered at her. "Are you serious?"

"Well, that's what Sally's letter was about. Inviting her mother to the wedding." A sudden realization struck her. "And the letter that went to Mother had money Sally sent for train fare."

"Now, that's funny." He slapped the table and guffawed. After leaning the chair back on two legs, he shook his head. "'Cept you don't see it that way, do you?"

"I do not."

"How so? Just tell your mother the truth." He leaned forward.

"Have you told Sally her mother isn't comin'?"

She stiffened. "No! I completely forgot." Becky sighed. "What a mess I've made of everything."

"Well, that seems to be the first thing you need to do."

"No, the first thing is I need to figure out what to do about my mother."

"Oh, well, you'll have a nice visit and a good laugh over it." He toyed with his coffee cup. "Assuming she has a sense of humor."

"Mother has a heart condition. Her doctor warned her not to worry. She isn't to have any surprises. Or shocks."

"Too bad you didn't know that before you mixed up the letters."

Another shot to her heart. As if she hadn't already chastised herself. She should have sent a simple letter saying she'd arrived safely. Waited a week and sent another with more information. But no, she had to save three cents and say it all at once.

All, of course, except about her father's death.

What would that do to her mother when she arrived in town expecting to see him?

I cannot wait until we are all together again.

Sounded like a prime opportunity for disaster.

He studied her face. "You didn't tell her your father is dead, did you?"

She shook her head. "I couldn't find the words. I thought that might be best told in a separate letter. After I find out who killed him."

A frown marred Zeke's usually complacent face. "The law is lookin' into that. These are dangerous times. You're best off out of it."

"But that's just it. The sheriff isn't looking. He has other things on his mind. Like sitting outside the mercantile and talking to people passing by."

"A goodly part of his job is to keep the peace. And folks tend not to steal or kill folks they know. 'Community relations,' he calls it."

"Sounds like you already talked to him about that."

A blush crept up his neck. "I did. We had a few beeves rustled earlier this year. I confronted him one day and asked why he didn't spend more time in the saddle and less time on his—" A deeper shade of crimson colored his ears. "Well, you know what I mean."

"And that's when he said he was working on community relations?"

"Right." He leaned back in his chair and crossed one leg over the other. "Crime has dropped since he was elected two years ago. And he found the rustlers."

"I will find who killed my father. But my more urgent problem is my mother."

"Send her a telegram and tell her you're not gettin' married. Explain the mix-up."

"She's already left New York."

"What are you goin' to do?"

The exact question she hoped he'd ask. "I don't want to give her a huge shock. So I thought I'd just get married."

"To who?"

She batted her eyes at him, hating herself for turning into a simpering female. So totally unlike her true nature. But men seemed to like that kind of thing. "Why you, of course."

If she'd smacked him with a porcupine, she couldn't have surprised him more.

Marry her?

Marry anybody, for that matter?

Not that the thought hadn't crossed his mind once or twice over the years, especially with his brothers weddin' and havin' children of their own, fillin' his parents' home with laughter and joy.

And it wasn't as if he didn't feel some kind of attraction to this Eastern filly. He did. When she didn't make him too mad.

Well, most of the time, if he was honest with himself.

Which he usually wasn't.

But seriously, shouldn't they have some formal courtin' first, an understandin'? Under other circumstances, he'd write to her mother and ask for permission. Wait another month or so while the letters traveled, then he'd get down on one knee—confound it, Becky Campbell was the most cantankerous female—no, person—he'd ever met.

Stealin' all the fun leadin' up to a weddin'. It was like lettin' the air out of a balloon before handin' it over to a child.

He shook his head. "Even if I had those kinds of thoughts for you, that would be no way to do it."

"Oh, I don't want to marry you for real."

Her words stung like hornets on a rampage, buzzin' around his head. He wished he could jump in the river like he did that time he accidentally roused a nest. Maybe then he could wash her words out of his mind. Instead, he stared for a long moment, workin' up the spit so he could get his tongue unstuck from the roof of his cotton mouth. "Well, thank you very much."

"No. I've got it all worked out, you see."

"I'm sure you do." She seemed to have most everythin' figured out. Find the man who killed her father. Make a profitable business of the mine. Tell the sheriff how to do his job. Fake a marriage, so she didn't upset her mother. "Well, I've waited this long for the right woman to come along. I'm not about to wed for convenience."

"Not convenience. And it won't be real."

"You're right, it won't be. I don't know what folks do in New York City." He scrunched up his face at these last three words. "But out here in Silver Valley, marriage is serious. We wed for life."

Her bottom lip trembled.

Now he'd gone and made her cry. He was such an idiot. He sighed. "Forgive me. I shouldn't have said that."

Becky lifted her chin and stared at him. "I don't think we need to worry about that. I suspect my mother won't live long. The news, the journey, and this country will be the death of her."

"But what if she does live? Do we keep lyin' to her? What will happen when she learns the truth?"

"I'll cross that bridge when I come to it."

"And in the meantime, you 'spect me to pretend I'm your husband when I'm not?"

She tilted her head in question. "Would marrying me be such a burden?"

He considered her words. And the implication behind them. In truth, marryin' her would make him a happy man—if her heart was in it. Marryin' her would mean he could plan for a family. Buy more land. More beeves. Never wake up alone again—heat rushed up his cheeks at the images generated by that thought.

He stood and put a few feet between them, hopin' the distance would clear his head.

It didn't. Thinkin' about bein' married to Becky caused his heart to jump and skip like a calf let out of the barn in the spring.

He shook his head. Best to let those thoughts loose.

There was no way he was marryin' her.

He locked eyes with her. She stared at him, waitin' for his answer.

What to say? And how to say it? As tactfully as possible. He sure didn't want to hurt her. Or alienate her. Or abandon her. She already had enough of that in her life. But he wouldn't be used or made a fool of either.

A deep breath gave him another second or two to formulate the answer. "No, it wouldn't be such a burden to marry you." She exhaled as though his answer were a lifeline. "But if we married, it would have to be for the right reasons."

As if they would ever marry for real. But if they did … yes, it would be for the right reasons. But that wasn't their situation. And might never be.

She wasn't cut out to be a cowboy's wife.

How many times had his head tried to tell his heart the truth of that?

She waved off his words like a fly buzzin' around a pie at a church social. "I'll arrange a fake preacher to speak the words over us."

"What about witnesses? You can't ask Sally. She'll know different." He studied her. Wherever did she get such a plottin' mind? "Or will you lie to her?"

"This is getting more complicated by the minute. A pretend wedding seemed so simple yesterday." She sighed. "No, I can't lie to her. She's my friend." She planted her hands on her hips. "What would you suggest?"

He didn't really want any part of what she was plannin'. But he surely couldn't leave her to her own devices. What if she thought she was fake marryin' some other man who tricked her into a real weddin'? "I think the fake preacher might work. But how can we convince Pastor Obermeyer to let us use the church if he's not officiatin'?"

"Are you trying to scuttle my plans?" She shook her head. "Fine. We won't get married at the church. Mother wouldn't really expect that, anyway." She paced the small cabin. "So where could we have a wedding that won't draw attention from people? Yet will look real?" She paused and snapped her fingers. "I know. We could get married here."

Zeke looked around, his nose wrinklin'. "Here? Might be fine to sleep in and to feed us in, but would your mother put up with you gettin' married here?"

"No." Her shoulders slumped. "And knowing Mother, if she found out where we were having the wedding, she'd take over, and that would ruin everything."

He hooked his heel over the chair rung. "Seems to me if we want to trick your mother, we need to take into consideration how she thinks. What about your parents? Did they love each other?"

"Mother doesn't talk much about it. But Papa said she fell madly, hopelessly, impossibly in love with him. And he with her. They married three weeks after they first met. But Papa was gone so much, I think they hardly knew each other. Then I came along, and she was busy with me."

"But she stuck with him."

"She had few choices. And neither did he. A woman abandoning her husband is looked down upon by society. She had the money, the position, the introductions into the right places. He had the wit, the charm, the panache to find the next adventure."

He hadn't considered how a miner's daughter looked and sounded so refined. "So your family is rich?"

"I wouldn't say rich. Comfortable."

"So here we are again. You with the money. Me with the wit and the charm and little else. Do you want the same kind of marriage your parents had?"

"No." She sighed, her eyes closed.

What he wouldn't give to be able to see what she saw. Then her eyes snapped open, and she caught him starin'. He tore his gaze away. If he didn't look at her, maybe he wouldn't wish things could be different. Not hugely different. Just a little. Like if she said she cottoned to him. That this could be a real marriage. He'd make it work. He knew he could. He would—he snapped back to the real world. What was he thinkin'?

And was that the tiniest hint of a smile liftin' one corner of her mouth? Could she read his mind?

She sipped her coffee, one brow archin' up. "I can make you an offer you can't refuse."

"I doubt it."

"Half ownership in the Becky Mae."

"Why?"

"I don't want to kill my mother."

He licked dry lips. Despite the unpleasant thoughts about lyin' to Mrs. Campbell, the idea of bein' in partnership with Becky wasn't such a hardship. He peered at her. "So you'd give me half of your mine? Make us equal partners?"

She nodded. "Equal partners."

"We'd have to agree on everythin' from now on." Like that would ever happen. Aha! Did a flicker of uncertainty just cross her face? "No more doin' what you want when it comes to the mine."

"O-kay."

Now she didn't sound quite so sure of herself. Time for the kill shot. The thing that would blow her crazy plan sky high. "And since not only your mother but everybody around will believe you're married, how are you goin' to prove we're not?" He tossed her the most lascivious grin he could conjure. "'Specially if I say we consummated the marriage."

"You wouldn't."

"Maybe I would. Maybe I wouldn't." He was enjoying this.

"Why would you force me to stay in a marriage that was a sham?" Becky cocked her head, then snapped her fingers. "Of course. The money."

"What money?"

"You need money." She stood and planted her hands flat on the table between them. "That's why I'm offering you half of the mine. So you can spend it on your precious beeves."

Her mockin' tone tore at his gut, but he refused to admit the hurt. "And I would jump at your offer because you're makin' so much money grubbin' in the dirt for silver." He leaned across the table. "Why do you think you're even showin' a tiny profit?"

She blinked a couple of times, then plunked down in her chair. "Because you and the men work hard. Because I cut expenses as much as I could. Because—"

"Because I stopped takin' wages a month ago."

Had he slapped her, he didn't think she'd be more shocked. Her face lost all color, her mouth gaped open, and her hands clenched and relaxed several times. He wished he'd kept his big mouth shut.

"You're lying."

He shrugged. "I can prove it."

She glanced at the ledger on the other end of the table. "If you're telling the truth, I'm going to pay you every penny I owe. I will not live on charity."

"It's not charity to make sure you're eatin' enough to keep body and soul together." His voice swelled with emotion, but he swallowed it back. Accordin' to his mother, there was a thin line between compassion and pride, and it all depended on who took the credit. "It's not charity to buy the tools the diggers need. It's not charity to pay the mercantile account."

"I'd have figured out a way to keep going."

"How? By askin' your mother for money? You'd choke on a stick of dynamite before that would happen."

She glanced around the small shack as though seeking an escape. "I don't know. But I wouldn't do that."

He exhaled. "If you really want my input, I've got some ideas to increase production and cut costs. Maybe even enough for me to buy the water rights I need to irrigate my land."

She sighed, then nodded. "So we have a deal? You agree to pretend we're married for my mother's sake. You don't tell people we—we consummated the marriage. Then after she leaves, you get an annulment. Blame it on me. Tell them we didn't—you know—have our wedding night. Nobody will have a problem believing I'm—whatever the term is for a woman who won't—won't—you know."

Her cheeks flamed again. Yes, he knew what she meant. And he wouldn't make her say it. Because if one thing was true, it was that Miss Becky Campbell was much too passionate a woman to be … that way.

He nodded. "I'll go along."

She offered her hand as if they were makin' some kind of business deal.

Fine. He'd play this farce through to the end.

He shook her hand, and a lightnin' bolt raced up his arm. She didn't pull away like he thought she might. Instead, she left her fingers nestled in his like they belonged there.

If only.

His heart screamed at him to tell her how he really felt about her.

If he listened to his heart, he'd race into town the next mornin' and marry her right away.

But his heart did nothin' but get him into trouble.

CHAPTER 16

On Tuesday morning, after the diggers finished breakfast, Zeke hung around the kitchen as if he had something on his mind. Becky dropped the dirty dishes into the pan and added soap and hot water from the kettle to the cool from the well in preparation for cleaning up.

As she plunged her hands into the water and scrubbed the plates, she glanced over her shoulder. "What's got you thinking?"

He looked up from his coffee mug. "Who says I'm thinkin'?"

"The little worry knot in the middle of your forehead."

He sat back in his chair and tipped it on its hind legs. "You can read me like a book."

"Should know the man I'm going to marry."

The chair *thunk*ed back on all fours. "Not for real, though."

She shrugged and turned back to her task. "As far as my mother is concerned, it will be." She paused and wiped her hands on her apron. "So what's really on your mind?"

"We talked to pretty much ever'body from town at the Fourth of July party, but we don't know any more about who killed your father or who is behind these accidents now than we did before."

"Agreed. So what will we do about it?" She pulled out the bench and sat at the table. "If people won't talk, they won't talk."

"I just think somebody knows somethin', but they don't know they know it. Or they don't know it's important."

"We can't follow everybody around and keep dropping clues, hoping they'll catch on. If it ever comes to trial, the judge will toss the case out because we tainted the witnesses, the jurors, or both."

"So where do we start?"

She leaned forward, her heart racing. "I'm convinced that the murder and the accidents are the work of one person."

"Can't see my way out of it. This is a small town. It would be a mighty big coincidence for a killer and somebody else to be operatin' independently, don't you think?"

"How about our men? Miguel and Dakota have been involved in almost every accident." She held up a hand when he started to speak. "'Involved' may not be the best word. What I mean is, they've been victim to every incident. They could have been killed or badly injured. Maybe they haven't put two and two together that the accidents and my father's death are connected. If we can convince them that the next time somebody might die, maybe they'll open up."

He steepled his fingers and nodded. "We can remind them that the law can't hang a man more than once, so if the killer is the person behind these accidents, he won't stop if one of them gets in the way. They'll die just like your father did."

"Good idea. Because all these crimes have one thing in common."

"What's that?"

"The mine."

He peered at her. "You're right. Your father was killed at the mine. All the accidents were here. I was nabbed when I followed a man into the mine."

She exhaled. "Maybe I should just go away. Leave the mine to whoever wants it."

"You are the legal owner. Your father died for this piece of land. If you up and quit, you'll be sayin' his death was of no account. Is that what you want?"

She shook her head, the empty place in her heart since learning of his passing growing ever bigger. "No. I want to prove he knew what he was doing when he bought this claim. And after talking to the land agent, I'm even more convinced that whoever is behind this doesn't want to do it legally. My father gave that person a chance by not registering the claim right away. By traveling to Denver to confirm it was still a freehold claim."

"Right." Zeke crossed one leg over the other. "If this man wanted the claim, he should have—could have—bought it outright. Seems like he's more willin' to spend time tryin' to drive us off than in gettin' the land legally."

"Which means we need to keep going. Ask questions. Make suggestions if need be. Hound the sheriff until he does something."

"Then let's continue what we started on the Fourth today. I have to go into town to the blacksmith. My horse threw a shoe. We can go in the wagon and pick up the supplies I'd normally get tomorrow. That'll save me a trip. We can visit people where they work, not in a party where they might be afraid somebody will overhear. Maybe they'll be more likely to open up."

She smiled. "Sounds like a plan. Now go get some work done at the mine while I finish these dishes. Maybe ask Miguel and Dakota if they know something. I'll meet you outside in about a half hour."

He left, and she completed her tasks, finally hanging her apron on the nail inside the door. Her heart raced in time with her thoughts, which was just plain silly.

After all, this was just a ride to town to investigate her father's murder.

∞

Zeke paced back and forth in front of the wagon and the two horses hitched to the traces. This was just another ride to town for supplies. And shoein'. Nothin' new. Nothin' different. He'd done this a hundred times before.

So why couldn't he sit still? Why did it seem every minute was at least an hour long? She'd said thirty minutes. Why, that had to be—

She stepped out of the door of the shack, purse in one hand, hat in the other. A different dress than the one she'd worn to make breakfast. And was her hair pinned higher? With those little curly things hangin' down in front of her ears? Ringlets, he thought his sisters called them.

Swallowin' his nervousness back like a hunk of poorly chewed meat, he hurried around the wagon to help her board. Light as a feather, she was gettin' better at this and didn't hardly need his help, but he liked the feel of his hands around her waist. And the smile she always bestowed on him as she slid across the seat. Why, that would scare a thundercloud plumb into the next county.

The trip to town was short—far too short for his likin'—and more than once he slowed the horses with a tiny twitch on the reins. Despite the fact their upcomin' weddin' wasn't real, simply spendin' time with her was a joy. Almost right away, Becky started fidgetin' beside him, and he released his hold a mite to encourage the animals onward. When they got within a quarter mile of Silver Valley, they either smelled water or remembered the handful of oats he usually provided, and they picked up their pace until they were just about lopin'. Becky laughed and clasped her hat with one hand, giftin' him with a sight and a sound that lifted his heart even higher.

If he could be the one to make her squeal with delight every day for the rest of their lives, he'd die a happy man.

But right now, all she wanted from him was help gettin' answers to questions about the connection between her father's death and the things happenin' at the mine.

And the only thing she needed him for was to convince her mother she was gettin' married, when in fact she really wasn't.

Short term and temporary.

If she had her way.

While Zeke tied the horses to the hitching rail and scooped a couple of handfuls of grain out of a sack in the back of the wagon, holding it for them until they slobbered most of it up—the rest fell to the ground, where a couple of birds flew in and argued over the bounty—Becky pondered what he'd told her along the way.

While both Miguel and Dakota denied any knowledge about the incidents—in fact, Miguel had insisted they were accidents—after Zeke had asked more questions, Dakota had revealed an important piece of information. The night before the cave-in, he'd dreamed he and Miguel were in the tunnel, and somebody was trying to dig through the roof, except it fell in and buried them. He'd awakened in a sweat, then gone for a walk to work off the horrible visions. While he hadn't noticed anything odd at the time, the next morning, he'd been unable to find his pickaxe. He'd accused Miguel—in a lighthearted fashion—of hiding it, as the two often played practical jokes on each other. Miguel had denied it, and on a later trip to the privy, he'd found it leaning against the wall.

When Zeke had told her this, he'd suggested that perhaps the dream had actually come as the result of Dakota hearing the sound of the digging that weakened the support beams and that the culprit had skedaddled—his words, not hers—when he'd heard Dakota coming out to clear his head.

All of this made sense, not because Becky understood the scientific reasoning behind it, but because she'd experienced similar situations herself. A party her parents once held had turned into a crazy, circus-like, fantastical event in her six-year-old brain. A dream that her house was burning down when she was about thirteen had been spawned by her candle tipping over and smoldering on the rug, filling her room with smoke. And more recently, she'd dreamt her cat—which had died when she was ten—had found its way from the city to her shack. When she'd awakened, the growls and rumbles of a mountain lion outside her window had kept her from sleep for several hours.

Zeke swiped his hands on his pants legs, then held them toward her. She didn't really need his help getting down, but there was something comforting in his hands holding her aloft an extra heartbeat before settling her lightly on the ground. Perhaps her father used to toss her in the air and catch her when she was a child. Had she laughed and giggled? Begged him for more? Her memories of him were sparse, and she hated to lose even a single one. Perhaps when she saw her mother next, she'd ask.

Then again, maybe not. If the shock of learning her husband was dead didn't kill her, months or even years might pass before her mother was able to talk about him.

She exhaled and looked around when Zeke released her. "First I need to go talk to Sally. Tell her about the letters. Then we'll continue our investigation."

He nodded. "Good. I'll get the supplies I came for, and I'll meet you here in about—how long will you need?"

"Let's say fifteen minutes. If I'm not back here by then, come looking for my body in the alley behind the mercantile." She softened her words with a smile. "Hopefully you won't have to bury me beside my father. That would surely kill my mother."

He tipped his hat, his hazel-green eyes full of something she couldn't quite discern. Pity? Sympathy? Compassion?

She tapped her parasol against her leg, then exhaled. "Here I go."

Becky strode toward the mercantile to deliver the bad news to the first—and perhaps only—friend she'd managed to make in town. Once she explained the situation, would she be on her own again?

When she entered the general store, Sally came around the counter and gripped her in a fierce hug. "Oh, it's so good to see you. Haven't set eyes on you in a dog's age."

Becky returned the hug, hoping this wasn't the last one her friend bestowed on her. She swallowed hard, leaving her mouth far too dry. "I have some bad news." In search of a quiet corner, she glanced around the store. "Can we sit a minute?"

Sally nodded, her smile now replaced with a frown. "Over by the checkerboard."

Becky sat in the same chair Zeke had occupied the first time she met him. Flipping through the pages of the Bloomingdale's catalog. Buying a range and a table for his parents for their anniversary. Most cowboys would be drinking and gambling their earnings away, but not him.

Why hadn't she seen his worth much sooner?

Probably because she'd been so full of her plans and ideas for what her new life would look like. And at the time, those hadn't included him.

But now she couldn't imagine a future without him.

Sally settled into the chair opposite, and Becky began her explanation. "I mixed up our letters. I put my letter in the envelope addressed to your mother. And your letter in my envelope."

Sally's eyes filled. "But I'm getting married in—" She closed her eyes a moment, counting on her fingers, then opened them. "In six days. Not enough time for a letter to go to New York, is it?" She straightened. "I could send a telegram. But she still wouldn't have time to get here." Her shoulders slumped. "So my mother isn't coming for my wedding?"

"I'm so sorry. But no. My mother is coming. She thinks I'm marrying your George, apparently."

"Well, that sure is bad news." Sally hung her head and sighed. "But that won't stop me gettin' married." She looked up. "I wonder what your mother thought when she saw the money."

"Mortified, I'm sure. Likely thought I figured to bribe her to come here."

Sally giggled, such a welcome sound considering the news Becky had just delivered. The girl really was a gem. "And what about the part of somebody else writing the letter for you?"

"No wonder her response was such a jumble." Becky didn't want to ask the next question, but she had to know. "Can you ever forgive me?"

Sally gripped Becky's hands across the checkerboard. "Forgive you? But we're best friends. I love you. This won't change a thing. Except now you're going to have to walk me down the aisle."

A lump formed in Becky's throat. "After the mess I made of things, you'd want me to do that for you?"

"Well, it should be somebody who knows me and loves me. I guess I could ask George's father to do it, but I'd be right pleased if you would."

Becky exhaled all the worry from inside. "I'd be proud as a peacock to escort you to the altar."

Sally jumped up and rounded the table, pulling Becky up, then gripping her close again. When she stepped back and held her by the shoulders, tears glistened. "Now, I got to get back to work. Maybe on my next half day off, we could decide what you'll wear to my weddin'."

Becky's outfit was the least of her worries. In the space of ten minutes, she'd gone from potentially losing her only friend to taking an honored place in the wedding party.

If only she could solve all her problems so easily.

She waved goodbye to Sally and returned to meet Zeke at the wagon.

As she neared, he tipped his hat to her. "Glad to see you survived."

"Sally is fine. She's such a sweet girl. She's asked me to walk her down the aisle."

Zeke whistled. "And you were worried about dyin' today."

"Not seriously. It was a figure of speech." She squinted up at him, the early morning sun creating a halo-like effect around his head. "Where shall we begin?"

He quirked his chin toward the mercantile. "There's the sheriff."

Of course. He'd be sitting in his usual spot outside the store. Not enough crime to keep him busy, apparently.

She nodded. "Might as well get it over with." She clenched her fists. "I have a lot to say to that man." He laid a hand on her arm, sending a tingling sensation all the way to her shoulder. She sighed. "What?"

"Let me do the talkin' this time. You can ask questions at our next stop."

"Why?" She already knew the answer but couldn't resist putting him on the spot.

"Because we want him talkin', not bristlin' up like a porcupine." He grinned. "After all, he does keep folks in line. Keeps most of the riff raff out of town. Means I don't have to shoot every varmint that crosses my path, so I have more time for minin' and ranchin'."

Becky studied his face a moment, memorizing the lines, the sunbaked crinkles at the corners of his eyes, the laugh lines around his mouth. Were his lips as soft as they looked? Heat filled her cheeks, and she lifted her gaze to meet his. A tiny smile lifted his lips. As if he read her thoughts.

She tossed him a curt nod, then concentrated on smoothing wrinkles in her skirt. "Fine. Let's go."

He offered his arm, which she refused. Better to remind him this was all business.

Nothing more.

Despite the fact her heart threatened to bust out like a chick from an egg.

Zeke chewed the inside of his cheek to keep from laughin'. She was as transparent as a fine piece of crystal—but nowhere near as breakable. He 'spected if he actually laughed aloud at her reaction when he'd caught her starin', she'd slap his face and storm away.

Then burst into tears the moment she was alone.

Not that he had any intention of pushin' her that far. Just far enough so she'd come to her senses and realize that the feelin's conflictin' inside her like vegetables in a stew pot were natural and to be allowed.

Which was probably also good advice for himself.

But right now, he had a murderer to find. Else Becky would never allow her guard to drop so she could get on with her life. And give him some room in it.

As they walked up, Sheriff Fremont paused in his tall tale about huntin' down some dangerous gunman in a long past time. "Howdy, Zeke. Miss Campbell." His eyes narrowed as he studied her, perhaps expectin' she would tear a strip up one side of him and down the other as she had last time. "Fine day."

Becky stiffened beside him, her shoulders rigid. He risked a glance. Her nostrils flared as if she'd just run a mile, and her fists clenched and relaxed. Perhaps she envisioned poppin' the lousy lawman a good one.

He nodded. "Sheriff." He took in the other three men gathered on chairs and a barrel to gab away the morning. "Boys. Mind if we talk to the sheriff a bit?"

Amidst much scrapin' of boots and chair legs on the warped boardwalk, nods to Becky, and promises to catch up later, the three left.

The sheriff turned back to him. "What's stuck in your craw?"

Zeke gestured for Becky to sit on a vacant chair while he took the other. At first, she hesitated, but he threw her a nod and a tip of his head, and she perched on the front corner of the seat. There was so much room left over, he had half a mind to rent out the space.

Instead, he addressed the lawman. "Sheriff, Becky and me are lookin' into her father's death."

The sheriff drew himself up in his chair. "Well, you know I'm gonna find that killer."

Becky forced a smile that didn't quite meet her eyes. "We appreciate all you have on your plate, Sheriff. We thought we could relieve you of some of your responsibilities."

If the lawman detected the heavy note of sarcasm in her voice that almost drowned in the honey tone, he didn't give any indication. Then again, she was good. She could go on the stage, she was that convincin'.

Zeke sat forward, elbows on his knees. "We'd like to have your blessin' to ask questions. Maybe see if anybody knows anythin'."

Becky went rigid beside him again. He hadn't mentioned he'd

be takin' this line.

But the sheriff took the bait hook, line, and sinker, as Zeke had hoped he would. The man sat back in his chair and folded his hands in his lap, relaxed and as un'spectin' as a baby. "I think that would be fine. So long as you promise to keep me informed."

"Of course. Any suggestions where we should start?"

The lawman pushed his hat back and swiped at his forehead with a kerchief. A quick dab at his tin badge and he was ready to talk. "No clues out at the mine. I already gave Miss Campbell here her father's personal effects. Nothing in them. Talked with most folks in town. Nobody had a beef with him. Seemed everybody liked him."

Becky's exhaled response was so low only Zeke heard. "Not everybody, apparently."

The sheriff continued. "Don't know what you think you'll learn. Must'a been a crazed lunatic passin' through town."

Zeke nodded and remained silent. Better to let the lawman do the talkin' right now. Never know what they might learn.

"'Course, Robbie Campbell was one of them land speculators. Asked around town before he picked his claim. Went out and talked with the prospectors out there. Made quite the pest of himself, so I hear."

When Becky opened her mouth to speak, Zeke nudged her foot. She stared at him but clamped her lips shut. He crossed his arms loosely over his chest. "Anybody in particular?"

"The fellow on the uphill side of him, Arthur Wilson. Complained to me that Campbell was pokin' around his place. I asked Campbell, but he denied it." The sheriff tipped his head to one side. "Suggested maybe Wilson saw somebody else. The same fella who came back and killed Campbell, do you think?"

"Maybe." Zeke stood. Becky wouldn't sit still—or quiet—too much longer. Best they get a move on. "Thank you for the information." He nodded to Becky. "Shall we go? I'm sure the sheriff has things to do."

The lawman took the hint and stood, hitchin' up his pants and straightenin' his hat. "I do. Nice to see you both."

After he tipped his hat to them, he sauntered down the boardwalk, pausin' to help a woman with a package, then stoppin' to chat with a couple of old-timers sittin' outside the barbershop.

Zeke chuckled. "Community relations."

She rose, then fisted her hands on her hips. "Where to now?"

"Let's check at the land office."

"We already talked to Wilkerson at the celebration."

"Thought we might take a look at the records. Might prompt a memory or two on his part."

Becky glanced back to where the sheriff now perched on a railin' outside the saloon. "He said something that was important, but I can't for the life of me figure out what it was."

"Nothin' he hadn't said before."

"Right. But today, the way he said it, it's nagging at me." She shook her head. "I just don't know what it is."

"Sometimes you need to let it go. It'll float to the surface."

They crossed the street to the land claim office, slowin' to allow a wagon to pass before reachin' the other side. The door to the office stood partially ajar, and when they stepped inside, Wilkerson sat, feet on the corner of his desk, fannin' himself with a sheaf of papers.

He stood and smiled. "Greetings. Are you here to sell your claim, Miss Campbell? I have several willin' buyers, I can assure you. Best price paid. You'd likely get back most of your investment."

Zeke's fingers itched to wipe the smarmy grin from the man's face, but he held his temper. And his tongue. "We're here to ask a few questions about her father's death, as well as anythin' else you can tell us about his claim."

"Don't know nothin' about his death. I was just as surprised as ever'body else, let me tell you." Sweat beaded on his forehead, and he swiped at it with a white handkerchief he pulled from his jacket pocket. "I'm just an honest man tryin' to make an honest livin'. I sell claims, buy claims, and hope to make a little profit from both transactions. But I'll help any way I can."

Becky sat at one of the two chairs across the desk from him. This time she took in more real estate than she had prior, Zeke noted. "How did my father choose his claim?"

Wilkerson sat. "When he came here to see what was available, he told me he was lookin' for a small mine. Somethin' he could manage on his own. I suggested he go up there along the creek. So he did."

Zeke planted a foot on the other chair and leaned on his knee. "Then what?"

Wilkerson shrugged. "He came back about three days later and said he'd found the perfect place. But it looked like somebody had already done some work there, so he wanted to be sure the claim was available. It was. He filed for it."

Becky leaned forward. "Did he see anybody there?"

Wilkerson shook his head. "Nope. Introduced himself to Arthur Wilson up the hill and said he saw some old-timers doin' some pannin' in the creek, but that was it."

Zeke considered the information. "Is it possible the gold panners felt he was musclin' in on their territory?"

"Don't think so. They usually move on after a day or so. Nobody else has had any trouble."

Becky played with the string on her bag. Zeke held back a grin. Transparent as glass.

"Has anybody been in asking about claims in the area?"

Wilkerson nodded to her. "Sure. Lots of people. It's a minin' town."

Zeke cleared his throat. "She means anybody unusual. Or suspicious."

The land agent scratched his chin. "Well, now that you mention it." He shook his head. "Nah, he wouldn't do somethin' like that."

Zeke straightened. "Who?"

"Well, George down at the post office was in a few times.

Strange, since he seems an unlikely miner."

Unlikely or not, if George was somehow involved, for Becky's sake, he needed to find out.

The man was marryin' her friend in less than a week.

As Becky hurried back across the street, the heels of her boots keeping time with her racing heart, one question remained at the forefront of her mind: was her best friend marrying a murderer?

When she arrived at the post office, she stopped so suddenly that Zeke bumped into her from behind. She caught herself on the post holding the roof cover in place.

"Sorry. After runnin' over here like a stampedin' bull, that sudden stop caught me off guard." He peered at her, concern threading his features. "You calm enough to go in there?"

"I must know if he is involved in any way. Sally—"

"Is a sensible woman who surely wouldn't engage herself to a killer."

"But if he sweet-talked her?"

"George? You obviously don't know the man." He tipped his hat back on his head. "I know him. He hardly opens his mouth at all. Not to sing in church. Not when I buy a stamp or pick up a package. I 'spect Sally is the one who asked him to marry her."

Of all the nerve. She pierced him with her sternest look. One her mother would surely approve. "I'll have you know, he's the sweetest, most romantic man in town. Why, when he proposed, he packed a picnic lunch, took Sally out for a lovely drive, and got down on one knee holding flowers and a ring."

He grinned. "Gives me some ideas. Want to take a drive right now?"

"Well, don't think I'd fall for that kind of thing. Besides, we're already engaged and don't need that kind of foolishness."

His smile fell away, landing at her feet like a sack of horseshoes, and his shoulders slumped almost to his knees.

If she didn't know better, she'd say her words hurt him.

But he was simply fooling with her.

Wasn't he?

And if he wasn't, what did that say about him?

Or about her, since an ache gnawed in her chest like a chipmunk on a chestnut?

She didn't want to know the answer. She whirled around and headed inside, pausing in the doorway to allow her eyes to adjust to the semi-gloom. George Newman, a shade over his eyes and sleeve garters in place to keep his shirt cuffs clean, perched on a stool behind the brass bars of his cage. He looked up, offering a tentative smile as she entered.

She crossed the office, Zeke close on her heels. Like a shadow. "George, I need to ask you a question."

A single nod was his only response.

"Did you ask about land claims?"

Another nod.

"Why?"

George glanced from her to Zeke, who now stood beside her, then back to her. "Heard somebody sayin' maybe they wanted to buy one. For an investment."

"Were you thinking about mining?" She looked around. "Seems you have a good job right here."

"Thought maybe I could sell the land later."

"Why?" She clenched her fists inside her gloves.

"If it proved to bear silver, it would be worth more than I paid for it."

"Was it my father's claim?" Apparently, Robbie Campbell wasn't the only mining speculator in town.

He swallowed hard, his Adam's apple bobbing. "And the one on the other side."

"Arthur Wilson's claim?"

"No. The one south of your father's." He shuffled several papers, his hands shaking. "Wasn't doin' nothin' wrong."

Legally, the man was right. She gripped the edge of the counter. "Who was talking about this?"

He blinked a couple of times. "Your neighbor. Arthur Wilson."

She knew her much-too-inquisitive neighbor wasn't all he presented himself to be. She gritted her teeth. "What was he saying?"

George dropped his gaze and flushed. "Before your pa died, he was at the saloon one night braggin' on and on about findin' a huge vein of silver. Well, none of us believed him. He was always sayin' how much he was findin', but we never saw evidence of it."

Zeke nodded. "Now that you mention it, I heard him myself a few times."

Becky knew these kinds of men. Always talked bigger and richer and better than anybody else. "So he's a braggart. Knowing that, why would you take anything he said seriously?"

"He come in with silver nuggets big as peas in a little sack. Had at least ten dollars' worth. Bought drinks all around."

Becky leaned on the counter. Getting the story from this man was like pulling teeth. "And then what?"

"I figured maybe I could buy up land near him and take my chances. Thinkin' about gettin' hitched to Sally, and I wanted to support her right."

She prodded again. "Completely understandable. What else did Arthur say?"

"Well, the boys was askin' about his claim, and he let slip—after a few more drinks—that the vein of silver didn't quite belong to him. 'Sort of' was how he put it. So I thought maybe he found a vein in his own mine that traveled out into another claim."

Zeke's brow drew down. "And that claim wasn't for sale, right? It belonged to Becky's father. Did Arthur happen to mention anything about him?"

George shook his head. "But he said he was a-gonna get the silver no matter what."

Becky wrapped her arms around herself as a shiver ran from her head to her toes.

No matter what.

Sounded like a threat.

One Arthur Wilson may well have made good on.

Half an hour later, Becky sauntered up the wooden boardwalk. She couldn't think of anybody else in town who might have information relevant to their investigation, and Zeke waited for her in front of the mercantile.

Still, she had one more errand to complete before heading back to the claim.

And a discussion with Arthur Wilson.

As she neared the saloon, her folded lace parasol tapping on the boardwalk, a lanky man in a starched collar stepped through the doorway, thumbs tucked into his waistcoat pockets. His well-polished boots, newer-looking felt hat, and black suit bespoke wealth. The way his eyes raked over her suggested a barely bridled lewdness.

She slowed. Maybe this was the man she needed.

She nodded in response when he tipped the brim of his hat with a forefinger. He stepped aside as she neared. "Miss."

"Thank you, sir." She peered up at him. "You're a stranger in town, aren't you?"

"Yes, miss. Arrived yesterday on the stage." He studied her a moment. "I detect from your accent that you aren't long here yourself."

"New York. City, that is."

"I thought I heard culture and breeding. Both rarities in these parts. As I'm sure you're well aware."

"Are you staying long?"

He patted his jacket pocket. "So long as I keep winning."

A gambler. She swallowed down the sour taste rising in her throat, then snapped her parasol open to shield her from prying eyes of passersby. "Do you enjoy practical jokes?"

"So long as I'm not on the receiving end. What did you have in mind?"

She clutched her purse and rattled it for good measure. "I have a small sack of silver nuggets. I would like to play a joke on a friend. He keeps teasing me something awful about being a spinster, so the last time he did, I told him if he was so concerned, he should marry me. I bet him he didn't have the nerve."

"Doesn't seem a man would need much courage to marry you." He eyed her up and down. "In fact, I'd take on a sure bet like that any day."

She dropped her gaze and batted her eyelashes—that was at least the second time since coming to Silver Valley she'd employed that particular gambit. "Thank you, sir. I knew you were a gentleman." She lowered her voice and leaned toward him. "Would you pretend to be a preacher and come to the park next Sunday afternoon? That's where and when I told him we'd marry." She dug into her reticule and pulled out the sack. "Will this be enough?"

He hefted his payment in the palm of his hand. "What time do you want me there?"

"One o'clock."

He held out his hand. "Frank Jackson. And I should at least know the name of the woman for whom I'm not going to perform a real wedding ceremony."

She chuckled. "Becky Campbell. Pleasure doing business with you."

"And I with you."

He dipped his head, then headed for the hotel, tossing and catching the sack as though it were a ball before taking a left and disappearing from sight.

Good. One more item off her list of things to do.

Now, Arthur Wilson.

And he'd best thank his lucky stars she was in a good mood.

∞

Zeke wasn't certain what Becky was up to, but she sure as shootin' had somethin' flittin' through that female brain of hers.

When she approached and awaited his assistance into the wagon, he hesitated. "Who was that man?"

She glanced back. "What man?"

"The one you were talkin' to?"

She snapped her parasol shut. "Just some business for the wedding."

He held her gaze a long moment. That conversation, includin' the parasol and the battin' of the eyes thing—oh yes, he'd seen that—screamed to him somethin' more than weddin' stuff. Didn't Becky trust him enough to tell him the full truth?

Was this man her secret?

Well-dressed. Good lookin' in a worldly sort of way. Comin' out of the saloon.

So why didn't she simply marry that man?

When she stared back at him, a tiny smile liftin' her mouth, eyes battin' like a calf in a snowstorm, he gave up.

Fine, let her have her secrets.

Prob'ly for the best this weddin' wasn't the real thing.

He shrugged. "Ready to go home?"

"Not quite." Becky's voice tightened, and her eyes narrowed as she focused on the barbershop across the street.

Arthur Wilson exited onto the boardwalk, a silver-handled walkin' stick keepin' time with his steps. With a glance in their direction, the man turned on his heel and hurried in the opposite direction.

Becky glanced both ways, then darted across the street. Now what?

He chased her down and grasped her arm. "Where are you goin'?"

She pulled away. "After him."

"You can't confront him by yourself."

"Watch me. Or join me."

He wasn't about to let her talk to a possible murderer on her own, so he gripped her arm and followed in the man's wake. Wilson glanced over his shoulder, eyes wide, then quickened his pace. At the corner, he missed the step and fell heavily onto the street, landin' on his side, his stick fallin' beside him.

He yelped and grabbed his left shoulder. "Help. I think I've broken my arm."

Several townspeople gathered around him, tryin' to pull him to his feet, which brought about more groans and complaints of pain.

Zeke pushed through the crowd with Becky on his heels. "Step aside. Let me in." He knelt beside the man. "Stop wrigglin' like a trout on a line." When Wilson complied, Zeke ran a practiced hand up and down his arm. "Nothin' broken. Shoulder's dislocated."

He shifted his weight, pressed his free knee into Wilson's shoulder, then brought the man's arm straight out from his body. "You gotta relax. I won't make any sudden moves, but if you resist, it's gonna hurt a lot more."

Sweat gathered on Wilson's top lip and forehead, but he nodded, his mouth pressed tight as a bear trap.

He gripped the man's forearm in two hands and pulled gently. When Wilson screamed, Zeke encouraged him. "That's it. One more second." A soft *thunk*, then Wilson's eyes closed and he relaxed. "Got it."

Becky hovered over them. "Can he talk?"

Wilson breathed through his mouth. "Of course, I can talk. I'm injured, not drunk or dead."

"Why did you run?"

"I was late to my next appointment."

"We heard talk you found a vein of silver leading from your mine to my father's."

Wilson laughed. "Who told you that? An old drunk in the saloon?"

Zeke pressed against the man's shoulder, resultin' in a sharp intake of breath and a glare. "Why do you think it was somebody in the saloon? Because that's where you do most of your boastin'?"

"Can't believe half what people say."

Becky nudged his boot with her toe. "So which half of what you say shouldn't I believe?"

He jabbed a thumb into his chest. "Me? Honest as a church mouse."

"That's poor as a church mouse, honest as a preacher." Zeke stood and brushed off his knees. "Which is it?"

Wilson struggled into a sittin' position, cradlin' his hand in his lap. Sweat matted his hair, and his white lips bespoke his pain. "Whatever you heard is a lie."

Becky grabbed Zeke's arm, then pointed at the varmint sittin' in the street. "What's that?"

Zeke followed her gesture but didn't notice anythin' out of the ordinary. "What?"

Wilson glanced from one to the other, then struggled to tuck his hand inside his jacket.

But Becky persisted. "On his hand. A ring."

Wilson resisted when Zeke gripped his wrist. "It's nothing. It's mine."

Zeke held the man's arm aloft despite his protests and moans of pain. "Recognize it?"

"Yes." She yanked the ring from the miner's hand. "Now I remember what the sheriff said that bothered me. He gave me my father's personal effects, but his ring wasn't amongst them." She held the gold band with a blue stone in the palm of her hand, where the sun picked up the ring of diamonds around the jewel. "My mother gave him this when I was born." She turned the ring and extended it to him. "Her initials. 'MC.' His. 'RC.' And mine. 'RMC.' 'R' for Rebecca."

Zeke gestured to a bystander. "Get the sheriff."

Wilson snatched up his walkin' stick and swiped at Zeke,

catchin' him behind the knees and knockin' his feet out from under him. Zeke fell to the street, clutchin' at his legs, as Wilson rained blow after blow on his shoulders, arms, and back. Zeke rolled into the fetal position, tuckin' his chin against his chest, and scrambled away from his attacker.

When he finally got out of reach, he jumped to his feet, fists at the ready.

But Wilson lay prone in the dust, slack fingers cuppin' his weapon.

What the—?

Becky stood over the man, her parasol held like a baseball bat and a grin as wide as Kansas lightin' her face. "I've wanted to do that for a long time."

Sheriff Fremont hurried across the street. "What is going on here?"

"He killed my father. He's wearing his ring." She held it out to him. "And he knew about silver in my father's mine."

The sheriff slipped manacles on the unconscious man's wrists. "A couple of you men grab his arms and legs." Wilson screamed when they picked him up, and the sheriff stopped them. "Take him by the jacket. Although the noose won't be as gentle with him."

Becky snorted. "He surely didn't worry about treating my father right."

Zeke gripped her hand. She was right in what she said, and in fact, she echoed his own sentiments, but good thing the law didn't work that way. Maybe he should have a talk with her about grace and mercy.

Seemed she'd known precious little of either in her life.

CHAPTER 17

The chance to talk to Becky didn't come until three days later. Miguel and Dakota decided to go to town for a beer, leavin' Zeke and Becky in the kitchen after dinner. Actually, he gave them each a dollar—out of her earshot, of course—and asked them to leave for a few hours.

He finished his coffee while she washed up the dishes and put the kitchen in order. When she removed her apron, he set his cup down. "Want to go for a ride?"

"In the middle of the week?" She glanced around the room. "I don't know—"

"Come on. You can spare a couple of hours."

She sighed. "It would feel decadent."

He held out a hand, gratified when she slipped hers into his. "We can ride double to the ranch, then we'll get you a mount."

While he checked the girth and talked to his gelding, Becky changed into her skirt pants and donned a hat. He boosted her up into position behind the saddle, then mounted, enjoyin' the feel of her arms around his waist. A gentle lope brought them too soon to the barn, where he dismounted and helped her down. She slid into his embrace as neatly as if she planned it, and they stood touchin' for what seemed a lifetime.

Her nose—freckled by the sun—came almost to the top button of his shirt, and he longed to pull her against him and kiss her until they were both breathless. He envisioned sweepin' her backward into a grand dip, enjoyin' the weight of her body in his arms. Savorin' the taste of her lips, soft and yieldin' and—

But she stepped away, and he dragged his thoughts back to

the here and now. He cleared his throat while she made a show of smoothin' wrinkles from her skirt thing. "I'll get you that same paint you rode last time."

She didn't meet his gaze or speak, lickin' her lips although they didn't look dry. They looked—*never mind. Get on with it.*

Within minutes, their mounts loped across the yard, Zeke headin' for a rise in the land where they could look out over the valley below. Wildflowers dotted the green prairie grass, and cicadas and crickets joined in a chirrupin' harmony that never seemed to end. The wind against his face and knowin' a beautiful woman rode beside him was enough to fill his heart with a joy that threatened to drown him, and he had to remind himself to breathe.

At the top of the hill, he slowed, then stopped his mount, and she did the same. Her paint, always eager to run, breathed heavily and tossed its head a couple of times before settlin' down to graze on the tender grasses nestled under the aspen grove.

He dismounted, then helped her down, releasin' her quicker than he wanted. He had some serious talkin' to do, and he didn't want his fleshly desires—and he had many of those—in the way right now. If things went well, there'd be plenty of time for that later. After he brought her around to his way of thinkin'.

He untied the saddle roll and shook it out onto the ground, gesturin' for her to sit. She did, and he sank down beside her but not quite touchin'. He exhaled deeply. "Sure am glad the sheriff was there to arrest Wilson."

She folded her hands in her lap and stared out over the valley. "Me too. He finally got the chance to do his job."

"And that move with the parasol. You saved my skin."

She chuckled. "You'd have done the same thing if you were in my place."

"Don't usually carry such a thing."

"Well, with a shovel, then."

He nodded. "I love this view."

"I can see why. It's as if the whole world is spread out before you."

"Always reminds me of God when I'm up here."

She twisted slightly to look at him. "How so?"

"The green of the grass down there reminds me of His provision for my cattle. The water is like the Fountain of Life. The trees recollect the verse in the Bible about the trees of the field clappin' their hands for joy."

With the sun beamin' down on them, they talked about important things, like plans for the mine. And unimportant things, too, like the day they met at the mercantile.

Although, for him, that was a landmark day.

Then they returned to capturin' Wilson and how she felt about that.

At this, her eyes grew teary. "I came here to be with my father, only to find I never could really catch up with him."

He nodded. "Ever feel like you spent your whole life tryin' to be good enough for him to stay?"

"Yes."

"His need to always be somewhere else wasn't about you."

Her fingers knotted. "That's what Mother said." She stared out over the land spreadin' below them. "I know it here—" She pointed to her head. "But not here." A forefinger on her heart. "If only I could know for sure."

"Seems to me he wanted you with him. Why else would he name his mine after you?"

She thought on that for a while. "Makes sense. I never thought of it that way."

"Sure. He loved you and your mother. Always came back, didn't he?"

"Yes. Eventually."

"And another thing."

"What's that?"

"Your father isn't the only one who loves you."

"Oh, I know that."

Her answer surprised him. Did she already suspect his other

reason for bringin' her here?

Becky giggled. The look on Zeke's face was priceless. If she had one of those new-fangled camera boxes, she would take a picture. Or if she had a mirror, she could show him. His mouth hung open. His brow creased. And what happened to his color? It was as if all the blood drained out of him.

Goodness, she'd best not leave him in suspense a moment longer. The poor man might have apoplexy. "My mother also loves me. In her own way."

"And somebody else too."

She sobered and stared at her hands in her lap. When had they grown so red and chapped? Seemed as if she always had them in water. Or dirt. Or under a hen or holding a broom. Several nails were chipped, and she couldn't recall the last time she wore gloves. When her hands trembled, she wrung them together. All she really wanted was to feel the rough callouses of Zeke's palm against hers. His fingers entwined around her much-smaller digits. There was something comforting, strong, yet gentle about this man whose presence sent her heart galloping and her thoughts careening.

When the silence between them lingered, she looked up. A smile tickled his lips, and instead of looking away, he held her gaze as though willing her to read his mind.

But he was an open book, as transparent as glass. She knew exactly what he wanted.

A wife to cook, clean, help him on the ranch, have children. A wife to stand by his side through tornadoes. Through harsh winters and hot summers. Through floods and droughts. Through life and death.

Until death us do part.

But that wasn't her. They both knew the many reasons for that. Which meant that another would eventually take her place in Zeke's affections.

But Becky's internal reaction to that fact shook her. Already, she disliked this other woman whom she'd never met and likely never would. Already, an ache formed in the pit of her stomach.

His tongue flicked over his bottom lip, and he stared out over the valley. "I love this land."

A lump formed in her throat, and she forced her words past it. "I know."

He turned to her. "I never wanted to do anything else but follow in my parents' and grandparents' footsteps."

"I can see why."

"Always wanted to be a rancher."

"I see that. And you fit in this land."

"But now, there's something I want more. And I have to be true to my heart, Becky."

This time, the lump almost choked her. She clung to his hands and waited for the bad news. Because surely after such a soul-baring pronouncement, there had to be bad news.

When he just stared at her with that sincere, almost apologetic expression on his face, she snatched her hands from his and tucked them under her arms. He was too honest and true. He couldn't pretend something he didn't feel. He was going to pull out of their fake wedding plans, leaving her to deal with her mother, with the mine, alone.

Bad news, indeed.

Her mother was as good as dead.

As were her own chances for happiness. For love. For a future in this land.

"I know this is probably comin' as a shock to you."

To say the least. But it's my own fault. I didn't realize until now what he meant to me.

She closed her eyes, fighting back the tears. She would not let him see her cry. She raised her head when he stood and walked over to his horse, dug in the saddle bag, and returned.

But instead of sitting again, he knelt and removed his hat. His bottom lip trembled, and his eyes appeared wet, as if he'd gotten a speck of dust in there. He reached for her hand and gripped as though she were pulling him from quicksand while holding the other hand out, palm up.

"Truth is, I love somebody more than this life. And I want to spend the rest of my life with her."

Nestled in his palm, a ring. Old, by the looks of it. With two diamonds. Miner's cut, if she wasn't mistaken.

"Rebecca Mae, will you do me the honor of becomin' my wife?"

The next day, Becky paused in front of the mercantile to gather stray tendrils of hair under her hat, then hurried inside. She'd have talked to Sally last evening, but common sense and a desire to spend as much time with Zeke as was proper had brought her to the decision to wait and tell Sally today.

Then she'd go looking for Frank Jackson and tell him their deal was off.

Thankfully, this early in the morning—the store had just opened, it being five past eight—there weren't any customers around.

Sally turned from a shelf she filled with cans of beans. "Good morning, Becky. You're out and about early."

Becky leaned on the counter. "I couldn't wait to share my good news. And you're the person I wanted to tell first."

Her friend's eyebrows raised. "Do tell."

"Zeke asked me to marry him."

Sally reached across the scarred wooden plank separating them and crushed her to her chest, squealing and laughing in her ear. "Oh, that's such good news. Have you set a date? How did he ask you?" She held Becky at arm's length. "Who will be your witnesses? Will you have the weddin' while your mother is here?"

Becky held up a hand. "Slow down. I can't answer all those questions at the same time. You're talking a mile a minute!"

Mr. Dixon peeked through the curtain leading to the rear of the store. "Everythin' all right here, Sally?" He spied Becky and smiled. "Ah, good mornin'. Heard raised voices and couldn't make out the words, so thought I'd best check."

Becky nodded to the elderly man. "I was just telling Sally that Zeke asked me to marry him."

Sally twirled and did a two-step in place. "And she said 'yes.'" She peered at Becky. "You did say yes, didn't you? There isn't another man in these parts worth marrying." She smiled coyly. "Apart from Mr. D, that is, and George."

"I said yes."

Another squeal and Mr. D shrank back inside the partition, chuckling and shaking his head.

"Will you and Zeke honor us by getting married at the same time?" Sally clapped her hands. "Oh, say you will. You're like a sister to me, and sisters have double weddings all the time in those happily-ever-after stories I hear about."

"I'll check with Zeke, but I think he'd be happy to do that."

Sally's brow turned down. "But now we have a real problem."

Becky tipped her head. "What's that?"

"If'n you're gettin' married, too, who is gonna walk me down the aisle?"

The tension eased from Becky's shoulders. "We'll figure that all out."

"But you'll need a dress. And a hat. And flowers."

"I don't have money for a wedding dress."

"I have a dress."

At the voice from behind them, Becky turned. Mrs. Dixon stood in the doorway leading to the back room. "If you're willing, you can have my wedding dress. We had sons, no daughters. I think it should fit with only a few alterations." She tugged on her shop apron. "Of course, it might be too old-fashioned for you."

Becky glanced from one woman to the other. "But Sally—"

Her friend shook her head. "The pastor's wife gave me her dress. Such a pretty green it is too."

"And flowers?"

Mrs. D patted her hand. "From my garden, dear. Already promised Sally she could take what she wanted. You too. I have roses that just came into bloom. Pale cream. Should look right proper."

Seemed these two already had her future planned.

CHAPTER 18

Matilda's head snapped up as the stage took a curve in the road. Through eyes bleary from lack of sleep and an excess of dust and heat, she stared at the surrounding landscape. So unlike the city, to be sure. Rolling hills in the foreground, dotted with small greenery that turned out to be cacti once they drew closer. In the background, mountain peaks rose to great heights, their white caps gleaming in the sunlight like flaming spears trying to pierce the clouds.

Perhaps she should write poetry, so inspiring was this view.

She smiled to herself. Her Robbie would be surprised at her reaction to what she once thought a rough and untamed land.

Surely it was. But also … beautiful. Mesmerizing. She caught herself wondering whether the mountains were lavender or mauve. Whether the sky was cerulean or cornflower. Or the cacti were olive or moss. A veritable palette of colors, to be certain.

No wonder he loved it so much.

She peered through the curtained windows and the cloud of dust generated by the team of four horses pulling their conveyance so valiantly and with such great haste. A small shack drew into view, smoke drifting from its chimney. As they passed, she spied a woman hanging clothes on a line at the rear of the dwelling, a cauldron atop a fire, and two children playing in the dirt.

She shuddered. Was this the kind of life Becky was getting herself into? No matter how lovely the land in general, survival would be hard and prospering even more difficult.

Still, if anybody could do it, Robbie Campbell's daughter could.

A crack of the whip over the horses' hindquarters and a shout from the driver atop the stage drew her attention. "Silver Valley comin' up. Silver Valley."

Matilda settled back against the horsehair bench. Finally, they were here. And all in one piece, although her backside protested the jolting ride from the train station in Old Colorado City where they'd disembarked. Perhaps she should have spent the extra money for a private carriage.

If she could have found one.

Another ten minutes, and the stage slowed. Matilda removed her hat, tucked in several stray tendrils that escaped the French knot she'd arranged this morning—goodness, was that just today?—then donned her hat again, snugging it to her scalp with three long pins.

She nudged Polly, who still dozed beside her. "We're here."

Polly lifted her head and opened her eyes. "Where?"

"Silver Valley."

At those two words, her new friend snapped awake as though a doctor had given her a magic potion. Polly fussed with her hair, then smoothed her wrinkled dress. "Oh my. I must look a right mess. Sally will hardly recognize me."

Matilda patted her hand. "Never fear. Just as you'd know her anywhere, she'll know you as soon as she sets eyes on you." She pulled a compact from her reticule. "You've a smudge of dirt on your nose."

Polly cleaned up as much as possible in the cramped vehicle and handed back the mirror as the stage drew to a stop. The driver hopped down and opened the door, extending a hand for his two passengers.

Matilda smiled and nodded, slipping several coins into his free hand. "From my traveling companion and myself."

He tipped his hat, dust dribbling off as he did so. "Thank you, ma'am." He bowed to Polly, who likely hadn't enjoyed much courtesy in her life. "And to you, too, ma'am."

Polly tittered as they stood on the boardwalk. "Oh my, such a nice man, I'm sure."

Matilda glanced at the several onlookers gathered near the store, looking for the face she most wanted to see.

Who materialized from the back of the group as though called into existence with her wish, her hand raised in greeting. "Mother!"

Matilda's heart stuttered at the sight of her daughter pushing through the people. She looked fine enough. Healthy. A smile lighting her from within.

Matilda gathered Rebecca into her arms and held her close. If she let go, perhaps this would prove a dream she'd awaken from too soon. Or a mirage that would disappear like a vapor in the wind. Although thinner than when she'd left the city, her daughter stood straighter and stronger than before. Or was that merely an illusion of the inner strength she must have garnered to survive—and choose—this land?

When she finally released her, Rebecca pressed against her for a couple more heartbeats, warming this mother's heart at her child's choice to continue the contact. When she straightened, Rebecca held her by the arms and beamed at her. An inner joy emanated. Whatever her daughter had discovered, she wanted some of it.

But where was—she glanced over Rebecca's shoulder. No Robbie. If he was able, he'd be here. "Your father?"

Her daughter's smile slipped away, and Matilda regretted being the cause. At a touch on her arm, she turned. Polly. She'd completely forgotten her. She drew her friend forward. "Rebecca, this is Polly. She's—"

"Sally's mother?"

"Yes, but—"

Rebecca turned to a small boy hovering nearby. "Go and get Miss Sally from the mercantile. Tell her she must come." She turned back to Polly. "And please, call me Becky."

Matilda held back the automatic words of reproach at such a common name. How many times—but this was her daughter's life. And her daughter should be able to choose the name others would call her by. "Becky." She tried it on for size. "I like it. Fits better here."

Becky pulled Polly close. "Oh, Sally will be so happy. She thought you wouldn't come because you didn't get the right letter."

Polly frowned. "I came because I was concerned my daughter was in some kind of trouble. That letter didn't sound nothin' like her."

"Because she got my letter." Matilda hugged Becky close. "We figured it out almost right away."

Becky held her mother at arm's length. "But how did you meet?"

"On the train." Matilda smoothed a strand of her daughter's hair. "I thought you were marrying somebody totally unsuitable. Imagine my joy when we discovered the mix-up. To learn you're not getting married."

"Oh, yes, I am."

"To George?"

Sally joined their group. "Surely not. Because I'm a-marryin' him." She grabbed her mother and pulled her close. "Oh, Ma, it's so good to see you. When Becky told me about the letters, I just was heartbroken that you wouldn't be here for my weddin'. And here you are."

"Here I am. So you aren't in any trouble?"

"Trouble?" Sally giggled. "Not unless being head over heels in love is trouble, I'm not."

"I thought you was sendin' me a secret code. That's why I came. Wasn't about to let you down. Got me a job on the train to pay my way. That's where I met Matilda here."

"Seemed we had plenty in common." Matilda smiled at each girl. "Daughters who ran away."

Becky shook her head. "I wasn't running away, Mother. I thought I was, at the time. But now I figured out I was running *to* something."

∞

An hour and three cups of tea in the hotel café later, Matilda was just about caught up on all her daughter's news. The mine. The town. Zeke, a most suitable young man, it happened. A landowner with plenty of potential. Sally and her beau.

Now there was but one topic to be broached. After seeing her daughter's reaction to her previous unanswered question, she despised the idea of even bringing it up. However, there was no way to avoid it.

She set her teacup down. "Tell me about your father."

Becky sighed. "He died. Before I arrived."

"I suspected as much when I didn't hear from him for so long. He was always faithful. With his letters. His gifts. His love." Her breath caught. Where were her pills? She handed her drawstring purse to Becky. "My medicine."

Polly leaned forward. "Shall I send for the doctor?"

Matilda waved off the suggestion. "No, I'll be fine in a minute." When Becky passed her the container, she placed a tablet under her tongue. "Good. That will take effect in a couple of minutes." She sat back in her chair. "How did he die?"

Becky's mouth worked, but no words came out. Matilda looked to Sally. "Well?"

"He was killed, ma'am."

"Killed. But who—?"

Her daughter's shoulders slumped. "His neighbor, Arthur Wilson. He's in jail. He wanted the silver in Papa's mine."

Now Matilda's own words came back to haunt her. How many times had she told him that his adventures would be the death of them both? She wished she could snatch them back. But it was too late. "I see." She exhaled as the miracle drug eased her chest pains. "When you didn't mention him in your letter, I knew something was wrong." She patted Becky's hand. "He would be so proud to know you're carrying on the mine."

"Do you really think so?"

"Absolutely. He loved this country. He told me so in his letters. And I can see why. It is beautiful. Makes one believe anything is possible."

Polly reached over and touched Matilda's hand. "I'm so sorry for your loss."

Matilda nodded, her bottom lip quivering. "It's good to have a friend with me at such a time. Thank you. But I guess in my heart of hearts, I knew something like this was bound to happen at some point. He loved adventure so much, and adventure carries risk." Her eyes glistened. "But he also loved to come home." She patted Becky's arm. "To you. And to me."

Sally's mouth turned down. "I sure hate that your bad news takes away from your good news, Mrs. Campbell."

Matilda dug in her reticule for a handkerchief and dabbed at her eyes. "Thank you."

Sally stood. "Well, Becky, you and your ma prob'ly want some time alone." She reached for her mother. "Ma, walk me back to work. I'll show you where you'll bed down while you're here."

"So when is the weddin'?" Polly adjusted her hat. "And I want to see your dress."

"Next Sunday. Double wedding."

Matilda smiled. "How fun. I've never been to a double wedding." She leaned over to Becky. "When do I meet your young man?"

"Soon. I'll take you there once we leave here. He's looking forward to meeting you, then we'll take you to his parents' home."

Matilda raised an eyebrow. "Oh, I'm not staying with you?"

Becky chuckled. "My shack is very small. And I don't have all the—the modern conveniences to which you are accustomed. Zeke's parents live in a real house. And his mother said you can stay as long as you like."

"Good. But I have something to do first."

"What's that?"

"I want to arrange a dinner here for you and Zeke and his family, and for Sally and Polly and George and his family."

Sally grinned. "We'll fill this room up and then some. But that will cost a pretty penny."

Determined to embrace the joys life left to her, Matilda waggled her fingers at Sally. "No worries. I have plenty of pretty pennies. And dollars. And I'm going to spend it on family and friends."

If what the doctor said was true, she might not have too many months left.

And she'd spend every one of them surrounded by those she loved.

Any minute now, Becky expected her mother to begin The Lecture.

The one that started with "not throwing her life away" and included chapters about expectations, family honor, the benefits of living in the city, and probably some she'd not heard before.

In fact, for the entire ride from town to the mine, courtesy of Mr. D, she thought her mother would speak.

Instead, the woman gripped the edge of the seat, planted her feet firmly, and remained silent beside the older man while Becky rode in the wagon bed.

As they pulled into the yard, Matilda's shoulders stiffened, and her voice sounded strained. "What a lovely river. But does it get high in the spring?"

Mr. D. slowed the horses. "Not usually. It's pretty steep through here, so the water flows good. Unless it backs up downriver, closer to town. But folks around here tend to keep an eye on that."

Becky looked around her property, trying to see it through her mother's eyes. Dust everywhere. Sunbaked rock. Shabby cabin with tattered curtains that she'd never gotten around to replacing. She blinked a couple of times, then surveyed her domain once more. Over there, in the cleft of those rocks, lupines struggled for a foothold. Across the river, mountain ash trees, covered in berries, promised jelly for her and food for the birds come winter. In that lodgepole pine, a chipmunk chased its mate amongst the branches.

Beauty everywhere. She had nothing to be ashamed of.

Becky pointed to the pale lavender and pink lupine buds. "Mother, see the flowers?"

Her mother's face relaxed. "I do. They're lovely. Like a bouquet in the finest florist shop in New York."

Approaching the house, they admired an eagle soaring high overhead and the perfect little plot of ground for Becky's garden next year.

As the wagon rolled to a stop, Zeke emerged from the mine, his face covered in dust, his clothes almost white. He brushed them off as he hurried toward them.

"Is that your young man?"

By her mother's tone of voice, Becky couldn't tell what she thought. But as much as Becky wished he'd taken the time to clean up before their arrival, her heart almost burst with love and admiration. And something else. A desire to be with him. In the biblical sense. She pushed those thoughts aside as heat rushed to her cheeks. They'd wed in only four days.

"Yes, it is. That's Zeke."

Who tipped the brim of his hat to Becky's mother. "Mrs. Campbell, welcome to the Becky Mae Mine."

Her mother smiled at him. "Thank you. I'm expecting the grand tour."

"Which you shall have."

Zeke extended his hands to assist her mother to the ground, which she accepted. He showed her where to place her feet, explaining as patiently as he'd done with her. Becky came around the wagon to help if needed, but he had things under control, and soon her mother stood on solid ground once more.

Zeke peered up at the driver. "Thanks, Mr. D. I owe you a favor."

The shopkeeper waved off the words. "Not a'tall. Happy to

be of assistance." He nodded to Becky and her mother. "See you ladies soon."

He clicked his tongue, the horse leaned into the traces, and the wagon rumbled down the road.

Zeke grabbed Becky around the waist and twirled her. "I've got great news."

When she was so dizzy her head spun, she smacked him on the back. "Unhand me."

He set her down but gripped her hands. "Found a vein that looks like the mother lode."

"Really?" Becky squeezed Zeke's hands, then turned to her mother. "Isn't that wonderful? Papa knew the mine would pay off."

Her mother patted her on the arm. "Sounds like a grand beginning to your new life."

Zeke smiled at her mother. "Would you like a tour now?"

Matilda quirked her chin in the direction of the tunnel. "In there?"

"Don't worry." He held out his arm. "I'll be with you."

Becky's mother glanced at the shack. "Well, the mine looks safer than the cabin, to be sure."

He laughed along with her, then turned to Becky. "I'll bring her back in a few minutes. Sure you gals have plenty to catch up on."

Gals. Becky gritted her teeth at his casual address for her mother. Surely she'd have something to say about that. But Mother beamed up at Zeke as though he hung the moon.

She shrugged the tension from her shoulders. Everything would be fine. Her fiancé was well on his way to captivating her mother.

No easy task.

But if Zeke thought he could exclude her from a moment as important as this one, he had another thing coming. She ran after them. "I want to see this silver you found!"

As they rode back into town that evening for Matilda's celebration dinner—every detail arranged and confirmed before she'd agreed to go to the mine earlier—Becky's mother and Zeke chatted as easily as old friends while Becky relaxed in the wagon bed. Sitting on a bale of hay with an old horse blanket for cushioning, the rocking of the wagon almost lulled her to sleep.

Or perhaps the peace in her heart was the cause.

When a coyote trotted across in front of them, her mother gasped. "I've heard of them but have never seen one before except in a book."

Zeke gestured to the hills on either side of the road. "The place is crawlin' with them. They keep the prairie dogs under control."

"And that's a good thing?"

"Sure. Those varmints dig tunnels that weaken the surface. A body could be ridin' along and suddenly his horse steps into a hole. He could end up breakin' through and crackin' a leg."

"Have you had to shoot a horse before?"

"Unfortunately, yes." Zeke pressed his lips together. "Awful waste. Always hate havin' to do it."

"I've heard of racehorses being put down for that same reason."

He nodded. "All their weight is on their legs. And they don't lie down much. So it's hard for them to heal properly."

"A hard land."

"Yes."

"Tell me about your ranch."

He shared how his family had owned the land for the past three generations, having moved west during the War of 1812. How they'd traded milk cows in Pennsylvania for longhorns in Texas, then driven the animals west, settling in Silver Valley because of the water, grazing, and gentler winters. Talked about his parents and siblings, their families.

She nodded when he finished. "I can see you love this land almost as much as you love my daughter."

"Yes, ma'am, that's a fact."

"My husband wasn't a city man, you know. He loved

adventure. He loved action. But he loved me more. He gave up his dreams to marry me. Agreed to settle down. Live life under my terms." Mother shook her head. "But I saw that inside, he was dying. So after Becky was born, I released him to do what he really wanted."

Zeke drew back on the reins as they rounded a bend. "You must have really loved him."

"I did. He hated leaving us, but I knew that when he came back, he'd be happy to stay for a few months, and then he'd be off on the next adventure."

Becky swallowed hard as her mother's words hung in the air between the three of them. She hadn't known that about her father. Or her mother. Both had made huge sacrifices for love.

Her earthly father hadn't left her.

He hadn't found her wanting.

He hadn't been looking for something better.

Her mother had loved him enough to release him to be himself.

Becky pushed back tears as her mother stood, water glass in hand in lieu of champagne. "I'd like to propose a toast to the happy couple." She glanced around at the beaming faces surrounding her. George's family, Zeke's family, Sally, and Polly. Even Mr. and Mrs. D, and the sheriff too. "Happy couples, I mean."

George pulled Sally into a sideways hug. "Hear, hear, as the hoity-toities say."

Mother sent him a mock glare. "I'll have you know I used to be one of those hoity-toities you're so quick to disparage, young man."

The room went silent for a couple of heartbeats, then her mother laughed, and the rest joined in. Joy diffused what could have been a tense moment.

Becky elbowed Zeke and spoke in a loud whisper while tossing her mother a wink. "Do you see how bossy she is?"

He nodded.

"Well, I'm just like her in many ways."

"Not in every way, though. Just the important ones."

She chuckled. "Mother? Why don't you go ahead with your toast?"

Her mother cleared her throat softly. "I pray your marriage will be overflowing with love and passion. The way mine was." Her cheeks colored. "And for many more years than I had."

Zeke's father stood. "And I pray their marriage will be steadfast."

George's father was next. "May they have more mornings where they don't want to get out of bed than nights spent sleeping alone."

George jabbed his father's arm. "Pa."

By this time, everybody was laughing and teasing the couples. Becky's face heated with the veiled innuendos regarding the pleasures of marital life. If this kept up, she and Zeke might have to elope before the actual date. Winks, nudges, and nods implied that the physical side of marriage could compensate for the hardships and hard work required for survival in this land.

Mrs. Graumann shook her head. "Don't listen to all that foolishness. Sure and all, that stuff is good when everythin' else is good. But otherwise, it's only icin' on a moldy cake."

After another round of laughter, they settled in to enjoy dessert: a fine dried-apple pie with hand-churned ice cream and plenty of coffee. While Becky loved being surrounded by family and future friends, her thoughts returned to her father and the apprehension of his killer. Knowing Wilson was in jail awaiting the circuit court judge gave her some comfort, but until the man was convicted, she'd have no closure in the matter.

Zeke reached across the table and touched her hand. "A penny for your thoughts?"

She forced a smile. "I didn't know I was marrying a man wasteful enough to toss his money about."

He squeezed her hand, the grip a comfort. "I'm thinkin' it's your father."

She nodded. "I know he'd be happy for me too. I just wish I'd known how he felt about me before this. I always thought I wasn't good enough. That he left because of me."

"It's the way he was created. To explore, to discover. In another time, he'd have sailed with Columbus. Or crossed the country with Lewis and Clark. Or maybe, a hundred years from now, he'd go to the moon."

Sally leaned over from her chair beside Becky. "He'd be so proud of you. I know he would. All he ever talked about was when he hit it rich, he'd send for you and your mother."

"You never said you knew him."

"Only in passin', you understand. At church. In the mercantile." Her eyes widened, and her mouth formed an 'O.' "I only just remembered—" She shook her head. "It's probably not important."

Becky's hands trembled, and she dropped them into her lap. "What?"

"I only just remembered the last time I seen him. He didn't see me, though."

"Where was he?"

"In an alley next to the mercantile. I'd just closed up shop. I was goin' to meet George at the park for a little—well, you know." Her neck and face pinked. "It was startin' to rain, so I hurried along, my head down. I heard voices, so I slowed. Your pa was facin' me, and the man he was arguin' with had his back to me so I couldn't see his face."

Becky shivered. Why would her father meet somebody in an alley? This didn't sound like the man she remembered. "What were they talking about?"

"I heard the other man say your pa better not get in the way or he'd wind up in a box—"

She gasped. "What?"

"And your pa said something about doin' the right thing."

Now, that was more like her papa. Becky tensed, glancing down the table. Conversations near them hushed and heads turned their way as Sally continued her narrative.

"Your father said that this man should do right." She shrugged. "I thought at the time that maybe he'd tried to pick your father's pocket, but then I seen his walking stick. And I thought a man with money like that didn't need to steal."

"What was it about the stick that made you think that?"

"Why, the great big old silver handle on it. Big as a baseball, it was."

The sheriff slapped a hand on the table, making Sally jump. "That's it. That's what we needed."

Becky set her fork aside as almost complete silence fell among the guests. "For what?"

"Well, we had the circumstantial evidence against Wilson. He had your father's ring."

Zeke leaned forward. "And he bragged about a silver vein that ran under another claim."

"Right." The sheriff crossed his arms over his chest. "As I said, circumstantial. With the right jury, we might convict on that alone. But having an eye witness come upon their argument. Hear Wilson threaten Mr. Campbell. See the walking stick. Well, I'd say this is the evidence that will put the nail in Wilson's coffin."

CHAPTER 19

This is it. Just walk down that aisle and become Mrs. Zeke Graumann. You can do it.

Becky checked her reflection in the looking glass one more time. Sally hovered by the door, weaving her fingers together. Mr. D stood at attention, ready to walk her to her groom. Mr. Graumann stood just inside the doorway, waiting to do the honors for his future daughter-in-law.

But Becky's feet seemed frozen to the floor.

Which made no sense at all. She didn't have second thoughts about marrying Zeke. If anything, she wished they'd done it before now. And she knew he didn't have any concerns. Nothing struck her as off or strange.

Except for that one niggling thought she'd forgotten something.

But what?

Between her mother, Mrs. D, and the ladies of the town, they'd pulled together the something old, something new, something borrowed, and something blue for both brides. The church service this morning had been abbreviated, and several women had volunteered to decorate the sanctuary while the bridal party returned home to dress for the event. Fresh flowers now dotted the pews, ribbons hung from the kerosene lanterns on the walls, and a large basket filled with roses and daisies replaced the lectern Reverend Obermeyer usually stood behind.

All seemed in order.

Still … She shook off her concerns and tossed a smile to her friend. "Ready?"

"More than."

With Sally leading the way, Becky followed, her arm looped through Mr. Graumann's. The small church was standing room only, with the mothers of the brides seated in the front pew, side by side.

Becky fastened her eyes on her intended, who grinned and winked at her. Although she walked in time with the wedding march, the faces in the pews appeared as a blur—likely because of tears gathering in the corners of her eyes. Oh, if she cried now, her nose would be red and her eyes puffy.

What a way to start her marriage.

After the brides were deposited with their grooms, Reverend Obermeyer began reading the definition of love from First Corinthians. Becky clenched her toes and breathed through her nose—last-minute instructions from the pastor's wife to prevent fainting—and marveled at how Zeke fulfilled this Scripture.

Each had just faced their intended to repeat their vows after the pastor when a commotion at the door stopped the ceremony.

A man strode down the center aisle toward them, his loud voice filling the church. "You told me the wedding was in the park. Imagine my surprise when there wasn't nobody there but a couple of kids and a dog."

A collective, indignant gasp came from the witnesses, then stunned silence.

But Becky's heart sank to the toes of her borrowed shoes.

That's what she'd forgotten.

To call off the fake minister.

She opened her mouth, but no sound came out.

Meanwhile, Frank Jackson reached the altar. Eyeing the preacher top to bottom, he leaned close to her and spoke just above a whisper. "He looks pretty authentic, but something ain't quite right about him." Turning to Reverend Obermeyer, he raised his voice. "You can leave now. She already paid me, and I'm gonna hold up my end of the bargain."

Zeke helped his wife into their wagon, then settled beside her on the seat. He flicked the reins, and they followed the entourage headed toward the park for the potluck meal put on by the church ladies.

He grinned at Becky. "I wish I could have taken one of those new-fangled photographs of the look on your face when that scoundrel came into the church."

She twisted in her seat and waved back at her mother, who rode in a pony cart along with the banker's son. "You could have knocked me over with a feather. I had the feeling I was forgetting something but couldn't for the life of me remember what it was."

"And to think I almost went along with that crazy plan."

"Almost?" She jabbed him in the ribs. "You did go along. Apparently owning half the Becky Mae was enticement enough."

"Nothin' compared to havin' the real thing, though." He tipped his head toward an envelope she held in her hand. "What's that?"

"Something Mother gave me as we walked out of the ceremony. She said it was from Papa and her." Her voice broke. "She gave one like it to Sally too."

"What was in theirs?"

"The deed to a house here in town. With enough bedrooms, she said, to have the pitter-patter of little feet on the stairs for many years to come."

He whistled. "I'd like to have seen George's face."

"Red as a beet." Becky laughed. "And Sally's too."

The soft tinkle of her joy filled his heart with somethin' indescribable. Peace, maybe. Contentment.

Love. That's what it was.

He pulled on the reins, and the wagon halted. "You gonna open it?"

"Want me to?"

"Got to sometime. Might as well be now. Hope it's not a house, though."

"Why not?"

"I'm hopin' you'll agree to build up there on the hill overlookin' the valley."

"Where you proposed?"

"Yep."

She planted a kiss on his cheek, and he turned his face for more of that sweetness, with which she readily complied.

When they came up breathless, he exhaled. "Whoo-ee. How long we gotta stay at this here reception thing?"

She poked him in the arm. "Why? Do you have somewhere else you need to be?"

"Got us a room at the hotel. Way in the back. Paid for two nights for the other three rooms around it too. For privacy, you understand."

She grinned as she tore open the envelope. "You think of every—oh, my."

"A house?"

"No. Better. Our future."

She held up the paper for him to see.

Water rights for his part of the ranch. In perpetuity.

Becky stared at the western horizon from the same park beyond the town limits, where just a few weeks prior she'd celebrated the nation's birthday. This was not the wedding reception she'd anticipated. Sure, her mother was here. And most of the town. And her best friend and her mother.

But the grooms, the pastor, the sheriff, and the deputy were missing.

She held a hand to shade her eyes, hoping and praying for some sign of their return. A dust plume. Pounding hooves. A messenger sent ahead with word.

She turned back to the gathering behind her. Knots and

groupings of folks, voices lowered, speculating on what was happening beyond their view. While everybody including the town's deputy and the sheriff had been at the wedding and reception, Arthur Wilson, murderer, had escaped jail by prying open his cell's lock with the prong of his belt.

If not for one of the Graumann boys noticing his horse missing from the hitching rail, Wilson could have gotten more than a thirty-minute lead on the posse the sheriff quickly assembled. Although he—and the brides—tried to talk them out of it, neither Zeke nor George were satisfied to stay behind.

Three hours later, and still no sign of them.

She returned to her vigil, eyes straining in the bright sunlight to pick out something, anything, against the backdrop of sand and cactus.

Wait. What was that? A tiny bit of dust near the horizon. Her breath caught in her throat. Could it be? She closed her eyes, willing them closer, faster. She clasped her hands below her chin and prayed. "God, please bring them all home safely. Even Arthur Wilson. Please, God."

She stared at the horizon. Yes, that was dust. And tiny, dark specks nearing the town. But were they bringing good news?

Or sad?

A small boy raced past, his dog close behind. He skidded to a stop. "They're a-comin' back."

The remaining townsfolk surged around and past her like a tidal wave, carrying her in their wake, not stopping until they reached the edge of the town. She panted in the heat, her dress too warm and her shoes too tight. A headache threatened behind her eyes, and sweat snaked its way down her back, her neck, her bosom, and her arms.

The sheriff, identified quickly by his black stallion, led the way. Zeke on his gelding followed close behind, leading a painted pony by a rope. A large sack of something flopped about on the pack pony's back.

No, not a sack.

A body.

Becky did a quick head count. Four.

She must be mistaken. She counted again. Four.

But five had gone out.

She scanned the men. Where was George?

Sally joined her. "Do you see them?"

What to say to her friend? A new bride of just three hours, and perhaps a widow already? She couldn't form the words to accompany her thoughts. And even if she had, she wouldn't have been able to speak them.

The concept was simply too horrible.

A hundred yards out, the sheriff held up a hand, and the posse slowed from a gallop to a lope. She focused on Zeke's face. Seemingly fine, he sat upright in the saddle, yet a pang of guilt threaded her heart because somebody—perhaps George—wasn't.

At another signal from the sheriff, the posse slowed again to a walk, and the horses, heads drooping, snorted and snickered at each other, straining at the bit. The sheriff dismounted and tied his horse to the hitching rail outside the jail. Zeke urged his mount to the far side of the sheriff's and handed him the lead rope. The lawman tied the pack pony beyond Becky's view.

Sally unsuccessfully stifled a sob, creating a hiccupping sound instead. "No. It's not—it can't be."

Becky gripped her arm. "Wait until they come to us."

But Sally broke free and trotted across the street, her borrowed wedding dress flapping around her ankles, kicking up small cyclones of dust that the wind carried away. She went first to the pack pony, then to the sheriff.

After a few words, she folded her hands together and returned to Becky. "It's not George."

Sally's words unleashed a torrent of tears, and Becky pulled her close. "Oh, I was so scared for you. But where is he?"

Sally's voice, muffled by tears, emotion, and Becky's shoulder, cracked. "George is out there helpin' a homesteader. Said I'd understand. Wilson is the one on the pack pony. The posse shot him dead after he broke into the house and pistol-whipped the rancher. The rancher's wife is expectin' their first child, and her husband was still groggy. Seems George owed the man a favor and offered to stay until the doctor arrived." Her brow pulled down. "I'll give him what-for when I see him. Plumb scared me into gray hair before my time."

"So when will he be here?"

"Should be on his way now. The doctor was coming from Durango."

Becky linked her elbow through Sally's to cross the street. On the other side, Zeke waited with open arms.

She hurried to him and held him close. "This better not be an indication of our future together."

"How so?"

"You taking off at the first sign of trouble."

He chuckled. "Well, at least I ran toward the problem, not away from it." He glanced toward the body. "It's sad, though. We didn't want to shoot him, but he didn't give us any choice. Stood in the doorway with a gun in one hand and his arm around the wife."

"Sounds as if he preferred to go that way than at the end of a rope."

His smile slipped away. "Yep. A sad endin' for a man."

At a touch on her arm, Becky turned. Wilkerson, the land agent, stood beside her. "Just heard Wilson is dead."

Zeke nodded. "Yes, he is."

"Follow me."

She glanced at Zeke, who shrugged, so she fell into step behind the land agent as he led the way to his office. Inside, he opened his ledgers and pulled a form from a pigeonhole in the desk. After scratching some words on the paper, he slid it across the desk.

Becky picked it up. "What is this?"

"The deed to Wilson's claim. In perpetuity. Seems like after all the trouble he caused, it's the least I can do." He completed another form and passed it over. "And here's a revised deed to your mine. In perpetuity." He grinned. "A weddin' gift."

"But what about Wilson's heirs? Don't they rightfully own his mine?"

"Don't think he had any, and if he did, it doesn't matter. He bought a lifetime interest only, just like your pa did. And now I'm givin' it to you."

She thanked the man and turned to leave, then stopped. "If what Wilson believed about the vein of silver is true, whoever owns these two claims could become very rich."

His gaze never wavered. "Yes, ma'am."

"You could have kept it and been a rich man."

"Like I said, I'm no miner."

She returned to the desk, leaned across, and kissed him on the cheek. "You're a good man, Tom Wilkerson."

He shook his head. "No, ma'am, I'm not. A good man would'a given you your father's claim without charge."

"You had every right."

"Mebbe so. But that didn't make it right. It's been eatin' at my conscience ever since."

"You could have given the money back."

He nodded toward the deed. "I could, but I think this is more justice than your father ever got."

CHAPTER 20

A month later, Zeke helped Becky down from the wagon. She giggled and twisted in his arms when he didn't set her feet on the ground right away, holdin' her tight against him. "Stop squirmin'. You're like a big old trout on a line."

"Let me walk."

"Nope. A new bride in her first home doesn't just walk in. She gets carried over the threshold."

He carried her up the steps and onto the veranda of their brand-new home, built on his land by his brothers as a weddin' gift. And not a minute too soon either. If he didn't soon have some privacy with his new bride, he would bust. Livin' in his mother's house, with Becky's mother down the hall and his parents next door, was downright painful.

At the door, he balanced her between the door jamb and his hip while he lifted the latch. Then he pushed the oak slab open with his foot before steppin' through and settin' her down gently as a baby chick. "Welcome to your home, Mrs. Graumann."

She curtsied. "Thank you, Mr. Graumann."

They wandered through the rooms, enjoyin' the space and the peace and quiet.

In the kitchen, Becky paused. "Seems a shame that there won't be much cooking going on in this wonderful room."

He leaned against the door jamb and crossed his arms over his chest. "And why won't there be much cookin' goin' on? A man has to eat, doesn't he?"

She strolled through the area, runnin' a finger along the top of the new range, across the hand-hewn kitchen table and handmade chairs, and rearrangin' a coffee mug on a shelf.

Women.

She turned to face him. "We'll be busy at the mine. While Wilson was a scoundrel, he was right about that vein of silver. It's going to pan out for months."

"Speakin' of the mine, I think we should rename it."

Her head snapped up. "What did you have in mind?"

"Double Jeopardy. For the two times we almost didn't live long enough to fall in love and get married."

She laughed. "Only two times? Seems like more."

He held out a hand and counted on his fingers. "Well, there was the time you got lost in the mine, and I had to rescue you."

"I wasn't in any danger of dying then."

Zeke tipped his head to one side. "Really? If I hadn't found you? You seemed pretty scared."

"Okay, I'll let you count that one." She crossed the room and lifted his middle finger alongside his index finger. "And there's the time when you were kidnapped and tied to a tree, and *I* had to rescue you." She snuggled against him. "Seems like we're even."

"Oh, we're very even." He ran his hands up and down her back. "I'd like to get even more even with you if you're feelin' accommodatin'."

She looked up at him. "Is that what you call it out here?"

"Well, what do you call it?"

She mashed her cheek into his chest. "Accommodating is a fine word. And yes, I am." She raised her face and pursed her lips, then stepped out of his embrace. "But I don't want to be reminded of almost losing you."

He nodded, buryin' his face in her hair. "You're right. The Becky Mae is just fine."

"We could call the other one Double Jeopardy. To remind us how we almost missed the biggest blessing in our lives."

He led her toward their brand-new bedroom. "I like the sound of that. And let's name the ranch Double Blessing."

If he had any say in it, they'd enjoy that kind of favor the rest of their lives.

A double blessing.

AUTHOR'S NOTE

Dear Readers,

Thank you so much for taking time to read *Double Jeopardy*. I would love to know your thoughts about the story, including the historical details, the characters, and the ending. Feel free to email me at donna@historythrutheages.com. And I'd also cherish your input by leaving a review at Amazon.com, Goodreads.com, BarnesandNoble.com, Smashwords.com, and anywhere else you usually leave reviews.

The town of Silver Valley is loosely based on the still-Wild West towns of Durango and Silverton in southwest Colorado. A beautiful yet harsh part of the state, it takes strong people with stronger resolve and faith to make a go of it there. Silver mining sustained Colorado for many years after the gold ran out and before its other resources—including water, lumber, and land—were recognized.

I pray you have many exciting adventures, and remember: His story is the only one worth telling.

In Christ,

Donna

CPSIA information can be obtained
at www.ICGtesting.com
Printed in the USA
FSHW010625040120
65713FS